DEATH ZONES

Simon Pasternak

DEATH
ZONES

Translated from Danish by
Martin Aitken

Harvill Secker
LONDON

1 3 5 7 9 10 8 6 4 2

Harvill Secker, an imprint of Vintage,
20 Vauxhall Bridge Road,
London SW1V 2SA

Harvill Secker is part of the Penguin Random House group of companies
whose addresses can be found at global.penguinrandomhouse.com

Penguin
Random House
UK

This publication was assisted by a grant from the Danish Arts Foundation

DANISH ARTS FOUNDATION

Published with the support of the Culture Programme of the European Union

This project has been funded with support from the European Commission. This
publication reflects the views only of the author, and the Commission cannot be held
responsible for any use which may be made of the information contained therein

www.vintage-books.co.uk

A CIP catalogue record for this book is available from the British Library

ISBN 9781846558504

Text design by Richard Marston

Typeset in India by Thomson Digital Pvt Ltd, Noida, Delhi

Printed and bound in Great Britain by Clays Ltd, St Ives plc

Penguin Random House is committed to a sustainable future
for our business, our readers and our planet. This book is made
from Forest Stewardship Council® certified paper.

MIX
Paper from
responsible sources
FSC® C018179

To Mikael, my maternal grandfather

Henceforth, in the death zones, all people are fair game.

Curt von Gottberg
SS- und Polizeiführer, Belorussia
1 August 1943

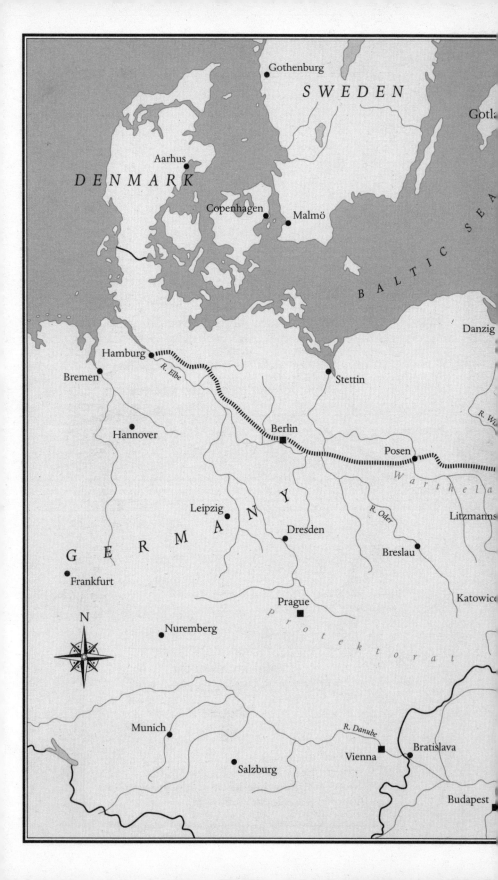

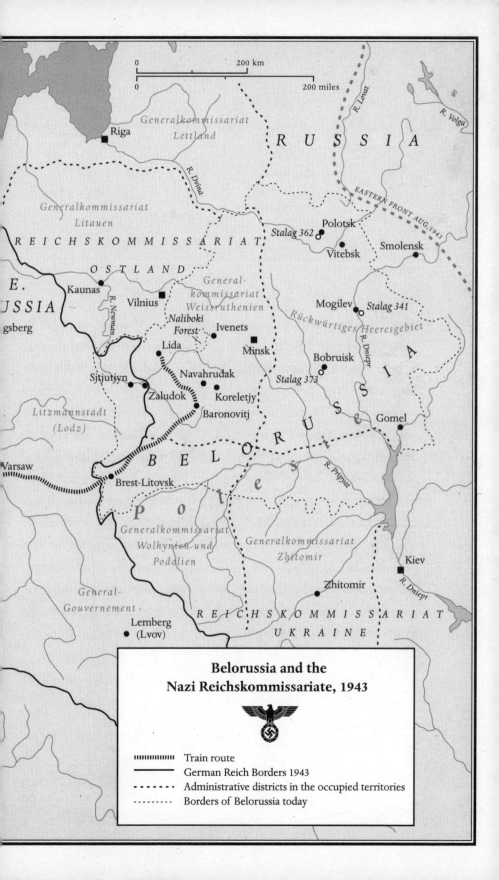

Belorussia and the
Nazi Reichskommissariate, 1943

Train route
German Reich Borders 1943
Administrative districts in the occupied territories
Borders of Belorussia today

Death Zones takes place in the summer of 1943, in what is today known as Belarus, at the time most commonly Belorussia, a land whose borders during the course of the twentieth century were fluid and which carried many names. With various demarcations, it has belonged to Tsarist Russia (until 1917), the German Empire (1917–18), the Soviet Union (1918–20), Poland (1920–39), and the Soviet Union again, as the Soviet Socialist Republic of Belorussia (1939–41 and 1944–91). Under the German occupation (1941–44) it was divided into a region of civil administration, the *Generalkommissariat Weissruthenien,* and the *Rückwärtiges Heeresgebiet Mitte,* administered by the Wehrmacht. *Death Zones* is fiction, and many of the events described in it did not occur. Some, however, did. A number of the characters were real people (here, the reader is referred to the notes at the end of the book).

STEINER

Letters

Lida, 4 July 1943

Letter 7

Dear Eline

Thank you for the honey. I wonder if it might be drawn from
our secret place on the heath, the abandoned beehives in the
hollow, down near the banks of the Alster, the ones we found on
our last night together? I like to think so. 'And yet, how much
he says who utters "night", for from this word deep grief and
meaning pour, like heavy honey from the honeycomb.'

To think it is eleven months now since we bade each other
farewell at the station and Manfred and I departed for the
unknown . . . Belorussia . . .

The jar is here on my desk, amid case files and topographic
maps. It shall be our little secret, untouched by this raging war.
Now and then I pick it up and unscrew the lid, allowing the
fragrance of ~~fragrant of summer~~ the smell ~~now and then I must
breathe in its scent of balmy, luxurious summer~~ I must take in
its scent of balmy, luxurious summer. I pretend ~~that it is your
flaxen hair . . . fragrant . . .~~

I put the fountain pen down on the desk and read the last lines again. The jar of honey is next to the typewriter, on top of the case files concerning the killing of the Jew, Feigl. My work, my predicament: the dogfight between SS officers Heinz Breker and Sigmund Kindler.

I unscrew the lid of the jar, smell the solidified wax, the creamy white crust. It smells of nothing. I dip a finger, sweeping it round in an arc, then draw it out to lick. It tastes of honey, not of summer. Certainly not of Eline's hair.

I toss the letter into the wastepaper basket, draw the typewriter towards me once more and turn the paper bearing my official letterhead into the carriage:

Heinrich Hoffmann

Oberleutnant der Polizei

GK Weissruthenien

Case No. LZ 512-A, - GHETTO LIDA/A. Feigl, in conclusion
cc: Hptstführer S. Kindler, Hptstführer H. Breker

The investigation instituted by SS-Hauptsturmführer Sigmund Kindler as to the deceased individual identified as Jozef Feigl, a Jew . . .

My cigarette lies smouldering in the ashtray.

After a long moment of indecision, I continue:

It is therefore to be concluded that the shots that killed the Jew Jozef Feigl were fired by SS-Hauptsturmführer Heinz Breker, attached to SS-Dienststelle Lida. Pursuant to regulations re. impunity within the administrative boundaries

of the Reichskommissariat Ostland, the case is deemed not
to be encompassed by sections 211 or 212 of the German
Penal Code. Charges will not be brought.
    Case closed.

H.H. Oberleutnant d.P., Lida District

I remove the paper from the typewriter and furnish it with my stamp, *Heinrich Hoffmann, Oberleutnant d. Polizei.* I place the report in the case file, only to be struck by doubt. I have to telephone Manfred.

Eline's brother. He is SS, and knows the hierarchy better than I. No answer.

Today is his big day. He will be strutting about, barking at his minions, peering at their buttons and boots, inspecting weapons, making sure the streets are swept clean. The Obergruppenführer is coming. Dr Hubert Steiner, Manfred's mentor, the man who taught him his trade.

I uncap my pen and start again, in an elaborate hand:

Lida, 4 July 1943

Letter 7

My dearest E!

Thank you for the honey. Such memories! 'And yet, how much he says who utters "night", for from this word deep grief and meaning pour, like heavy honey from the honeycomb.'

Damn it! I drum my fingers on the desk, remove my spectacles and draw my hands across my face, jump to my feet and go to the window. Falkowska Street is festooned with bunting, lined with flags at this end, where the road veers off towards Minsk. Manfred has had a grandstand erected opposite, in front of the yellow and white railway station from the Tsarist days, columns and capitals in operetta style. Three men drag cables, rigging up the loudspeaker system, while the orchestra sits perspiring in their chairs, the brass of their instruments gleaming in their laps. Perhaps Manfred hopes the Obergruppenführer's wife, the actress, will do a turn. A truck appears and the guard of honour spill out, in black parade uniforms with red and white emblems. I open the window. The heat, the dust and the noise smother me in an instant. But Manfred is nowhere to be seen.

I call for my adjutant. Wäspli appears immediately, his stout figure constrained by tight uniform. I wonder if his letters to his fiancée are as poorly lyrical as my own. Or perhaps he is already married? I know nothing about him. He flutters his fat, bustling hands.

'Has Hauptsturmführer Breker's transfer come through yet?' I ask.

'I think so.'

'Think?'

'My friend said—'

'Find out,' I say.

We stand for a moment, in spite of the matter's conclusion. I make a vague gesture and he withdraws. I return to my desk, open the bottom drawer and produce the Hungarian cognac and a small glass.

I telephone Manfred again.

I picture it ringing in his empty office in the hospital on the road to Vilnius.

Still no answer.

I curse.

— — —

Wäspli returns.

'Yes?' I demand.

'He said the papers are being processed . . .'

'But did he know?'

He smiles nervously.

No.

When he closes the door behind him I remove the portrait of the Führer from the wall behind the desk and turn the combination, open the safe, take the report on the killing of Feigl from the folder, repeat the case number to myself, then place the report back, underneath Eline's letters. I take out the bundle and smell the ribbon. It smells of musty papers.

I close the safe and rehang the portrait.

I type the case number, the main particulars, and assign the new report the same number as the one in the box behind me: LZ 512–A.

I leave out Breker.

I leave out the witness, Finckelstein.

I conclude:

```
Whether Jozef Feigl was the victim of an accident or a
premeditated act cannot be ascertained. However, since no
evidence has been found to indicate an internal dispute
between Jews, the case is deemed not to be encompassed by
sections 211 or 212 of the German Penal Code.
    Case closed.
                          H.H. Oberleutnant d.P., Lida District
```

My right hand trembles as I stub out my cigarette and snatch the paper from the carriage.

I cross over to the window. The sky is full of dust, a haze.
I curse.
Again.

− − −

This is Belorussia, the Lida ghetto, case number LZ 512–A, –
GHETTO LIDA/A. Feigl:

SS-Hauptsturmführer Sigmund Kindler has charge of the ghetto
workshops. He claims his share, though is by no means greedy:
six per cent of the intake, before the entries are made in the books.
He protects a Jew who makes little birds from wood shavings:
Feigl. Kindler sends them to his children in Kiel as Christmas
decorations. They are fine and delicate, miracles of life. Feigl looks
like a bird himself. There is some measure of contact between
them. He brings gifts for Feigl's wife, small items that can be
turned into capital. Feigl is accorded privileges. They make him
vulnerable. He bears the mark of Kindler. SS-Hauptsturmführer
Heinz Breker works outside the ghetto. He is a friend of
Manfred's. They are boisterous, fond of hunting the hare – by
which they mean partisans – and throw raucous parties, with
excessive amounts of champagne. Kindler gets drunk and calls
Breker's wife a Bavarian whore. Breker threatens to shoot him like
a dog, a suitable end for a Holsteiner such as him. He draws his
P38, bellowing and frothing from his fat mouth, exposing the gap
between his front teeth. Others intervene. The two of them square
off like a pair of bulls, same size, same rage, same rank: equals.
Breker puts a bullet through Feigl one night when Feigl is with his
birds. Kindler demands a police investigation. I am the police.

The legalities are fiendishly complex, and yet brutally straight-
forward. The German Penal Code applies within both the Reich
and the occupied territories. But if the perpetrator is German

and the victim Jewish or local, the provisions of sections 211 and 212 concerning murder and manslaughter do not apply. If both perpetrator and victim are of the same *racial value* – German–German, Jew–Jew, Russian–Russian, Pole–Pole, Pole–Jew, Russian–Pole and various other combinations – then the stipulations *do* apply. Thus, any matter may potentially be made the object of investigation. I have a witness, Finckelstein, who saw the killing take place. He sat only a metre away, painting wings. Breker stuck his arm through the window and fired his 9mm into the room. *His head was almost blown off*, Finckelstein stated. Breker must have discharged a whole round into the vertebrae of the scrawny man's neck. I have the blood-spattered birds in evidence bags. Autopsy is out of the question, but there are six bullets in the workbench and I have a reliable witness. I picked five fragments of bone, Feigl's, from his throat and hand, tiny shards of organic shrapnel. I end up with two reports.

The truth for Kindler. A lie for Breker.

I don't know who ranks highest in the real hierarchy.

If I deliver the wrong report, it could destroy me.

I need Manfred. He will know what to do. Kindler keeps on at me for a verdict.

I telephone Manfred again.

The adjutant says *something has happened*.

He won't say what.

When I look out of the window again, people are running.

– – –

Lida, 4 July 1943
Letter 7

Honey, dearest!
  Thank you for the par

Manfred flings open the door.

He is pure energy, crackling electricity in his black uniform. He gives me a handshake, a slap on the back, a forceful embrace. When eventually he steps back I see he is fuming.

My eyes focus on his small head, his puckered mouth.

'My car's outside,' he says.

'What's happened?' I ask.

He is already at the desk, telephone receiver in hand. He pauses, stares at the letter to Eline. He sees the jar. He opens it, dabs a finger in the honey and puts it in his mouth.

'Tell me what's happened, for Christ's sake!' I snap at him.

'What?'

'Manfred!'

'Steiner,' he says quietly. 'A reconnaissance plane spotted something north-east of Stützpunkt 43 . . . on his route . . . Gisela is with him . . .'

North-east of Stützpunkt 43

Manfred's command vehicle bumps along the dirt road. I have asked him about Breker and Kindler, but have received only monosyllables in reply. Manfred picks at his teeth with a small ivory toothpick. It is stiflingly hot. A machine gunner is positioned at the front of the vehicle, his hand on the MG's grip. There are four trucks behind us. Abruptly, the heavens open, a downpour, lightning leaping over the landscape. Manfred has Weber with him, a former forensics officer from Cologne, now regimental clerk. He keeps a small travelling case tucked under his right arm. His instruments? Manfred must fear the worst.

Weber's slight frame trembles. He drops his cigarette.

I grind it underfoot and offer him my Efkas. He says something, without taking one. It's cold now, visibility close to zero.

We pass Stützpunkt 43, heavily guarded by what appears to be Waffen-SS in camouflage and waterproof capes, the *Leibstandarte*. I thought they were further east, at the main front, Kursk. Are things moving that fast? Are the Russians already here in Belorussia, emerging from the forests in their heavy boots, with their Asiatic brains, their primitive battle cries? Our soldiers jump down from the trucks, man the flak, draw out the net. Men mill in the trenches and on the ridge, controlling the road. Hedgehogs are positioned further out, towards the swamps, the *puszcza*, the void.

Rain lashes at the tarp.

Manfred has left us. Weber shivers with cold.

We bide our time, waiting for it to end.

'Partisans,' Manfred says when eventually he returns and climbs back into the vehicle. 'Several attacks today.'

He raps his knuckles against the driver's helmet and we set off.

We are silent as we leave the last of the positions behind us and draw away into the terrain along an elevated gravel track. Nothing but green, broken only by white trunks as the fog rises after the rain.

– – –

Manfred jumps out.

Squeezing through the tarp, I see the burning vehicles, the dead strewn about, stripped naked, hanging from the vehicles, sprawled on the roadsides, heads submerged in ditchwater. It must have looked like a massacre from the air; black plumes rising up from the explosions, and flesh-coloured lumps.

Dogs sweep across a nearby field, jowls red with blood. They must come from the woods or the little village of broken-down farms a few hundred metres away. Our own dogs are in a frenzy, but will not be released. Not yet.

I bend down. There's an ID tag in the mud.

3rd SS-Panzer Division. Totenkopf. Steiner's division.

Everything else is gone: weapons, uniforms.

Manfred releases the safety catch of his PPK and fires into the air. He shouts out an order, points towards the running dogs with his gun. The machine gunner removes his leather helmet and waves it back at him. He looks dim-witted: big ears, small face, blinking eyes. He unleashes a round in the direction of the hurtling animals: jets of blood burst from their flesh, bullets ricochet off the vehicles, water leaping from the puddles. One of the dead is hit and the volley wrenches the corpse upwards, tearing it asunder.

I run up to him.

He hears nothing. I climb onto the footplate and slap him hard in the face.

'For God's sake, man! Stop!'

He turns his head towards me, shoulder wrenching from the recoil as he carries on firing, oblivious.

Then abruptly he stops and laughs.

His gums are receded, teeth brown with rot.

He can't be more than eighteen or nineteen years old.

Manfred is standing on a small mound.

He is waving at me frantically.

– – –

The open staff car smoulders, a shining black Mercedes in a ditch, behind it a trail of erratic skid marks in the wet clay. Manfred stands at the edge, looking down into the vehicle. There is a man in the passenger seat.

Something has hit him in the head, just above his shirt collar.

A large piece of shrapnel.

Leaning forward, I recognise the front teeth of Hauptsturmführer Heinz Breker. His distinctive gap.

I look up at Manfred. His eyes are fixed on something behind my back.

– – –

She is lying face-up in white fur, a feather boa slung around her neck. A white hat with a long red plume lies a metre away. Her white stockings are torn at the calves, her legs are alabaster, knickers at her ankles.

Her throat is taut, head turned to the side.

But I know who she is.

Frau Steiner, the actress. Gisela, née Lestrange. I saw her once at the Staatstheater in Hamburg, in '41. Steiner, the SS general, smoking, in the front row. Braying and bragging. The society couple from the pages of *Illustrierte*. Beauty and the Beast of Minsk. She was Gretchen in *Faust*. Who could forget her doll's face, her porcelain legs?

> *Bin ich doch so jung, so jung!*
> *Und soll schon sterben!*
> *Schön war ich auch, und das war mein Verderben.*
> *Nah war der Freund, nun ist er fern*

> *I'm still so young,*
> *So very young, and must so early die!*
> *Fair was I once, hence hath my ruin sprung,*
> *My love is now distant, he then was nigh . . .*

Fern? Or was it *weit?*

> *Nah war der Freund, nun ist er . . .*

Weit. It's *weit*. Afar, not distant.

Why did he bring her here, to the very edge of the world, in this grotesque finery?

Weber has unpacked his little case, laying his instruments out on a tartan blanket as if he were on a picnic. He sits on his haunches, stirring plaster of Paris in a small receptacle.

He has already put stakes in the ground and drawn twine between them, marking out the scene.

His cheeks have regained some colour. He is whistling.

I go towards him. He raises a hand.

'Don't touch anything,' he says.

'I've seen crime scenes before,' I tell him.

He carries on, head down, spreading the plaster of Paris evenly in a footprint. The grass has been trampled flat. There must have been quite a number of them, all come to look. The turf beneath her, visible between her legs, has been churned up where they manhandled her, turning her this way and that.

And then they gave her to the dogs.

When they were finished, they gave her to the dogs.

I go over to the other side.

Stare at her.

Her body, her face.

What is left, on a bed of white feathers.

The dog handlers are next to arrive, their charges straining at the leash. Manfred stands with his back turned, pointing towards a cluster of smallholdings a couple of hundred metres up the hill: coordinates 54° 15′ N, 26° 30′ E. The map says *Belize*.

– – –

'Why was the escort so small?' I ask. 'When the place is swarming with partisans?'

Manfred says nothing. He is standing at the kitchen window in the largest of the farmhouses. Hands on the windowsill, he leans forward and peers out into the yard. Two Sturmmänner are at the well, struggling with the long, stripped pole of the well sweep, pressing down on it with all their weight. I stand next to him and watch as eventually it tips and the rope quivers taut. There is something heavy at the other end. A moment later it is hoisted into view: a mottled pig, blood running from the snout, blood and water.

'Where is Steiner?' says Manfred, staring at the bloated animal. 'And where the hell are the locals?'

He turns round and scans the kitchen: a great clay oven, wooden tubs, tables, shelves stacked with tin plates. The icon has been taken, only a tallow candle remains in the empty niche. He throws up his arms. He knows as well as I do that they flee into the forests as soon as they catch wind of us.

He goes over to the stove. There's a loaf in the oven. He bends down and pats his hand on the crust.

'Still warm,' he says, and breaks off a chunk. 'Want some?'

– – –

'There's someone here,' a voice shouts from the garden.

We dash outside, down the step, kick open the gate into the tall grass, insects swarming in the air, heavy with the fusty smell of dungheap.

A trail has been tramped down in the grass. The beehives hum at the very bottom of the garden, as the ground slopes away, into wild rhubarb, a stream.

We hear shots, two or three: a shotgun. Manfred points to the right. Two Sturmmänner peel away behind the great leaves of the rhubarb. Two more go back in the other direction, in single file, releasing the safety catches of their carbines. Manfred slaps my face – *Wake up, for Christ's sake!* – then jabs a finger towards the hill, to the left of the shimmering grey barn.

Crouching down, we approach, taking position with our backs to the wall next to the barn door. Manfred steps swiftly into the open doorway, legs apart, firing arm extended, sweeping right to left, and back.

No one. A horse stands harnessed to a cart covered by a tarpaulin. It tosses its head and snorts.

I walk up to it, run my hand through its mane, pull aside the tarp. Inside are barrels of fish, lashed down securely. Manfred is ransacking the place, already over on the other side.

'Here!'

Standing beside him I can see the whole valley; the span of a ridge, a gulley, a river below. A man in a white smock is running through the tall grass, leaving a trail behind him of trampled sheaths and seed heads. His left hand holds a shotgun, and he is lugging a large bundle under his right arm. His stride is plunging and awkward, and yet he is getting away. Behind him, from both sides, our men close in. Ahead of him on the ridge stands Michael, the stumpy Oberscharführer from the Schwabenland, braced, a long iron bar, a crowbar perhaps, in his right hand. They lock eyes at the same moment. The running man looks back over his shoulder, and Michael descends the sandy slope in short, shuffling strides, directly into the man's blind spot.

In a moment they will meet.

Michael places one foot in front of the other, twists his hip, and draws back the crowbar with both hands.

Now.

I turn away.

– – –

I don't know who found the pulley and the chain.

The man is laid out on the straw in the stable, his feet bound, the chain slung over a beam. They hoist him up. His upper face has been obliterated. Only the lower jaw remains; shattered teeth and a gaping, blood-filled cavity at the throat. The man drips blood and a thick, dark liquid. The white smock is a mess.

Let him hang there.

Hang there and talk to himself.

Michael stands leaning against his crowbar, as if for a photograph.

'What do we do with this one, Manfred?'

Michael's even stumpier brother, Hans, has his hand on the head of a little girl in a white dress. She is perhaps five or six years old, and her hair has been put up in a white cap. Her face is smeared with blood, her dress spattered, from left to right.

Reconstruction: The girl was the bundle under the man's arm, the reason he was running so awkwardly. Michael was standing to his right, and when the crowbar impacted against the man's head, brain matter was ejected onto his daughter in this diagonal pattern.

'I thought she was . . .' Hans says when nobody answers. 'Only then she came to all of a sudden and went off down the hill . . . like a little machine . . .'

His voice trails off and he grins sheepishly. Like an idiot. Manfred turns towards me.

'What do you say, Heinrich? Fancy a bit of fatherhood?'

He steps up to the girl, unties the little ribbon under her chin. Her thick, yellow hair tumbles into his open hand. She rolls her eyes up like a doll.

'You've always wanted a daughter, haven't you? You're about the right age for it. And you'll never get anywhere with my sister . . .'

The girl stares into space. She is out of her senses, as though in another world. A blow to the head?

Her little hand slips into Manfred's. Her other hand is clenched. There is something in it.

A striped candy stick. She does not look at her father. Does she even know he is dangling there, his insides dripping?

– – –

'What do you say?' says Manfred. 'You've always been such a good person, Heinrich. Heart of gold.'

I say nothing. I am enraged.

'Can't hear you, Heinrich!'

'I didn't say anything,' I reply. '*Nothing.*'

'Very well.'

Manfred lets go of the girl's hand and steps backwards, a single pace.

Now she is alone, in the middle of the room.

Everyone is silent.

Manfred is behind her. She turns round and gazes at us all.

'We can't do this,' says Hans. 'Not like this . . .'

Manfred glares at him.

'Then you take her,' he says.

'No, I—'

The girl says something in Belorussian. She begins to unwrap the tight cellophane from her candy stick. Her small fingers struggle. Manfred draws his PPK and steps behind her back. He holds the gun down between his legs, as though to conceal it. He racks the slide to load the chamber. The girl turns and looks up at him.

She puts out her hand with the sweet in it.

He stops mid-movement.

She speaks to him.

'What?' he blurts, spit spraying from his mouth. His eyes are bloodshot. He raises the gun. His hand trembles. 'What? What is it?'

'She asks . . .' says a Hiwi, a tall, dark-haired Belorussian I only notice now, his skin taut across the cheekbones, sockets black and empty, 'She asks if you would help her with, what is it called . . . the paper . . .'

'What?'

'That's what she said,' the Hiwi says. 'She can't get it off.'

Manfred steps forward, snatches the sweet from the girl's hand, but is unable to remove the wrapper, his pistol in the air. He puts it back in its holster, picks at the cellophane until eventually it comes off. He is furious. He gives the sweet back to her. She takes it and puts it in her mouth.

'*Khotite yvidet tjeloveka . . .*'

'What now?' Manfred splutters.

'She asks if we want to see the man.'

– – –

The Hiwi bends down to her. She says her name is Etke. She is six and three quarters. She has been to the market with her father. In Koreletjy. His name is Boris. Where is he? She speaks mechanically. Hans's little machine. The Hiwi's translation is a stutter. She walks through the stable, crosses a narrow path and enters a barn with a steeply sloping roof. She leads us through stalls, we come to a halt in front of a large mound of hay.

A grubby foot protrudes, a corner of a trouser leg, a crushed ankle sodden with blood.

Hiwis step past me, they pull away the hay to reveal the man's head. He is gagged. His side gapes open, a brown slop has seeped from the waist of his trousers.

'Is it him?' Manfred shouts from outside.

'Yes. It's Steiner.'

– – –

Manfred is shaking the girl when I come back out. The Hiwi who was translating shrugs. The girl is crying. I go up to Manfred and put a hand on his arm.

'Let me question her,' I say.

'You?'

He looks at my hand, astonished.

Michael freezes, cigarette lifted to his mouth.

'You won't get anything out of her that way. You can see that, surely?'

I take the girl by the hand and beckon to the interpreter. He comes over.

'Say something to her,' I tell him.

'Like what?' he asks. 'What should I say?'

'Anything at all.'

– – –

'Heinrich,' says Manfred.

He has sat down beside the girl in the back of the commando vehicle. I am standing next to the machine gunner at the front, watching the Hiwis torch the village. We can already hear the rumble of the flames, the frenzied crackling of shingled roofs.

As the driver pulls out onto the gravel track, the first windows shatter.

'Heinrich,' Manfred says again.

'Yes?'

'I want you to find him.'

'What do you mean? Find who?'

'Whoever did this . . .'

I twist round to look at him, my arm resting on the side of the vehicle, an Efka smoking between my fingers.

'This is a war, Manfred. Anyone could have done it. There's a whole Red Army out there, for crying out loud.'

'Now you're being silly, Heinrich. A single person did this, one person.'

'We're not in Hamburg now, Manfred, this is . . .'

The girl looks out on the burning village. The blood and grime on her face has begun to flake away. In a few hours, her home will be a smouldering ruin.

'This is what?' says Manfred. Then, when I fail to answer: 'I don't understand you, Heinrich. I'm doing you a favour.'

'A favour?'

I inhale the cigarette smoke deep into my lungs, surprised by the bitterness in my voice.

'That's right, a favour. Steiner's killer, if we find him, could be big for us. And you love Hamburg. Law and order, logic, justice. All that stuff.'

'That stuff?'

'Yes, that *stuff*. You can proceed however you like.'

'Logic, order . . . Look over there,' I say with a nod in the direction of Belize. 'Is that order, justice, *logic*? Destroying evidence, killing witnesses?'

'It's logic of a higher order.'

'A higher order? Oh, for God's sake . . .'

'You do the logic, I'll do the higher order.'

He smiles now. There's a gleam in his eye that I've seen before, back in our school philosophy society. The sweeping statements he used to love: *the neo-Kantians are a bunch of homosexuals, objectivity is for weaklings*. But I know him: he can turn in a heartbeat.

'No.'

'Stop the vehicle,' he says, leaning forward and placing a hand on the driver's shoulder. 'Clear off for a minute. You too,' he says with a nod to the machine gunner when the man fails to react.

The young Schütze pulls in to the side and both men climb out.

'Heinrich,' says Manfred. 'Do you seriously think you have a say in the matter?'

'Like with the Feigl case, you mean?' I stare out at the two men who stand waiting a short distance away. One of them searches his pockets, the other offers him a cigarette.

'Who the hell is Feigl?'

'The man with the wood-shaving birds, Kindler's Jew. It was Breker who shot him. But who cares? Another SS pantomime, a bloody . . .'

I realise I've gone too far.

'Say that again?' says Manfred. 'What are you getting at?'

'Nothing,' I say. 'Nothing. I'm sorry . . . I apologise, for God's sake!'

He smiles and places his hand on Etke's head.

'Good,' he says. 'So. When you find him, when we've got him, I'm going to kill him. And Heinrich . . .'

'What?'

'Don't get sentimental about the girl.'

'What do you mean?'

'You know what I mean.'

The girl

The girl is seated on a chair in my office. She holds her hands in her lap and looks down at them. Her dress is sticky and bloodied. My adjutant, Wäspli, comes in with a fresh glass of cordial. There was fear in his eyes when he saw her fifteen minutes ago, but he came back with a little paper parasol that he put in her drink like a cocktail. After that he went away. An interpreter from Manfred's unit just arrived, a stocky incarnation of *Volksdeutsch*, who extends his hand towards me and introduces himself. I nod a curt greeting and go over to the girl, squat down in front of her and ask the interpreter to translate:

'Etke . . . that's your name, isn't it?'

She looks away as she answers.

'What did she say?'

'She says she wants to go home . . .'

'Tell her she can't just yet . . . tell her that.'

The interpreter says some words in Belorussian, modulating his voice.

'She says she wants to go home to her mother *now* . . .'

She begins to cry.

'Hello!' I raise my voice. 'Listen. Little girl.'

The interpreter shakes her, she bites his hand, he recoils, I grip his fist as he draws back his arm, then after a brief tussle he shouts and I shove him away.

'Get out of here,' I yell at him.

– – –

My house in Suwalska Street.

It's boiling hot. The girl is seated on my sofa in the spacious drawing room facing the street. She swings her legs. Masja, my housekeeper, has washed her, she is clean and sweet-smelling. She must know something, but is she aware of it?

I am sitting by the window, my Efkas on the windowsill.

My Masja comes in, curtsies, though I have expressly forbidden her to curtsy, and sits down next to the girl. She smoothes the child's dress, and pecks her on the cheek.

The girl begins to sing a song, her voice wavering and frail.

What the hell am I supposed to do?

I go over to the bureau, open a drawer and find a notepad and pen.

'Translate for me, Masja,' I say, and sit down in a chair in front of them.

The girl fidgets with a little ribbon of her dress, then looks up at me and says something.

'She says . . .' Masja has difficulty finding the words. 'She asks, where is my father? Do you know?'

'Yes,' I reply, standing up again. I go over to the window, pull a cigarette out of the packet, light up and survey the dusty street. 'Yes, I do.'

– – –

Later that afternoon, the mortuary in
the basement of Manfred's hospital.

Further down the corridor is Manfred's secret room with the iron bed.

Weber has a camera with him.

Manfred and I are standing slightly back from the autopsy slab, he with his arms folded, while I lean against the tiled wall. A young SS-Schütze stands self-consciously over by the door. The pathologist, Dr Weiss, an SS physician Manfred has had flown in from the infirmary at Vibetsk, nods to the two Hiwis, who lift Steiner onto the terrazzo slab. They salute awkwardly and leave.

Weber takes a photograph.

Manfred has seeds in his hands, and asks if I want some.

I don't.

'Have you got a statement for me from the girl?' he asks.

'No. Not yet.'

The limbs of the Obergruppenführer are stiff, his jaw is dislocated, dentures gone, only blackened stumps remain in the lower jaw. His upper body is bare, his shoes and socks have been removed.

There are three entrance wounds in the chest, ringed with black residue.

The arms are locked at the elbow joints, right hand clasped. Incipient rigor mortis.

There is a brown discoloration at the crotch of his unbuttoned uniform trousers.

Manfred spits out the streaked hull of a sunflower seed.

'When, then?' he says.

'Give me a couple of days.'

'A couple of *days*?'

The Obergruppenführer's feet are old and gnarled, but the toenails neatly clipped and filed.

On the toe tag someone has written 1–233 in ink. The name will not be released until the propaganda department has concocted a death more heroic.

'If you want reliable information,' I whisper, 'then, yes.'

'Let's see what he's got in his hand first, shall we?' Weiss cuts in.

We nod. Weiss braces his legs, then grips the clasped hand, bending at the waist as he puts his strength into it, prising the fingers open.

'Empty,' he says. 'Nothing at all.'

The flash illuminates the room as Weber takes another photograph. Weiss glares at him.

His brow is moist with perspiration.

'Let us begin,' he says with a nod to the young Schütze, and the boy, his face a smatter of freckles and fiery red lips, notes down in shorthand: 'Deceased has three entrance wounds at the thorax, all sufficient to cause death . . .'

Weiss leans forward and smells the wounds.

'Shot at close range, gunpowder smell, abrasion rings. No further injuries to torso.'

He picks up a pair of scissors, proceeds to Steiner's feet and cuts open the trousers, removes them, stiffens.

'Come here, Hauptsturmführer,' he says softly. Then, when Manfred hesitates: 'Come here, please.'

Manfred steps over to the slab, his head recoils as he sees what Weiss is pointing at. They exchange brisk whispers, agitated. Weiss turns towards me.

'They've mutilated him,' he says. 'Cut off his—'

'This goes no further,' Manfred interrupts.

He darts towards the Schütze and tears the notepad from his hand.

'Out!' he commands.

The boy is at once seized with terror, his eyes wide, a bloom of red flushes his cheeks, a haemorrhage of embarrassment.

'You have seen nothing, you were never here,' says Manfred, spelling it out. 'Do you understand me?'

'Yes.'

'Sure?'

'Yes.'

'Good, now get out.'

The Schütze gathers his things, knocking over the carbine he has propped up in the corner by the window. The gun clatters against the tiled floor; he picks it up and scuttles away.

'You, too,' Manfred says to Weber. 'Leave the camera here.'

Manfred follows him out and locks the door behind him. Weiss has covered up the groin area with a piece of cloth.

'What?' I ask, but receive no answer. 'If I'm supposed to find out who did this, you'll have to tell me what happened.'

Neither of them speaks. Weiss has gone over to a table and starts arranging his instruments. Manfred pulls a cigarette from his breast pocket and lights up.

'Please refrain from smoking in here,' says Weiss.

'I smoke wherever I want,' Manfred replies. 'Now tell us what the hell they did to Hubert.'

Weiss picks out a pair of long, steel pincers. From a leather case he takes a head lamp and straps it on. He returns to the slab, switches on the lamp, adjusts the angle, and with the pincers proceeds to investigate Steiner's groin, its flaps of skin and lumps of coagulated blood.

'I *insist* you put out your cigarette,' he says. 'Smell is an important part of the procedure.'

Manfred hesitates for a second before furiously grinding the cigarette underfoot.

'And you're taking notes?' he says with a nod in my direction.

'Yes,' I reply.

'So what's the verdict?' Manfred says after I pick up the notepad from the windowsill.

'Well, it's certainly not *lege artis*,' Weiss says. 'There's been massive bleeding. Gaping wound at the scrotum. That's with a *c*—'

'I know how to spell it,' I tell him.

'Good . . . then let's proceed. Both testes absent. Were his testicles found at the scene?' Weiss inquires.

'No,' says Manfred. 'No, they were not.'

'This was done with a very sharp instrument indeed, probably a scalpel or a sharpened knife of some sort,' Weiss goes on. 'The wound edges are clean and precise, though as I said the incisions are not *lege artis*.'

'So will someone tell me what *lege artis* means,' Manfred says.

'We're dealing with an absence of surgical method,' Weiss replies without looking up, without irony, persisting with his pincers.

'No injuries to the remaining groin or thighs. And no injuries to the hands or arms that would accord with any struggle . . .'

Manfred steps closer, purses his lips.

'So what are you saying? That Steiner cut off his own balls?'

'I can't say for sure. But no, I shouldn't think so.'

Manfred tightens his jaw. Weiss continues the examination. He lifts the Obergruppenführer's penis with the pincers, his long face peering from all angles, a finger nudging his spectacles up the bridge of his nose.

'Severe injury to glans penis,' he says. 'Skin lacerated from glans, along corpus, almost as far as radix penis . . .'

'Weiss,' says Manfred, suddenly raising his hand. 'I want to know one thing.'

Weiss looks up.

'Yes?'

'What was the sequence?'

'Sequence?'

'Yes. Did they . . . mutilate him first and shoot him afterwards, or . . .'

'The massive bleeding would indicate . . .'

'Indicate . . . indicate!'

'They tortured him while he was still alive,' Weiss says. 'Any of the three shots to his chest would have killed him instantly and prevented such massive bleeding.'

We leave together. Manfred has already lit up.

He jabs a finger at me.

'I want that girl's statement *today*, Heinrich.'

— — —

Home, in front of the drawing-
room door, half an hour later.

They had run out of ribbons at the Nur für Deutsche shop, so I twist the brown paper bag into a little parcel before going in:

candy sticks, lollipops, sugar pearls. I clear my throat and open the door.

Etke is standing with her back to me, looking up at Masja, who shakes a record from its hard cardboard sleeve and puts it on the gramophone. She issues a brief instruction to the child, who then lifts the needle and places it on the revolving disc, to scratchy silence before the music comes on.

She turns and is startled to see me.

I am standing with the paper bag as a storm of violins starts up.

Strauss. *Die Frau ohne Schatten*, the woman without a shadow.

Emperors and the empresses.

I hold the paper bag out towards her.

'Tell her it's from her father,' I say to Masja. 'Tell her that she'll see him soon.'

– – –

INTERROGATION NOTES 1

We were at the market at Koreletjy . . . when we got back everything was quiet. Normally you can hear the dogs, but it was quiet. Then we heard shots and my daddy carried me up to the hayloft. We didn't have time to hide where we usually do.

Where do you usually hide?

In the tar kiln down by the stream, or we've got this sort of room . . . only my daddy says I'm not allowed to tell . . . Where is he?'

He's in the hospital . . .

When is he coming back?

Soon, if you help us. We need you to help us, so we can
help him.

(Note location. "Tar kiln". Interrogation suspended
17.45. Hstf. M. Schlosser contacted. Interrogation resumed
17.55)

— — —

INTERROGATION NOTES 2

Etke, tell me what happened when you came home from the
market at Koreletjy.

The men came and we hid in the hayloft. They didn't speak
Belorussian. One of them spoke Polish, like my uncle.

Did any of them speak Russian?

No. I could tell it wasn't Russian.

Could you see them?

Not at first. We could only hear them. There were a lot of
voices. They were very angry. I was frightened. But then I
heard Uncle Vitek. So then I crawled over.

Who's Uncle Vitek?

He lives out in the woods . . . with my cousins Pawel and
Ryszard. They're fighting for the Jews. My daddy says it's
because they like their women, and their gold jewellery.

Where does Uncle Vitek live?

In Koreletjy. Out in the woods. My aunt Anna lives in
Koreletjy with Karol and Agnezka.

What are they called besides Vitek and Anna?

Czapski.

(Note: Anna and Vitek Czapski, Koreletjy. Children Pawel
and Ryszard)

32

That's very good, Etke. We'll soon have your father out of
hospital, you'll see. Should we go back to what happened in
the barn? You said you crawled over. Over where, exactly?

We were in the hayloft. My daddy tried to drag me back,
but I wanted to say hello to Vitek, so I crawled over. I
was ever so quiet, because I wanted to surprise him, but
when I got there and could see them down below they were
hitting the man. He was bleeding, and I was too frightened
to say anything.

Who was the man?

He was tall, with grey hair. They'd taken his shirt off.
His face was all dirty (Note: victim Hubert Steiner). They
were hitting him and I couldn't see Vitek.

Wasn't he there?

They had scarves over their faces.

Scarves over their faces . . . all of them?

No, not the one with the knife. He had a sack on his head
with holes in for his eyes. He was at the back. He had this
big knife, like at the butcher's. He kept sharpening it. The
others were hitting the man, and shouting at him.

Could you hear what they were shouting?

No, I couldn't understand.

Did Uncle Vitek say anything?

No, only the one who was in charge. He kept saying the
same thing. There were two of them holding the tall German
and then he said a word and the German had to say it too,
only he couldn't. And every time he said it wrong he went up
and hit him very hard in the tummy.

Did you hear the word?

It was something with an S.

Something with an S?

Sjip or Sjibko. It sounded like _fast_ . . . something with spikes . . .

Spikes? Fast? How do you mean?

He spoke funny. Maybe it was Jew language.

Jew language?

I don't know, it sounded like the Jews at the market. My daddy says they killed Jesus. It wasn't Belorussian they spoke. It sounded so horrid . . .

(Note after conferring with interpreter: _Sjibkij_ or _Sjibko_ = fast, violent _Sjip_ = thorn or spike. As in roses, spiked shoes.)

It's important you think hard, Etke. What happened then?

They kept hitting the man. No one said anything. I was too frightened to move, I was scared to breathe. All I could hear was them hitting him, until the air went out of him. Like when Hanna snorts.

Hanna?

My horse.

And then what happened?

Then he took his shirt off.

Who?

The man. The one who was in charge. The man with the sack over his head. He was sweating. He had a drawing on his shoulder like I've seen in Koreletjy, the beggar Mirko has them as well.

What do you mean? Tattoos, is that it?

Yes, tattoos. He had them on his shoulder, and up above his bottom.

What did they look like?

Above his bottom he had two big scary eyes. I felt like they were looking at me. I thought they were going to find me. They were looking up at me when he leaned forward and used the knife . . .

He used the knife?

When he used the knife and did that to the man. He screamed. I've never heard anyone scream as loud as that. And then it was all quiet. I was afraid the bird had told them where I was.

The bird?

The one he had on his shoulder.

Did he have a tattoo of a bird on his shoulder?

Yes. And when he was finished he put his shirt on again, and then they all went away.

Do you remember what the bird looked like?

Do you want me to draw it?

Can you do that?

Yes.

And what did you do then?

Then we waited until we couldn't hear anything any more. My daddy wanted to hide him, but then we heard you coming. And then we ran.

(Note: We arrived no more than minutes after the perpetrators left the barn. Note: drawing attached.)

— — —

Notes, attached LZ-132-567-A-I (Steiner), cc Hstf. M. Schlosser

Prob. looking for a gang of mixed race, likely Jews, certainly three Poles, Vitek (father), Ryszard and Pawel (sons) Czapski, address Rosenberg Allée (formerly Boulevard Kalininogo) 12, Koreletjy (residents Anna (mother), Agnezka

(daughter), Karol (son) Czapski). Not known if household in
Belize is involved. Since witness heard no Russian, perps
most likely not Soviet partisans, though poss. Polish Armia
Krajova.

Re. group leader [henceforth perp.] 2 tattoos observed,
viz. one pair of eyes above loin, one cockerel/hen on shoulder
(drawing attached). Witness states "like Mirko in Koreletjy".
Perp. moreover observed speaking "Jew language" i.e. Yiddish.

Victim Hubert Steiner tortured. Witness believed him
subjected to a test, or else interrogated as to some matter
to which vict. unable or unwilling to provide satisfactory
answer.

Question: Why were perps masked? Afraid of witnesses? Or
WERE THEY UNKNOWN TO EACH OTHER?

— — —

Masja and Etke are by the brambles at the hedge. Etke picks
the berries quickly, in a skilled manner, and collects them in the
apron Masja has wound around her waist. I sit in the conservat-
ory and read the bible, searching for a specific passage. Every
now and then I look up and watch them.

It is a fine picture.

Etke has been sitting in here drawing for hours, the eyes and
the bird, over and over.

Now she is outside in the sun.

I see myself sitting, considering the picture.

Suddenly someone calls out to her from the left, from the
road. Masja points, getting to her feet.

I walk to the open door and see it is Manfred.

He rests his hand on Etke's head, strokes her hair, and gives
her something, a bag. Sweets, perhaps.

Majsa and Etke come inside, while Manfred takes the long way, round the outside of the house, to the front.

Masja is rosy-cheeked, flustered with excitement. The little girl holds her hand, and it is she who gives me the bag from Manfred.

'Herr Hauptsturmführer gave us this. He says he is to say hello from Aunt Anna.'

I hear her say the same to Etke. I cannot make out the words, only the name, *Dadja Anna*. I untie the ribbon around the bag and spread out the contents on the glass-topped table.

'What are they?' Masja asks, as curious as the girl.

They look like dried apple cores, the colour of pale flesh.

'Are they sweets?'

'No,' I say. 'They're not.'

They are larynges, rinsed in water. One adult, two smaller.

Aunt Anna, and the cousins Karol and Agnezka.

– – –

I close the French windows.

I had no idea what to say to Masja; I shouted at her and sent them away. Etke cried, Masja shielded her. Now Manfred is sitting in my wicker chair with his legs crossed.

He has lit another cigarette.

I am furious. Manfred picks up the bible from the table and weighs it in his hand.

'Spare me the sermon. I know what you're going to say,' he says.

'And what would that be?'

'That it's brutal and base, but you're a sentimental fool, Heinrich.'

'I gave you a crucial lead and you destroyed it, and now . . .'

'They knew nothing.'

'And that's something you can be sure of, is it?'

'As a matter of fact, it is. And if they did know anything, I'm sure this famous Uncle Vitek will come looking for them. We've got men posted in the building, so congratulations on a fine piece of work, Heinrich. But you need to give me more. We need more. *Spiked shoes*, Jew language . . . some beggar from Koreletjy with eyes on top of his arse . . . What's going on, Heinrich?'

'I think she's been very precise indeed. Anyway, she's a child, what more do you expect?'

I go over to him and take the bible from his hands. I look up the page I'd marked, find the verse and read it to him:

'*And the Gileadites took the passages of Jordan before the Ephraimites: and it was so, that when those Ephraimites which were escaped said, Let me go over; that the men of Gilead said unto him, Art thou an Ephraimite? If he said, Nay; Then said they unto him, Say now Shibboleth: and he said Sibboleth: for he could not frame to pronounce it right. Then they took him, and slew him at the passages of Jordan: and there fell at that time of the Ephraimites forty and two thousand.*'

'And what the hell has that got to do with anything?'

'The Book of Judges, chapter twelve, verses five and six. Etke says the leader wanted Steiner to say something with a *sjib* or *sjip* sound . . . She also said it was Jew language . . .'

'So what?'

'He didn't say *sjip* or *sjipko* – it was nothing to do with fast, or spiked shoes. What he said was *shibboleth*. And shibboleth is Hebrew and means ear of grain. Or river. But on top of that it's a sound too . . . *sji* . . .'

'Ear of grain? *Sji*?'

'It's a password, or a code. If you can say it, it means you're Jewish . . .'

'What are you on about?'

'Think, Manfred. Steiner's injuries.'

'What are you saying? Are you implying they circumcised him?'

'That's what I suspect, yes.'

Manfred jumps to his feet and walks over to the window. He throws up his hand.

'Like a . . . a fucking *Yid*?'

– – –

The jar is sealed with wax, with a glass lid. Dr Weiss holds it up for us to see, turning it in the light. He has removed a piece of the groin and the perineum with it, a swirl of flesh, a little whirlpool in the alcohol, and now we see the deep incision around the glans and along the shaft, the empty scrotum.

'Perhaps,' Weiss says. 'It's a possibility. I perform a number of circumcisions in Munich, at the hospital there, purely medical grounds, and I must say the commencement . . .'

Weiss puts the jar down on the table again, crouches down and points a finger at the penis head, his eyes swimming in the glass, finger grotesquely enlarged.

'The commencement, the manner of the initial incision, corresponds very closely to a circumcision. But then . . .'

'Then what?'

'Then we have sheer rage, the cuts are impure . . .'

We stand for a moment looking at the pale, purple organ in the jar. Weiss has affixed a label to the glass on which he has written *1–233* in ink, Steiner's code. To which cabinet of curiosities will it be consigned? Weiss's own study, perhaps?

Or will future medical students back home in Germany traipse along behind some consultant with his hands behind his back to be shown *Sexual punishment, Eastern Front*? Will they stand and scratch their necks and exchange whispers with their peers? Will they snigger? Will they ever know who it is? That this is Dr Hubert Steiner, the Obergruppenführer, the Beast of Minsk, with more than 70,000 dead Israelites on his calling card, teeth knocked out and a gag stuffed in his mouth, knees bleeding, ankles broken, three shots to the chest, mutilated by a Jew? Did he pray for his life? Should I demand it be seized as evidence? Should it be sent to Berlin for the state funeral, in its own casket of zinc?

'So what you're saying,' I venture, 'is that we're dealing with someone who is able to perform a circumcision, but who is not necessarily a surgeon?'

'That, I think, would be my conclusion,' says Weiss.

'A mohel?'

Manfred, silent until now. He is standing behind me with a cigarette in his hand. He drops it to the floor at the same instant and crushes it beneath the toe of his boot. He unbuttons his pistol holster, takes out his PPK, removes the magazine and checks its contents.

'What's a mohel?' I ask.

Manfred leaves without reply.

— — —

The ghetto is completely silent, broken only by the loudspeaker vehicle issuing Manfred's threats, thin and metallic. There is no one out on the cobbled streets, no one in the shops, or in the windows. No one, though 3,000 people inhabit these three streets, and it is usually a tumultuous bustle of life, of Jews.

I can see the trail Manfred has left behind him. They lie on their stomachs, arms stretched out, legs protruding through doorways, long streaks of blood spattered across the cobbles. Shots ring out, somewhere to my left, not far from Feigl's workshop.

– – –

Tovner's bakery, second floor.

There are three of them – two men and a woman – on their knees with their hands behind their necks, staring at the wall, staring at the floor. Two already lie to the far right, their blood issuing out into the room, trickling crimson. Manfred's voice is hysterical, he waves his PPK. Michael is seated on a chair. In front of him is a bottle. He wipes spit from his mouth with his thumb. Hans leans against the windowsill. Manfred fails to notice me; he goes up to the woman and puts the pistol to her neck.

'Where *is* he!'

The woman says nothing, she appears to be catatonic, the petrification that precedes death, this state without name, in which a person loses all bearings and becomes mute, as stupid as death itself.

She squeezes her eyes tight shut, as if she already feels the blow to her neck.

'*Where is he!*'

'Manfred,' I say.

He turns slowly towards me, his eyes distant. He smiles, turns back and pulls the trigger. The two men recoil as the projectile slams her head against the wall.

'Manfred, for God's sake!' I yell.

'*What?*' he says.

'This is meaningless,' I say, more subdued, and step towards him, making eye contact. 'These people know nothing. You don't even know what to ask them. We'll go to Koreletjy and look for those tattoos.'

He lowers his pistol, his body relaxes. Michael and Hans stare into space, impervious.

'You're right,' he says. 'Come on, let's go.'

Michael twists the lid back on the bottle and gets to his feet. Hans is already on his way down the stairs. Manfred raises his pistol again.

Two swift reports.

I slam the door as we leave.

Tattoos

Koreletjy

We find our man, Mad Mirko, behind the church in Koreletjy, a two-hour drive to the south.

His eyes radiate insanity, his face leathered by sun, a wrinkled landslide, mouth full of blackened gums. He gibbers and slurs, tosses his head, making sweeping, empty gestures with his hands, and then he sees an opening and is off in his flimsy shoes, a shuffle more than a run, around the back of the church. Michael drags him back by the arm, deposits him in front of us.

He smiles vacantly.

Hiwi: 'He wants to know if we've got four kopeks – four kopeks for a tallow candle?'

Manfred looks at me. I rummage in my pocket and produce a large, shiny Reichsmark. Mirko snatches the coin from my hand, and conceals it in the folds of his clothing. Michael steps towards him and I stop him with a flat hand against his chest:

'Give him some of that rotgut . . .' I say, nodding towards the bottle.

'What?'

'Do as he says,' says Manfred.

Michael hands him the bottle; Mirko tears it from his hand, downs the contents in one, belches, and glances sideways at us.

'Ask if we can see his tattoos,' I tell the Hiwi.

They exchange a few words, Mirko's face lights up, he lifts his coat and brown homespun shirt, unties the cord around his trousers. His belly is white as chalk, skin covered in grimy tattoos, towers, crucifixes, a grinning devil.

'What are they?' I ask the Hiwi.

'Vorkuta,' the Hiwi says.

'What?'

'Gulag . . . Siberia . . . these are prison tattoos. He's a thief, not political.'

The old man puts his hands out now, they too are tattooed, symbols etched across the backs of his hands, fingers and knuckles; even his wrists are covered. The Hiwi examines him.

'Fifteen years inside . . . four prisons.'

'How can you tell?'

'They write their history in the tattoos: the cross here is for the Peter and Paul Cathedral in Leningrad, before the Revolution . . .'

I take out the notepad with Etke's drawings in it, flick back through the pages until I find them: the eyes and the birds. I point, and nod to the Hiwi:

'Ask him if he knows what these mean . . .'

Mirko takes the notepad, turns it in his hands, clicks his tongue.

He begins to laugh.

'What's he saying?'

'Cockerel . . . It's a cockerel.'

'I can see that.'

The Hiwi asks him again, more words are exchanged.

'This tattoo is enforced,' says the Hiwi.

'Enforced?'

'Yes, how do you say, one of the strong inmates has carved it into his back with a razor blade, like the eyes . . . he is a sex slave, a slave of slaves,' he explains.

'What?'

'It means the man who killed Steiner was probably an untouchable.'

'A what?'

'An outcast – the lowest, humiliated.'

– – –

Manfred pulls up outside a whitewashed house, a few hundred metres from the edge of woods on the outskirts of Koreletjy.

He puts his finger to his lips, presses the handle down and shoves the door open with the toe of his boot when it sticks. We enter, into the cool air of a scullery, then stand and listen. Not a sound. Manfred nudges me on.

The kitchen is warm from summer. It smells of cardamom and lime.

At the rear, on the bench, concealed from the street and the scullery, sit two Sturmmänner. Manfred leans forward to one of them.

Etke's aunt stands with her back to us, whispers something to a girl who must be about seven or eight. The boy is tied to the table leg. In two strides, Manfred is over the Czapski woman, pulling down the zip at her back. The woman does not flinch. He exposes her shoulders, runs his hand along the shoulder blades. She is rigged up with wires. He slaps her buttock and she turns, her arm covering up her breasts, and I see her face is gnarled and bruised. There are some marks, burns perhaps, on her breastbone. Manfred has attached an explosive charge to her abdomen, fastened with a padlock. He lets go and nods to her, she pulls up her dress and watches him as he lifts up the blouse of the girl, Agniezka, who is in the same apparatus. The boy glances away when I look at him, he is no more than two or three years old but has already learned never to look a German in the eye. I turn my face to the two Sturmmänner, who shake their heads, one of them draws up his shoulders in a shrug and spreads out his arms, unable to stifle a snigger. The other one holds a detonator in a round, soft hand.

Manfred turns to me. He pats my cheek. *Come with me*, he whispers.

— — —

We are in the alley outside. Manfred slaps me on the shoulder and can keep quiet no longer:

'Heinrich, for Christ's sake. You didn't really think I'd killed them and cut out their gullets?'

'Actually, I did.'

'Jesus. I know you think we SS are thick, but not even we are that stupid. What does that tell me about you, I wonder?'

'About *me*?'

'That you're easily fooled. I give you a bag of pig's throats for your little girl, and straight away you've got me down as wiping out her entire family!'

'It seemed like the most likely scenario.'

'Exactly. And now you want me to believe we're looking for some perverse Jewish *zek* with a cockerel on his shoulder. Is that another likely scenario?'

'It may be.'

We go through the alley, its low walls backed by gardens, with vines crawling up the gable ends. Manfred pulls a packet of Efkas out of his breast pocket and offers me one. He cups his hands around the flame and he gives me a light.

'At Belize you said Steiner's escort was small,' he says. 'What did you mean, exactly?'

'Just what I said, a company, hardly more. And that parade vehicle. What was it for? Who were they trying to impress?'

'It got me wondering.'

'About what?'

He says nothing, but steps into a garden and returns a few moments later with a handful of peas.

'It got me wondering if it was all some kind of set-up.'

I shake my head as he offers me one.

'Is that what you think?'

'Steiner,' he says after a brief pause, 'Steiner taught me *everything*. I don't mean . . .'

He throws up his hand. At once his expression changes, becomes gentler:

'Not this . . . butchery . . . No, the *spiritual* side.'

'Spiritual? In Einsatzgruppe B?'

'What do you mean by that?'

'It's hardly a secret, what you did out there, Manfred.'

'You wouldn't understand, Heinrich.'

'What wouldn't I understand?'

'You wouldn't understand what it means to be *consistent*. Every truth is consistent . . . without mercy.'

He draws his weapon, holding it in the flat of his palm, curling his fingers around it. Then he raises his arm, and points the gun at me.

'Heinrich.'

'What?'

'You're not being fooled, are you?'

'How do you mean?'

'You have looked into who organised that escort, haven't you?'

'Yes.'

'And who was it?'

'It was you, Manfred.'

The pistol is still pointed at me. He weighs it in his hand, index finger on the trigger.

'Have you proposed?' he asks.

'What?'

'To my sister. Have you?'

'No . . .'

'Why not?'

'Put the gun away.'

'Have you?'

'Put it away. Now.'

'Don't you think I know?'

'Know what, Manfred?'

'It's so easy to get swallowed up by all this . . . *shit*. To lose one's grip. Are you losing your grip?'

'No.'

He sticks the semi-automatic back in its black holster and buttons down the flap.

'Then you must know you can't keep the girl.'

'What's the girl got to do with it?'

'Everything, Heinrich. Everything.'

He smiles.

He has tiny teeth. They look like baby teeth, white as chalk and almost transparent.

– – –

My office, Lida, police headquarters, the following afternoon.

Wäspli pours me a cup of scalding hot tea.

'They say Minsk. Minsk is the most likely place if you're looking for a *zek*, a Gulag prisoner. They've got most of the NKVD archive there, managed to save it. I've already made an appointment with them.'

'Good. Thank you, Wäspli.'

He turns to leave; he is fat around the hips, giving him a feminine curve under his grey uniform trousers and green jacket, making the black belt around his waist look anything but manly.

'There was something else,' I say.

'Oberleutnant?'

'The girl.'

'The girl?'

'Yes, our witness from Belize. Etke. What are we to do about her?'

Wäspli blushes, smiles stiffly and looks down at the desk.

'Or would you like to take care of her, Alfred?'

'What? Me?'

'No, perhaps not.'

When later he comes back I am unable to make eye contact with him, his soft hands fumble.

'Just sign here.'

I don't know how he found out her full name.

```
SURNAME(S): Steiger
FIRST NAME(S): Sophie  NICKNAME (WHERE APPLIC.): Etke
DESTINATION:
```

We glance up at each other as we consider the empty field.

'It has to be filled in by SS-Dienststelle Lida,' he says. 'They say they can come and collect her in two days.'

'All right, Wäspli. Thank you,' I say, and sign my name.

— — —

'Wäspli, come in here a minute.'

He enters with his briefcase, coat over his arm, ready to go.

He is still looking at the floor, blushing.

'Come here and have a drink with me.'

I pull open the drawer and take out another glass, twist off the cork and indicate the chair opposite.

'Sit down, it's good stuff, from Hungary . . .'

He sits down, perches on the edge with the glass in one hand.

'*Prost*, Wäspli . . .'

'*Prost*, Herr Oberleutnant.'

'Good, don't you think?'

'Very good indeed. French?'

'Hungarian . . .'

'Hungarian, yes, you said . . .'

What is it with him? He seems tense. He must be at least fifteen years older than me, and yet I have to draw everything out of him as though he were a schoolboy. He fingers the lip of the glass with his thumb. Are the older generation now afraid of us?

'Wäspli, what did you do exactly, in civilian life?' I ask, and we chink glasses. 'I'm assuming you weren't a policeman?'

'I was a clarinettist.'

'A clarinettist, indeed! Where?'

'Leipzig . . . the symphony orchestra.'

'Clarinettist! I'd never have guessed!'

'No, I suppose not . . .'

He continues to gaze into his drink, swirling the liquid around the glass with a slight movement of his hand.

'Are you married?'

'No, never got round to it.'

'Then who looks after your children?'

'Sorry?'

'Wäspli, look at me . . .'

He lifts his gaze, his face is large and loose, his open mouth seems too soft and fleshy for the delicate mouthpiece of a clarinet, its bamboo reed. I try to picture his large hands together with tone holes and finger keys, fumbling with the zip of a woman's dress, clasping her hips, unhooking a bra, patting a child on the head. What kind of a man is this?

'A joke, Wäspli, I'm sorry . . .'

'No, it was funny. You got me there . . . not married, who looks after the children, ha, ha . . .'

'Sometimes, Alfred,' I say, more seriously now, 'sometimes everything back home seems like another world entirely, wouldn't you say?'

'I beg your pardon, Oberleutnant?'

'Call me Heinrich, please. No need to stand on ceremony.'

I am being rather too loud, I swing my glass towards his, standing up to lean across the desk, and we drink to it, awkwardly as I insist we link arms.

'And sometimes we do things . . .' I say as we sit down again, '. . . things that perhaps might be hard to explain . . . but then, one has to distinguish, wouldn't you agree?'

'Indeed . . .'

'One must consider . . . the greater scheme of things . . .'

I almost bite off my tongue as I realise I am about to say *the higher order*, and trail off.

'I'm not sure I understand. Is the Oberleutnant dissatisfied with me?'

'No, not at all—'

'If I'm doing something wrong—'

'Wäspli, you're not doing anything wrong. Please don't think that.'

'Thank you, Herr Oberleutnant. You had me worried. If I'm honest, I'm not much of a soldier at heart . . .'

'You're doing a splendid job, Wäspli, and if there's anything you need, you know you can always come to me. Do you understand? Now, how about we find ourselves some dinner . . .'

'Yes. Thank you. But I'm afraid tonight's a bit . . .'

He pats his briefcase.

'To the telegraph office, yes. Work. Always work, am I right? I understand. Enjoy your evening, Wäspli.'

He gets to his feet, nods and leaves.

– – –

I do not go home. I amble through the streets, sit on a bench in the park with a bottle from the shop, watch the sparrows and the straight-shouldered women auxiliaries. They come here on their breaks, it's just below the civil commission offices, to smoke cigarettes in small clusters, their faces smooth and lustrous.

Dear E

   Thank you for the parcel. Today has been ~~strange~~ good.
   The weather too is go

I tear the page from the pad and take out Eline's photograph from my wallet. She insisted it was the one I had to take with me *to this raging war*. It is far too posed, taken at Mertesacker's studio on Alsterdamm; in semi-profile, her hair dyed red like the film star Zarah Leander, lips glistening black, with deep eyeshadow, too much rouge and lacquer; glancing away. It was taken just before the gala at the students' association last year, during the blackout, when she wore her big black dress with the puffed sleeves, like Leander's in *Die grosse Liebe*; she had been at the professor's sherry, her cheeks were flushed, and she kept flicking open her fan as we went up the stairs.

Do you think the miracle will happen, Heinrich?
How do you mean?
That life will be wonderful?

I turn the photograph over. The writing is scribbled hastily, a girlish hand.

The nymphs have left the golden forests
Kisses
E

I look at her again. Zarah Leander.

Dear Eline

   Today I signed a piece of paper and a child will die because of it. No, not just a child. She had a name. Etke. ~~Etke. Etke.~~

~~Etke.~~ I feel compelled to write and tell you this. I don't know how to

I place my hand over the page when a woman sits down next to me. She must have crept up from behind, I failed to notice her among the other auxiliaries. She is small, a telegraphist – the electric sparks on her sleeve. She stretches out her legs, points her brown laced shoes. She can't be more than twenty.

'Sorry,' she says. 'I didn't realise . . .'

'That's all right,' I tell her. 'It's nothing official.'

'Can I have a swig? What is it?'

'I'm not sure. Kirsch.'

'Kirsch?'

'Kirsch. It's quite acceptable.'

She puts the bottle to her mouth and takes a sip. She has a delicate mouth. Fine, broad cheekbones.

'Ugh,' she says.

'Ugh,' I say.

'Actually, I'm quite cross.'

'With me?'

'No, not with you. I don't even know you!'

'Who are you cross with, then?'

'Frida . . . the tall one over there, the one in red lipstick and gloves. She's got dry hands.'

She points. I can tell they are watching us.

'She says I've got a singular face. That's what she said. *Singular*. But that's the same as odd, isn't it? Can I ask you something; do you think she's right? . . . Go on, look at me!'

'I can't say.'

'Is it my chin? I know it's got a dimple in it . . .'

She holds her hand upright against her chin, dividing her face; the precise centre-parting of her hair, her small, blue eyes.

'It makes it look sort of . . .'

'Dimpled?'

'Exactly!'

I smile and put away the notepad in my jacket.

'You're making fun of me.'

'A bit, perhaps.'

'Am I being stupid?'

'No, I don't think you're being stupid.'

'Singular, then?'

'I wouldn't know.'

'You don't know much, do you, Herr!'

She pulls a packet of cigarettes from her breast pocket; it takes her a while to tap one out and light up.

'Were you writing to your sweetheart earlier?' she asks, picking a shred of tobacco from her lip.

'Yes.'

'Are you engaged?'

'Why do you ask?'

'So you aren't, then?'

'How can you tell?'

'I saw you were scribbling things out. Proper sweethearts know exactly what to write. The ones who are engaged; it's all . . . flowers, flowers, flowers and oh, my darling . . . alas, he's in Belgrade . . . While husbands, they just fill the page with what they've had for dinner and how are the kids. That's what Renate says anyway, and she should know, she's married. But you cross out. You must have run into problems! Maybe you want to finish with her? Is that what you want?'

'No, it certainly isn't.'

'You love her then? You'd say you loved her?'

'Yes.'

'So what's the problem?'

'There is no problem.'

'Oh, I get it . . . you're *that* type.'

'Who's fond of his sweetheart?'

'No, who wants to confide . . .'

'What do you mean by that?'

'Do you really think it'll make her happy? Knowing what's going on out here?'

She turns her face towards me, closes her eyes as if she is concentrating. She opens them again, and purses her lips.

'You can confide in me. I know how it is . . . come on, Herr Polizei . . . open up . . . it'll do you good. Then afterwards . . .'

'Afterwards?'

She smiles, lips curled back over small, white teeth.

'Yes, afterwards I can be . . . the one . . .'

Her head flies back but she makes no sound as the flat of my hand strikes her left cheekbone. I get to my feet, gather my things, and walk away. Her face is buried in her hands – one of her friends runs towards her as I turn my head to look back.

– – –

I am seething with rage and shame as I stop by the Nur für Deutsche and buy a bottle of Poire William, taking a swig even as I put the money on the counter. On Skzkolna Street I go into the Wehrmacht cinema in time for the early screening. The name NIRVANA can still be seen on the facade in Polish, Russian and Yiddish. The theatre is a hum of heat and boredom, flies. I drink, and skim through an abandoned copy of *Das Reich* before the film.

Bulletins from Kursk. The push is progressing well in the south. Hoth has achieved the targets, new names for us to learn, new crosses on the map; on the Northern Front we are encountering fierce resistance. Generaloberst Model must have his work cut out. I drink as the curtain goes up to newsreel clamour, endless marching. A Turkish general admires German weaponry at the Southern Front as I drink. A partisan operation in Minsk. I drink some more. They have bombed the cathedral at Cologne – it gapes to the skies.

I try to read my letter in the dark, and drink. It will never get past the censor.

Do you really think it will make her happy?

I jump to my feet and stride out.

– – –

The light is fading by the time I get back to the park. The woman is gone, the windows of the civil commission are dark, but I know people are at work inside. I go over to the guard and show him my ID.

'Telegraph service, I have an important message.'

Outside the telegraphists' room I pause and scribble the rest of my letter.

She is sitting second from the window at an exchange; the room is only half full.

'Send this,' I tell her. I am standing behind her now.

She turns, startled.

'You?'

She has a plaster across her eyebrow.

'Just send it. The address is Dimpfelweg 6, Hamburg.'

'Look what you did.'

'Send it. Not for my sake, but for hers, for ours. Her name is Eline. Do it.'

She reads the letter through.

'I can't send this, you know I can't.'

'Just send it!'

'I can't believe you're this naive – as well as beastly. You'll get me into trouble.'

'Do it now,' I hiss through my teeth.

'Or else you'll do what: hit me again?'

'No, or else I'll . . .'

I hesitate, taking in her small, round face with the plaster above her eye. Blood has seeped through it, forming a crisp scab on the gauze; her upper lip is swollen, and there's a bruise on her left cheek.

'Or else you'll what?' she says.

'Nothing. *Nothing*, I'm sorry!'

– – –

Down at the bridge over the pond,
fifteen minutes later.

Obscure reading of the waters: broken brow in the mouth of night. I fling the empty bottle out across the water, hear the splash in the darkness. I briefly consider throwing myself in, to crumple, *brow in mouth*, and stand indecisive at the flat-bedded basin, but this is a half-hearted pantomime. I am reeling drunk when I arrive at the officers' mess.

I have the veal tongue, and the Chablis.

Afterwards, my stomach begins to growl, a tight, squirming convulsion, intestines knotting together. I stagger outside, hook my arm around a lamp post, bend over and heave out the loam of my guts: speckled meat, and the yellow piss of the Chablis. My knees hit the ground, I am face down in my filth, stomach retching and pumping, out of control, spewing out my insides.

I see her there, in my vomit, in the barely digested meat, a face dissolved.

Etke.

— — —

Ach Bächlein, liebes Bächlein
Du meinst es so gut:
Ach Bächlein, aber weißt du
Wie Liebe tut?

Ah, brooklet, dear brook,
You may mean so well,
Ah, brooklet, but do you know,
How love casts its spell?

I wake up on my sofa to the crackle and stutter of the gramophone. I go over and lift the arm, turn the handle and place the needle at the point where the miller boy jumps into the brook. I do it again, listen to the piece over and over. I weep.

And then I begin to laugh.

Manfred is right. I lied to a little girl and coerced her into informing against her own family. As a result the family is killed, and now I cry over the girl; her small hands, her chubby face. The woman in the park was right. Confiding is a sentimental self-indulgence. I go over to the sideboard and remove the cork from the cognac with my teeth, and gulp it down.

I bellow:

'Long live sentimentality!'

– – –

They are asleep. The girl has climbed into bed with Masja, snuggled her little head into Masja's armpit, her arm across her abdomen, one leg dangling above the floor.

When I return from Minsk she will be gone.

I pull the door shut.

I will not speak her name.

I will never be able to tell Eline.

Truth is consistent. Without mercy.

I am already dressed for the journey. My car is waiting on the corner, engine running.

The night is still.

– – –

We drive along the highway to Minsk through thin darkness, the cold of night upon the landscape, houses passing by. Then: a turmoil of searchlights from a Stützpunkt; men digging, shovelling, hacking, it looks like anti-tank barrage, a lorry in a ditch, the roar and scream of axles from the RSO, writhing free of mud, two Wehrmacht soldiers gesticulating. A Hiwi puts a tin mug to his lips with both hands, drums a finger against his side; his eyes follow us, our little convoy waved on.

I have brought Manfred's interpreter, the tall Hiwi. I am driving. He takes a pouch from his jacket, crumbles some black tobacco in his hand, mahorka. He finds a scrap of newspaper in his pocket, *Das Reich*, smoothes it between his fingers and lays the tobacco out across the print. I watch him from the corner of my eye, tapping my fingers against the wheel as he rolls the paper tight. He licks Hitler's sleeve, stops in mid-movement, and sits there with his half-rolled cigarette.

He looks at me.

'I . . .' he says. 'Gospodin . . .'

'Have one of my Efkas,' I tell him.

I fumble in my breast pocket and pull out the packet. He takes one and lights up. The road is clear. We are going to Minsk, to the main archive. If our man with the cockerel on his shoulder is from the western Soviet Union he will be there. All we need is to find the J in his passport, *Jevrej*, Jew, a prison sentence for homosexuality – a perversion, a category. And they are good at categories, the Reds. Providing the documentation has not been destroyed, burned or rolled into mahorka. Providing the witnesses are not decomposing in some mass grave, theirs or ours.

'So . . .' I say.

'Gospodin?' says the Hiwi and lifts his hand.

'What's your name exactly?'

Something strikes me hard behind the ear, the front wing flies through the air.

I wrench the wheel.

– – –

They have got me by the legs, and pull me through the wet grass, my arms trailing limply behind. I try to kick out and receive a blow to the head. They roll me over, I find my pistol, sit up and pull the trigger, only it won't fire. I rack the slide, and then he is on top of me, knees in the grass, striking me with the flat of his hand.

'Gospodin, it's me! Semjon!'

'What?'

61

He snatches the pistol from my hand and puts a finger to his lips.

'Gospodin, we will look after you. Wait here.'

He hands me back the gun and gets to his feet, nods to another Hiwi, they release the safety catches on their own weapons. He points towards the road, our Kübelwagen is on fire. They vanish into the darkness.

My pulse is racing.

The woods are silent.

Only the roar of the fire.

My mind churns.

– – –

Shadows.

I check my weapon, my hands are shaking, I am unable to hold it.

It is between my legs.

Shadows.

I thrust out the magazine – it is empty. I find some loose cartridges in the grass, press them in, pushing down the spring. I pull back the slide, hear the round deploy into the chamber.

Etke.

I must have dropped my cigarettes.

I am shaking with cold.

– – –

He sits on his haunches, the tall Hiwi. His hand is on my shoulder.

He turns to someone I cannot see, and says something in Belorussian. He looks at me again.

'It was a mine. You are all right.'

When I fail to reply he takes a cigarette from his breast pocket. The paper has absorbed blood. He turns it between his fingers, then puts it between my lips. He lights it for me; I hold on to his hands.

It tastes of blood; blood and smoke.

'What did you say your name was?'

'Semjon, gospodin.'

'Why do you call me gospodin?'

'It means *master* . . .'

'Master?'

'Yes.'

'Semjon, do you have any children?'

'They are gone. Three chicks, gospodin. Three chicks that ran into the forest. Now they cannot find their way home.'

'Etke.'

'Etke, gospodin?'

'The girl from Belize. Could you take her?'

'Take her, gospodin?'

'Yes. Take care of her . . . let her live with . . . your family. Or . . .'

Semjon gets to his feet, picks up his rifle and slings it over his shoulder. He reaches his hand out to me.

'Come, gospodin.'

Minsk

The nurse holds safety pins between her lips, she presses my shoulder wound together and leads the roll of gauze under my arm, making a tight bandage and fastening it with the pins.

'We've run out of fasteners. Would you believe it?' she says and straightens up.

'Are you from Hamburg?' I ask.

'Why?'

She is over at the sink, rinsing her hands. She's a redhead – the knee stockings don't suit her – her hands are red too, her arms freckled.

'No reason,' I say. 'You sound Hamburgisch, that's all . . . and I haven't been back in Hamm in, what . . . eleven months now.'

'You're from Hamm?' she says, turning round to face me. 'You're joking?'

'No, I'm not. Deadly serious.'

'Whereabouts?'

'By the park, Süder . . . or rather, that's where I grew up. My mother lived there . . . she's dead now. What's it called . . .'

'Can't you remember where you live?'

'No . . . it's gone. A white building . . . five floors . . .'

'There are lots like that in Hamm.'

'Yes, but next to the park, what on earth is it called! By the sports fields . . . you must know.'

'Sievekings . . . ?'

'No, the other side.'

'Horner?'

'No. No, in the other direction.'

'Oh, that would be Hammer Steindamm . . .'

'Er . . . no.'

'Hammerhof . . .'

'No, that's not it either. Rumpffstrasse!'

'Rumpffstrasse?'

'Yes, number three, second floor . . . that was quite a job, wasn't it? Can you remember where *you* live?'

'I think so,' she says, and giggles.

'Did I hit my head?'

She produces a little torch from the pocket of her apron, holds it up to my eye, keeping the eye open with her fingers while she shines light into the pupil.

'Watch my finger,' she says, and moves it from side to side in front of my nose. My eyes follow, but the finger confuses me, my nose moves with it, only it doesn't, it stays put – it's my head that is swimming.

'My name's Gertrud,' she says. 'Gertrud Engeler. I live on Claudiusstrasse, number forty-one, in Hamm.'

'Hello, Gertrud Engeler,' I say.

– – –

Gertrud is gone. When I wake up in a bed two men are standing in the doorway of the room. One has his hair slicked down – he wears rimless spectacles, a suit. He holds a briefcase in his right hand. The other wears a uniform I have never seen before. It looks like the Luftwaffe, only with purple epaulettes and gold braid at the collar patches, trousers wide at the thigh, and white pointed boots with a Cuban heel. Are they spurs, making that tinkling sound? Who does he think he is?

'The Generalkommissar is expecting you,' says the man in the suit.

'Generalkommissar Kube?' I say. 'Expecting me?'

'Yes. You are Oberleutnant der Polizei, Heinrich Hoffmann, are you not?'

'Yes.'

'A car is waiting outside for you.'

– – –

I ask what this is about on the way to Generalkommissar Kube's residence in the centre of Minsk. We're going to the Kubepalast – one of the few remaining baroque palaces from the Tsarist days not to have been bombed.

The man in the bizarre uniform twists round to face me:

'My name is Grünfeldt. I am GK Kube's adjutant.'

'I see.'

'And that's Haber,' he says with a nod at the besuited man behind the wheel.

'And what would the Generalkommissar like to see me about?'

'All in due time,' Haber says. 'Hand me my cigarettes, would you, Erwin? They're in the glove compartment.'

Grünfeldt rummages around.

'Are you sure they're here?'

'Yes. Positive.'

'Well, I can't find them.'

Nothing more is said for the remainder of the journey.

– – –

The Kubepalast, ten minutes later.

In front of the building: a ring of Wehrmacht and SS, barbed wire, machine-gun posts and concrete security blocks – an obstacle course up the broad driveway to the main entrance. They wave us through. The partisan war is near.

Haber and Grünfeldt lead me down a long corridor, an endless foyer of sofas, marble, solemn paintings and hunting trophies – stags, wild boar, great salmon glistening with varnish, half-foxes with paws protruding from the walls. Grünfeldt, the uniformed adjutant, swivels on his heel. We stop in front of a door that must be three metres tall. He knocks, and a bellowed order comes from inside: *Enter!*

And there he sits, in this enormous room, the Generalkommissar Kube, Weissruthenien's German Tsar, with a napkin at his throat, knife and fork in hands, the table set for two. He throws out an arm and barks in falsetto:

'Be seated!'

I sit down.

The Generalkommissar says nothing further, bent over his pie. He is one of the old warriors, all blood and honour, one of the vociferous few who enjoy Hitler's confidence; he has plundered his Generalkommissariat, excels at finding slaves, but is protective of Jews, they say – a Jew lover. He bristles, and his trousers tighten, and yet he has the face of a boy, bright and fresh. He smells clean, of a beach in summer, is a non-smoker like the Führer, and a vegetarian. He offers me a piece of the pie; onion, it looks like. What does he want with me? My head hurts, I drink water poured from the jug and answer in monosyllables. I want to smoke. The table looms up, as if I were looking down the wrong end of a telescope, adjusting the lens. I feel sick.

'A shame about Obergruppenführer Steiner,' Kube says at last, dabbing the corners of his mouth with the napkin. 'A shame indeed.'

'Yes, Herr Generalkommissar,' I say. 'A shame.'

'And his wife . . . the lovely Gisela . . .'

'Yes. The lovely Gisela. A shame. Tragic.'

'Don't you want any pie?'

'No, thank you, Herr Generalkommissar. I'm not at all hungry.'

'It's very good, I can tell you. Leek and sour cream.'

'It looks delicious indeed, Herr Generalkommissar.'

He claps his small, white hands and immediately two young women enter, dressed in Bavarian costume, with thick hair, lederhosen and frilled blouses, displaying white bosoms, bare arms. They clear away the table. Kube rolls up his napkin and puts it through a napkin ring. The ring is of horn, mounted with silver bearing the engraving GK WEISSRUTHENIEN in Gothic lettering. He gets to his feet and goes over to the great stone fireplace.

A badger adorns the mantelpiece, mouth open, glistening with red varnish.

Kube's uniform is too tight across the back.

'A damned catastrophe,' he says. '*Damn* it . . .'

'Herr Generalkommissar?'

'Steiner, of course.'

'Of course. Indeed.'

'A good man, Steiner. Did you know him?'

'No, I'm afraid I never had the pleasure of meeting the Obergruppenführer.'

'Still, it may well turn out for the best.'

'I'm sorry, Herr Generalkommissar?'

He says nothing, but turns and looks at me, his round face, thin yellow hair.

'I understand Manfred Schlosser has got you leading the inquiry. Why did he not consult me?'

'I'm afraid I don't know, Herr Generalkommissar.'

'Do you understand our project here in Weissruthenien?'

'Project . . . Herr Generalkommissar . . .?'

'The idea behind . . . what we're doing here, our civilising mission?'

I look down at the table: a small flake of pastry, with some green leek. I dab it into my mouth with a finger. Kube seats himself again, folds his hands.

'Do you?'

'I think so, yes. Or . . . what exactly do you mean, Herr Generalkommissar?'

'We cannot do without men like Steiner.'

'No. It's tragic.'

'Hm. Yes, well. Tell me what you know.'

'We're proceeding from the hypothesis that the Obergruppenführer was killed by a partly Jewish band of partisans.'

'Jewish. Why's that?'

'He was subjected to what we think is a Jewish . . . ritual . . .'

'What the hell's that supposed to mean?'

'He was subjected to a ritual circumcision and died from loss of blood. The killing would seem to indicate a so-called crime of passion, in which the method employed is overdetermined and, well, *exaggerated*.'

Kube pushes away his napkin.

'In that case I assume retaliation has been initiated?'

'No. Only on a small scale.'

'For what reason?'

'Schlosser, Herr Generalkommissar. He wants to find the perpetrator first.'

'You mean he wants you to investigate this as if it were an ordinary killing?'

'Yes.'

'As though this were an ordinary *country*.'

'Yes.'

'Hmm.'

I clear my throat, gathering my courage. The room is filled with the smell of vegetables, and madness.

'Herr Generalkommissar, may I ask a question?'

'Fire away.'

'I think it might have been an act of vengeance . . . that is, not directed towards just any high-ranking SS officer as such, but specifically towards *Steiner* . . . the mutilation would seem to be suggestive of it . . . and . . .'

'Go on.'

'As far as I'm informed, Steiner was head of Einsatzkommando B . . .'

'That's classified, as you should know . . .'

'Indeed, but I thought that if I could see the march route for autumn '41 and spring '42, our perpetrator could be a survivor from one of the operations . . .'

'The map only?'

'Yes.'

'That's SD . . .'

'Yes. I'm sorry. It was foolish of me.'

'Very foolish. In fact, I think you have misunderstood the whole matter . . .'

'I beg your pardon?'

He folds his hands again; they look soft and delicate.

'The crux of the matter is this: Have you found out what Steiner was doing in Lida?'

'No.'

'He was supposed to be in Kursk on the 2nd together with his division. So what was he doing with his wife in a private car five hundred kilometres away?'

'I don't know the answer to that. All I know is that Hauptsturmführer Schlosser was expecting him.'

'I see. How do you mean, expecting him?'

'Well, there was a big reception planned. I don't understand—'

'No, you don't. But you will. And when you come up with your answer you report to me.'

'But Hauptsturmführer Schlosser . . .'

'Understood?'

'Yes, Herr Generalkommissar. Understood.'

'Now, you've got two days for your Jewish lead.'

– – –

They let him design the uniform himself, Grünfeldt tells me in the car on the way to NKVD's old prison and camp archives, Glavnoe Upravlenie Lagerei, GULag. He flutters his glossy white calfskin gloves. He looks like an idiot; the pheasant feathers, gold braid and sparkling buttons, his perfect nails. Are they varnished? On arrival I see this building too has been turned into a cinema for the Wehrmacht on leave from the front. NKVD set fire to the place in July of '41 when they moved out, but they had fireproofed the archive boxes in the basement themselves. If my theory is correct, we are looking for a local Jew dispatched to the Gulag for *bourgeois pederasty*, Article 121 of the Soviet Criminal Code, then returned to the partisan throng. In which case he must be here, inside NKVD's bureaucratic brain.

'They killed them all,' says Haber, running a long finger across his moustache after we have found an office and an assistant has provided us with the records.

'Who?' I ask.

'The inmates,' Grünfeldt says. 'They tossed hand grenades into the cells.'

'What are we looking for?' Haber asks, and yawns.

'A Jew, I think. Probably convicted of homosexual activity.'

'I see,' says Grünfeldt. 'Have we got a name?'

'No. We have nothing. Or rather . . .'

I pull out my wallet, remove Etke's drawing from the note section, and unfold it on the table. The cockerel and the two eyes.

'Ah,' says Haber. 'A rebus?'

'You could say. Prison tattoos.'

'Let's get started,' Haber says, and takes out the first bundle of documents.

— — —

Later, the same evening. Haber is perspiring. He drinks buttermilk from a large glass jug. The Hiwi, Semjon, translates. Grünfeldt takes notes. He smokes Semjon's mahorkas. They drink vodka.

My head is swimming.

We have found sixty-three candidates: Jews convicted of homosexuality.

'Here's another,' says Grünfeldt. 'What does it say, Ivan Abramovitj Henker, born 1899. Member of the Communist Party 1919. Convicted of Trotskyist conspiracy in '36. There's an addendum about Article 121 . . . No, he was shot.'

'Next,' says Haber. He clicks his tongue, a semicircle of milk on his upper lip.

'Christ,' says Grünfeldt. He gets to his feet and lifts his arms above his head, stretches his fingers, rolls his neck. 'I could do with some *pussy* . . .'

'That's enough,' I say.

'But I could,' says Grünfeldt.

'Have some buttermilk,' says Haber.

– – –

Later still. Grünfeldt is bored and fidgety. At one point he goes outside to stretch his legs, but Haber brings him back. After some heated words of reproval in the corridor, Grünfeldt comes back in and sits down.

The sky is light, though it is past 2 a.m. The town itself is dark and brooding; burnt-out buildings, blacked-out windows.

Haber stands with his hands clasped behind his back, looking out of the window. Semjon translates the dossiers for me, and I make notes.

'Semjon, do you think we're going to win?' Grünfeldt says all of a sudden.

His long legs are stretched out in front of him, feet on the table. We are down to eighty-seven candidates, but many of the archive boxes have yet to be opened.

'Gospodin?'

'Do you think we'll win Kursk? Do you think we'll break through?'

'I am only Semjon, gospodin. I know nothing.'

'An ignorant Belorussian, is that it?'

'Yes, gospodin. But I know one thing.'

'And what's that?' Haber asks from over by the window.

'No one is ever released from Gulag. So there is only one possibility. The man we are looking for was part of a penal unit.'

'A penal unit?' Grünfeldt says.

'Yes, released from Vorkuta to serve in a penal unit.'

'What are you suggesting?' I ask.

'That we try the camps. Maybe someone there fought alongside him . . . Or maybe the Hiwis. There are many Russian prisoners of war among us.'

'Jews as well?' Haber asks.

'No.'

'And you know that?'

'Yes.'

'How?' Haber persists.

'I just know.'

'I see,' says Haber.

He produces a cigar from a pocket of his jacket, bites off the end, and strikes a match on the windowsill.

'How might that be, exactly?'

'They cannot say *r* or *schji* . . .'

'*Sji?*'

'Yes, *schji* . . . and besides, they have this . . .'

'This what?'

'Well . . . *Jewishness.*'

Grünfeldt takes his feet off the table and the heels of his boots clack against the floor. He unscrews the cork from the vodka.

'Ah!' he says, wiping his mouth with the sleeve of his shirt. 'Interesting! Now, the Cabaret Moderne in Berlin. No, Haber, don't look at me like that! I was trying to become an actor, you know perfectly well! It didn't turn out terribly well. But I did write some sketches! Rather good ones at that, if I may say . . .'

He proceeds to hum a tune.

'"Kleiner Max"! Don't you know it? Well, it got them going, I can tell you, you should have seen the ladies . . . fanning away, and they were very particular, they wouldn't go for just any old thing. Anyway, why am I sitting here blathering on like this? What I wanted to say was: Irma Wagner, she was the one who sang it. Oh, was she athletic! Anyway her, what do you call it, impresario, was an Israelite. I wonder where he is now! A conceited Jew in a morning coat – painted face, falsetto voice, I hated him . . . and yet I loved him!'

'Erwin . . .' says Haber.

'But I did! Was that wrong too? Yes, all right, I know, I know. But anyway, the thing was I asked him one day, what it *was* about the Jews. Whether they were a people, even if they'd lived apart for thousands of years, if there was an *Ahasuerus*, an eternal Jew . . . if there was something peculiarly Jewish . . . not money or big noses, menorahs and all that, but something they themselves felt to be Jewish, and Steiner . . . it strikes me now that his name was Steiner . . . or was it *Stein* . . . how odd . . .'

'Get to the point, man!' Haber barks.

'Do you know what he said?'

'No,' I say. 'What did he say?'

'Put two Jews in a room with a hundred people and within two minutes they'll have found each other and be exchanging reminiscences, even if they've never met before!'

'And that would be peculiarly Jewish?' says Haber. 'That one Yid can recognise another? Hardly likely to get us anywhere, is it?'

'My words exactly!'

'Then what did he say?'

'He said: the Prussians are beaten dogs, the Jews are beaten cats!'

'What kind of nonsense is that?'

'That's what he said. The Prussians bear a grudge, they sneak away and will bite, whereas the Jews will be polite and *smile* . . . the Jews will smile. And it's true. Cats are . . . Egyptian, aren't they, like the Jews themselves. They're alien and can't survive on their own in the wild in Germany, they have to be fed. But the *dog*. The dog is a German animal . . . and the Germans *love* dogs!'

'I've seen a lot of Jews. Most were not smiling,' says Semjon across the table.

'Indeed, they've not got much to laugh about,' says Haber.

'Smiling cats, ha!' Grünfeldt exclaims with delight.

'There may be some truth in it,' Semjon goes on. 'I've seen many Jews beaten, but never a Jew who has laid a hand on a Christian. They just carry on their way, muttering their Jew language and sewing your trousers. That's why they're so *unsettling* . . . they're like water.'

'False as water . . .' Haber ponders.

'Schiller,' says Grünfeldt. 'Good old Schiller.'

'It's Shakespeare,' says Haber. 'Othello.'

'So it is. Well done, Haber! How clever you are!'

There is a lull. Grünfeldt studies his varnished nails. Haber returns to the table and opens another dossier.

'How many have we got now?' I ask, with a nod in the direction of Haber, who has been making the list.

'Eighty-seven Jews, of whom twenty-one we know for certain are dead. And of course none of them gave their real name, if whatshisface here is to be trusted,' he says, indicating Semjon. 'And they were in one of our camps.'

'Semjon,' I say. 'His name is Semjon.'

'Suit yourself,' says Haber.

'There you go again . . . work, work, work,' Grünfeldt says and pats his stomach with both hands. 'How about that pussy – Haber, what do you say?'

– – –

Haber drives, Semjon is in the passenger seat. Grünfeldt has his long fingers between the thighs of a skinny whore, her painted mouth opens in laughter, lips a small red heart, a kiss, a crude hallmark; jangling jewellery, plated metal and coloured glass, pale, flat bosom with blue veins, boa puffed at her throat. She babbles in Polish, Grünfeldt hands me the bottle and buries his face in hers, hands and glistening nails around her neck. He devours her with his undersized mouth and pointed tongue, slobbers, sucks at her as though sucking an egg, a partial vacuum. Haber watches them in the mirror and lights a cigarette.

'Let me out here,' I say.

'What? But what about the cabaret?' says Grünfeldt. 'I could have them sing "Kleiner Max" . . .'

'Just let me out,' I say.

'What about me, gospodin?' says Semjon.

77

'Do whatever you want,' I tell him as we pull up at a corner. I get out, and he follows. Haber revs the engine, the car tears off down the street.

I pull out an Efka and hand it to Semjon.

'Well, if it's all right with gospodin, I think I'll go for a walk,' he says.

'Let's say six o'clock tomorrow morning, shall we?'

We stand for a moment, then Semjon nods, turns and strides off on his long legs into the bright night.

I savour the cool air.

I asked Haber where the nurses live.

– – –

It is a two-winged building behind the hospital; to get in means scaling a fence and entering a dark garden area that smells sweetly of night and cold apples. The windows of the top floor are lit up. I sit down in grass wet with dew and wait, listen.

Nothing.

This rush of expectation. I can hear my heart beating.

I know where Gertrud lives. I could have gone the front way, shown my police ID; the security guard would have let me in. But this moment is irresistible: the particularly German smell of a residence hall, to climb a fence, to tap against a pane.

She opens the door in her nightdress, red hair heavy, her freckled skin transparent.

I reach a hand to her face, tuck a lock of hair behind her ear.

'Hello, Gertrud Engeler of Claudiusstrasse 41.'
'Hello, stranger of Rumpffstrasse 3.'

– – –

Her eyes are closed, she holds onto the headboard of the bed. I can see the beat of her pulse in the hollow of her neck.

She licks my ear, whispers, sings: *Casper, my darling, Casper, Casper, Casper.*

– – –

She lies in the light. She has to be up soon. She is beautiful, and almost orange; her lips *are* orange in the still light of morning. I scribble a note and leave it on the table.

Thanks for letting me be Casper.
Live well, H.

– – –

When I meet up with Grünfeldt, Haber and Semjon again outside the Kubepalast – the car packed and ready, permissions and permits signed by the Generalkommissar, who has arranged a three-motorcycle escort – I rummage in my briefcase and find a topographic map marked with a route, dates noted at various locations on the Einsatzgruppe's passage of death. Steiner's trace of slime through Belorussia in '41 and '42. Haber stares stiffly out of the window as I study the map. Grünfeldt is absorbed in some detail of his white gloves. Haber must have put it there. Grünfeldt is an idiot. Has he been through my notes as well? His payment will have to wait. What will he want in return?

Stalags

We take the lower-ranking prison camps first, the stalags. Haber drives, Grünfeldt sleeps, mouth open, while Semjon smokes my cigarettes in the back as we proceed through the sandy, uneven landscape due west of Minsk, passing silent peasants, mangy cattle, bald fields tended by no one, burnt-out vehicles in mid-terrain, rusting since '41 amid swaying poppies. But there are more recent wrecks too: pushed off the road into the ditches, the bodies of the hanged lining the way, a woman, chin at her chest, sweater pulled up over a branch, one shoe missing, the warning signs, *We are partisans, we shot at German soldiers*, in German and Russian around their necks – heavy, dangling peasant corpses. Machine-gun posts and fortified villages, more signs. The machine gunner in the sidecar next to us loads his weapon. *Danger, bandits! Closed for single vehicles 15:00 – 06:00 . . . Keep weapons at ready . . . Never drive alone.* More peasant women with scarves and downturned eyes, and then, a short distance away, at the fringe of the woods, a fire – a thick belt of smoke. We cross the border of Weissruthenien and enter the Rückwärtiges Heeresgebiet: here neither Kube nor Manfred has a say, this is the domain of Heeresgruppe Mitte, Wehrmacht.

On the third day of the Battle of Kursk we reach Mogilev and Dnepr. I read the bulletin of the day, handed to me by a captain of the Wehrmacht at a guarded bridge on the city's southern outskirts. Progress, progress, but nothing decisive; the loudest roar of steel and blood, Germany's fate concentrated in this bump at the front, this pulsating tumour. Everyone here is on edge, testy, 400 kilometres behind the main line.

An hour later I show my ID and the permit from Kube to the guard at Stalag 341.

A sergeant appears, a slice of buttered rye bread in his right hand, examines my identity card, wipes some onion and jellied stock from his mouth with his sleeve:

'Go ahead!'

We drive in through the barbed wire. The place is nothing but a field, like in '41 when we simply fenced them in and threw them items of food, and stood back to watch; hundreds of thousands scrabbling for a calf liver, a side of beef, a bucket of turnips, heads in the grass, they ate mud and beetles, their mouths full of soil. They had nothing, no huts, no wells, nothing, and they melted into the ground, began to eat each other, uniforms absorbed into the mud to rot. In the spring of '42 they came for those who were left, a couple of thousand at most, divided them among the camps, imported them into the Reich, shot them, experimented with the gas, offered them the chance to become Hiwis, and now there are three thousand here, pale shadows, labouring in this great workshop, repairing the Tiger tanks.

Problem: We have killed too many. How to find a witness who has seen our *zek* with the cockerel on his shoulder?

Haber sets up a chair and a small table on the assembly area in the middle of the camp and sits down. An SS guard announces roll call and prisoners appear from their work and fall into line. Grünfeldt opens a suitcase and places jars of pickled cucumber and tins of pâté on the table. Anyone who knows anything gets one.

The guard tightens his jaw, steps forward and thrusts the butt of his rifle against the skull of a prisoner who lunges for a tin.

Two hours: nothing. Three hours: nothing. Four hours: nothing.

No one has seen a *zek* with strange tattoos.

No one has any idea what we are talking about.

The ghosts reel away, the sun on their backs, streaks against grey soil.

— — —

Next afternoon. Stalag 373, on the
outskirts of Bobruisk, a former fortress.

I sit in the shade, in the splay of an embrasure, and look out over the flat land, doodling patterns on the topographic map while we wait for the roll call and for those in the sub-camps to come back. Steiner passed through more than seventy-five places: towns, villages, hamlets, holes in the ground, *shtetls*. Jews everywhere, any number could have a reason for vengeance, hidden from sight in the bushes, watching it all, the executions, the plundering. Is this a blind alley?

The assembly area in the inner
yard, early evening.

This camp is smaller, maybe a thousand prisoners, many of them Asian. I toss a tin of peaches into the throng from the top of the wall – *Made in the USA*, spoils from a downed Dakota. A fight breaks out. A man snatches it, twists free of his pursuers and runs, arm aloft, prize held high. He turns and dances backwards, jigging, yelling, whooping like a lunatic, a Red Indian, a Yankee plucking a baseball from the air. Two towers open fire from each end of the yard, savage ploughshares of steel. His sallow frame is ripped apart, the tin continues its flight. No one bothers with the corpse. Semjon steps down to the yard and collects the tin in the dirt, wipes the blood off on his trouser leg and stashes it in his cartridge pouch.

We are getting nowhere.

– – –

Two days later, Stalag 362, between Polotsk
and Vitebsk in the northern sector.

At the dividing line between Heeresgruppe Mitte and Heeresgruppe Nord, one half of the camp follows the slow, green course of the Dvina. The air is damp and unbearable, a hum. Haber fumbles under his collar and swears, Grünfeldt has disappeared again: what is he up to? Semjon stands with a boy, we are inside a workshop, a steaming heat. He is no more than fourteen, a stick insect, hands in the pockets of his oversized trousers, held up by braces over his bare chest, chocks of wood under his feet, rags wound around his ankles and calves, eyes red, the corners of his mouth inflamed by some infection. Semjon has produced a tin of Thüringer pâté from his bag.

The boy says:

83

'Khleb, Büchse njetu.'

He takes his too-large hand from his pocket, rubs his stomach in a circular movement, and coughs.

'What's that supposed to mean?' I ask.

'He does not want the tin,' Semjon says. 'It will make him sick.'

'What does he want instead?' I ask.

'Bread.'

'I see. Does he know anything?'

'He says he saw a *zek* a few months back, he had the same tattoos.'

The boy nods, though it is unlikely he understands what we are saying. He speaks again, to Semjon.

'He says he had two eyes on his back, just above the buttocks. He ran errands for him. He says he was from Vorkuta.'

'Vorkuta?'

'Yes. In the east. Gulag.'

'Ask if there was a cockerel on his back too.'

Semjon turns again to the boy, they gesticulate, a long exchange. The boy grins and bunches his left hand, drills the index finger of his right hand into his tightened fist. Semjon punches him hard on the cheek and the boy is propelled onto his backside on the floor.

'What does he say?' I ask.

'No. He said no.'

'Why did you hit him?'

'What?'

'Why did you *hit* him?'

'He said the prisoner was indecent . . . a faggot . . .'

'What else?'

'He joined up as a Hiwi. He is from the Asian republics, Turkmenistan, Kyrgyzstan, what do you call it . . . yellow.'

– – –

In the archive of the administration building. 'What?' is the response I get from the camp clerk when I ask if he remembers a *zek* with eyes tattooed in the small of his back who joined up with us. Kyrgyz, something like that. Grünefeldt laughs. He slaps his thigh. The Scharführer finds the names: 328 prisoners-of-war in Stalag 362 joined the Hiwis in '42 and '43.

I'm given the list. Semjon draws me aside once we are out.

He says nothing until we reach a cluster of trees.

'Gospodin . . .'

'What is it?'

'I can show you the Hiwis, but he cannot be with us . . .'

'Who?'

'They are difficult, the Hiwis. We are . . . secretive. And if the one we are looking for is an untouchable, they will never tell. And that one in his uniform . . .'

'What? Grünfeldt?'

'Yes . . . He is, how do you say, a turkey . . . cluck, cluck . . . a mad person . . .'

– – –

I watch the car disappear along the dusty road. Grünfeldt is in it, feet up on the dashboard. He has been given two hundred alcohol coupons for palm oil in the Mitte archive, a copy of the list of 328 names, and a job to do. *Find the Asian.* Vorkuta is a large camp, but two prisoners with identical prison tattoos, two untouchables, both preferring penal unit to forced labour? It can't be coincidence, they *must* know each other. I go inside and call Manfred. We agree that I can pick up his answer from the telegraph office at SS-Dienststelle Vitebsk.

We drive the forty-five kilometres to Vitebsk and wait; this place too bombed to oblivion, charred still, the fetid smell of '41. Haber has to call Kube; he locates the Wehrmacht staff headquarters – Soviet concrete – and leaves us.

Semjon and I find a leafy spot, a café behind the station. It is early evening; a man plays the violin, there are German women here, and tablecloths.

The heart-shaped leaves of the linden trees flutter in the breeze. A quiet rustle.

I need a bath.

We have a table to ourselves. A goods train passes through, an endless procession of great, grey tanks, Tigers, followed by troops, with their legs protruding from the open wagons.

No one waves.

They smoke.

– – –

Semjon offers me the opened tin of peaches.

They smell of sugar and America.

'The NKVD came and took my father and brother. The kolkhoz took our three cows. We ran away into the forests,' he tells me.

'I see.'

'What you people are doing is good. They treated us like we were not human at all.'

'And are you?' I say with a smile.

He turns his bony, oblong face towards me, and spits out a shred of tobacco.

He is not smiling.

'Our needs are small, gospodin.'

– – –

SS-Dienststelle Vitebsk, 21:00, I meet up with Haber again. I go in and pick up the list from Manfred and have the Scharführer make me out a receipt. Of the 328 Hiwis, 127 are confirmed dead, 52 are missing. The rest are divided between seven units, *Jägerbataillons*, combating the partisans, some are with Dirlewanger, in the Ukraine, Ostland and Weissruthenien, Rückwärtiges Heeresgebiet Mitte.

– – –

We drive through the nightfall. I have run out of cigarettes.

What Semjon shows me is folklore, a world of old, the shadow world of the Hiwis, in the barracks, the drinking joints, the holes in the ground draped with camouflage nets, the stables, this air of smoke, of gleaming eyes, a din of gambling and bottles, songs in mumbled language. They do not look at us, they hate us, they fear us, *the master race*; they are Russians, Estonians, Latvians, Lithuanians, Ukrainians, Romanians, yellow men.

Semjon translates, gesticulates, drinks, grins.

We cannot find our yellow man.

Maybe we are asking the wrong questions.

Maybe he is dead.

At two o'clock we run into SS-Jägerbataillon 502 some hundred kilometres south-west of Vitebsk, spread out over a wide area, south and east of the main road to Mogilev. The regular German troops are further ahead, on the other side of the birch wood.

The Hiwis bivouac here, in stables and hay barns, in tents and under tarps. We open the door of a barn.

The party is here.

I leave it to Semjon to deal with the many faces. Haber seats himself on one of the chairs they must have brought over from a nearby house. I sit down in a corner, in the hay, and pull off my boots.

It is warm here, I could sleep.

– – –

Flickering shadows, the stench of carbide lamps and sweat.

A grinning man is playing the accordion, his shoulders swaying, he grimaces like an imbecile. Is he singing?

On the ground a game is going on with sticks, but I can't work out if they are counters or if they are meant to be placed in some particular way, if that is the game, some kind of Mikado. They keep saying *trik-trak*, is that what it's called? I lie here as they toss their sticks, their hands swift. Is it fortune telling or gambling?

A door opens from a cowshed on the other side.

A girl, not more than thirteen or fourteen, spits semen into her hand.

Someone says *jevrejka*, Jewess.

Haber jumps to his feet, he speaks almost in a whisper, slaps a Hiwi hard in the face and drags the girl away by the hair.

Then suddenly it's quiet.

The abrupt, muffled report of a PPK outside in the night.

Haber comes back in and sits down again. He runs his hand through his hair.

I storm out with a lamp.

The girl is on her stomach behind an outhouse.

I sit down beside her, pull back her clothing to reveal her neck.

She is breathing, snapping at the air.

I take her hand in mine, but she does not react.

I hear her fade away, a whisper of life.

I stay with her.

Her darkness in the wet grass.

— — —

I clutch the photograph of Eline.

Her finery, her pout, all for me.

Do you think the miracle will happen?

How do you mean?

That life will be wonderful?

She still looks like Zarah Leander.

— — —

When I wake up, my limbs stiff, the body of the girl is gone.

Semjon is standing a short distance away, looking like he has only just seen me.

'Gospodin . . .'

I get to my feet and return the photo to my pocket.

'There was a girl here. Haber . . .'

'Here,' he says, handing me three packets of Efkas. 'Come, we must be getting on.'

We walk down the dusty gravel track behind the farm. A Kübelwagen comes the same way and blows its horn. We step aside. Grünfeldt jumps out, the vehicle still in motion, his spindly legs buckle beneath him and he stumbles forward, his arms flailing to find some balance. He falls headlong into the ditch, narrowly avoiding a birch tree.

The driver stops some ten metres further down the track and turns his head to look, mouth open.

'His name is Tulabajev! Turkestan Legion!' Grünfeldt shouts. 'We're flying out!'

The yellow man's friend

The Tante Ju rattles.

Haber reads Tulabajev's dossier. They have got him in an infirmary near Kiev.

'Does anyone know where Turkestan is?' he asks.

Semjon stares at his knees, Grünfeldt is a shade of green; we lurch into a wind pocket, the fuselage shudders. We are too far east, the main battle line is down below, a circle of fire, a seeping wound on the plain. The cabin wrenches, the clatter of flak fragmenting into scrap with each explosion.

I bang my knee on an ammunition box – my shoes squelch with blood.

My head screams.

The aircraft heels over.

The pilot gives the wing a pat on the landing strip twenty kilometres west of Kiev.

His goggles are pushed up onto his brow, leaving white rings on his sun-scorched face.

– – –

Infirmary Ia for internal medicine is housed in a manor, encircled by a bombed-out park, the lawns in flower, most of the trunks of the linden trees split to the root, charred. The whitewashed facade of the main house gleams.

Geese strut majestically, swanlike almost.

A new crematorium has been built behind the former stables.

Black smoke rises from its chimney.

'I'm going for a walk in the park,' Grünfeldt says. 'Maybe I can find some mushrooms . . .'

Semjon and I are led into a consulting room, a nurse with eczema on her hands dresses my knee. We are asked to follow along and enter what looks like a changing room; white tiles, benches. There are signs on the wall in Gothic lettering:

Remove all clothing! Wait until security staff arrive! Do not enter next sluice!

We place our clothes in two neat piles on one of the benches and wait.

Semjon's penis is long and heavy and he has thick crops of hair on his chest and back.

He looks human.

The two men who come in to collect us are wearing gas masks and one-piece suits of rubber-treated cotton reinforced from the shafts of their boots to the gloves and collar. Their eyes stare at us from behind circles of glass.

We are hosed down by hard jets of water. They sprinkle us with disinfectant powder that stings on the skin. We are hosed down again. Scalding water. One of them puts our clothes in a bag marked with a triangle with a circle around it. *For disinfection!*

They open another door. It gives with a sigh of suction from the rubber insulation strips and we are led into the *Next sluice*. Clean underwear and two rubber suits. One of the men jabs a rubber hand. They watch as we put them on, checking to make sure the suits are tight at the neck, hands, feet.

'Can you hear us?' one of them says.

I adjust my receiver, which gives out a high-pitched squeal – too much treble, interference.

'Yes!'

'Good. I am SS Doctor Severin Hildesheim.'

'Oberleutnant der Polizei, Heinrich Hoffmann,' I reply, and hold out my arm towards Semjon. 'And this is my interpreter. What's wrong with Tulabajev?'

'We don't know. But it makes you think.'

'About what?'

'About what a human is . . .'

'What do you mean?'

'The boundaries of zoology are unclear. Come.'

– – –

Tulabajev is liquid, a process. The receiver crackles.

He is lying on a bed, his entire body and head bandaged, only his lips and hands free. He is covered by a sheet, making the contours of his ravaged frame all the more pronounced; he is melting into the bed, melting out through the gauze, leaking a clear fluid.

'At first we thought it was gangrene,' Hildesheim says. 'Now we have no idea. Some Soviet weapon, perhaps, we know nothing. There have been several cases . . .'

'Is he conscious?' I ask, my eyes fixed on Tulabajev.

'Yes!'

I am startled by the loudness of his reply, and yet I did not see his lips move at all. Only his hands tremble, but I cannot tell if the reaction is conscious. And then they are still again. You could break a piece off his fingers, they are yellow and brittle as beeswax.

'Was that him?' I ask.

'Yes,' says Hildesheim. 'He can't control his voice, and his lungs are full of fluid. Sometimes he lies there shouting in his own language.'

'Is Tulabajev tattooed?'

'He was,' says Hildesheim. 'The small of his back. But they're gone now, the skin is completely destroyed . . .'

'What did they look like, do you recall?'

'Eyes. Two big eyes, on his lower back. Quite bizarre.'

My heart misses a beat.

I hand Etke's drawing of the cockerel to Semjon. 'Ask Tulabajev if he knows who has a tattoo like this.'

Tulabajev emits a savage growl as Semjon holds the drawing up in front of him. He sounds like someone drowning, a splutter of terror from the depths of his being, his eyes are bloodshot, pupils large and black. He is livid.

'He calls him Goga,' Semjon says a moment after.

'Goga?'

'That's what he calls him.'

'Goga *what*?'

'He was Prokhonov's slave in the camp . . . he doesn't know his real name.'

'Vorkuta?'

'Yes.'

'Was he Jewish? Ask him . . .'

'He doesn't know. But he is a Belorussian, from a village, a bend in the river, they had beehives . . . he always talked about them, he says. The bees . . .'

'Does he remember the name of this village?'

'No. He knew it once, but no longer. The wind has taken it.'

'The wind?'

'That's what he says. He says they joined up to get away from Prokhonov. He hasn't seen Goga since Christmas '41, Tula.'

Tulabajev has drifted into sleep again, his breathing is momentous, he mists up my mask.

'I don't think there's any more we can do,' says Hildesheimer, when after a while Tulabajev has failed to react.

It's not much, but we have something: a name, and a place. Someone called Goga from a bend in a river. We turn to leave.

'Zaludok!' Tulabajev cries from the bed. We are at his side in an instant.

'Was he from Zaludok?' I bark, but Tulabajev is no longer there. A deep, plunging gargle issues from his throat, like a stone tossed in a stagnant pool as its fetid waters close over it.

– – –

The flight back is uneventful. Haber and Semjon sleep, Grünfeldt reads *Illustrierte*, one long leg crossed over the other. On the cover, Zarah Leander's comely figure on its way in to some establishment in Berlin: black lips, glossy hair, white lace gloves, shapely ankles, black high heels. She holds up her long black train with both hands.

I sit with a large map showing Steiner's route and follow it with my finger. He was *not* at Zaludok in August '41 when the first massacre took place, but he did hold a meeting of his staff at its town hall when they liquidated the ghetto last May, killing two thirds and moving the rest to the ghetto in Sjtjutjyn. I flick through Haber's filing cards from Minsk. No Jews from Zaludok convicted of homosexuality, but then the records show only given addresses at the time of arrest. On the other hand, there was a wave of arrests running from September '39 to June '41 throughout the western part of the Belorussian Soviet Republic after the region passed from Polish control to the NKVD – the time we broke bread with Stalin. Fifty-two of the eighty-seven were arrested in that period.

Reconstruction: Our man, alias Goga, hails from Zaludok, he moves to somewhere bigger, Lida for instance. Seven of the arrests on our cards are from Lida, or Baranovitj, fourteen in all. He is deported to Vorkuta after the Soviets enter, is tormented and tortured, tattooed by force by a thief named Prokhonov, joins a penal unit along with other untouchables, among them Tulabajev, is dispatched into the fray, the Battle of Moscow, perhaps parachuted down behind our lines. Whatever, he ends up in the puszcza and starts looking into what has become of his family. Maybe they were wiped out in Zaludok by Einsatzgruppe B as early as August '41, while Steiner was holidaying at the casino in Baden. Maybe they survived the first selection, only to be killed the year after. Maybe Goga returns incognito to the town of his birth on that *exact* day, 8 May '42, when Steiner arrives to watch the last liquidation. Maybe he sees him standing on the steps, or seated at some sumptuous table, napkin around his bull's neck, sucking on crayfish tails and toasting the good life as the last of the Jews are lined up on the square and divided up into those who are to die and those who are to live.

Maybe.

We need his *real* name, a face.

– – –

I part company with Grünfeldt and Haber in the Kubepalast at Minsk after delivering a full report to Kube. He is irritable this time. Perhaps it is indigestion.

The truth

The door is open and the light switch doesn't work as I enter my house in Lida after 160 kilometres in a bumping, freezing cold car. It is almost three in the morning.

'Masja,' I whisper. 'Masja . . .'

Nothing. I leave the door ajar, it gives me some light. I go up the stairs.

'Masja, are you there?'

The switch doesn't work upstairs either. I follow the banister, find her door in the darkness, and knock. Nothing.

I open the door.

'Masja, for crying out loud . . . How many times have I told you . . .'

The window is wide open, curtains flapping, but she is not there. I go over and shut it. Her bed is made, it smells of her. Is she out somewhere having a good time? I stand and listen to the house.

Not a sound.

I go back down and lock the door, find some candles, then return upstairs to my bedroom. The flame provides only a flicker of light; everything else is dark and silent.

I blow out the candle and undress.

A noise.

I lunge for the chair where I hung my holster, and am lit up in the beam of a torch.

'Heinrich!'

'Who's there?' I blurt. 'Is that you, Manfred?'

'Yes.'

'For Christ's sake, you frightened the life out of me!'

'Etke,' he says.

'What?'

'Your little girl . . .'

'What about her?' I say, furious now.

'I have only one question for you, Heinrich. Did you know?'

'Know what? What are you talking about?'

— — —

Manfred's car was parked in the alley behind the house. They've sat me in the back, between the two Schwabenland brothers, Hans and Michael. I know where we are going. Manfred's domain: the white hospital.

We pull up in front of the shining building, another of Stalin's showcases, by the main road to Vilnius. Manfred seized the place on the very first day, 28 June '41, while the rest of them were busy plundering, arguing over their command cars, the sleek Mercedes, the Kübelwagen outside the country mansions, party headquarters and Izvestija's brown skyscraper; the yapping morons of the Ostministerium, the Reichskommissariat, the Four-Year Planners, paper tigers, army command, Gestapo, Ministry of the Economy, the agricultural experts, all with documents in hand, leather shoes already spattered with mud – all squabbling over the spoils, each with his own stick to draw a line in the dirt, to declare a kingdom, sandcastles, huffing and puffing to no avail. Manfred took the hospital, made one half an SS hospital and kept the rest for himself. Everything was there: operating rooms, wards, crematoriums, basements, where the mortuary is, as well as Manfred's special room with its steel hospital bed and white tiles, where one day I stumbled upon his book of instructions: *One prisoner had for instance made valuable confessions, but since he had swallowed a number of nails, precious time and resources had to be used on medical help and medicine. Such allocation of resources is inappropriate.*

We go in through the glass doors, the rotund brothers at my sides, not physically touching me, but close enough for me to feel their presence. We reach the great echoing hall, the staircase with its faded red carpet, the place humming with activity even though it is deepest night, a clatter of typewriters, a woman in uniform passing us as we proceed. My teeth are *not* chattering, but it is as if an electric current is running through my jaws, making them tremble. Are we going up or down? Office or basement? Am I, too, to be taken to the basement?

Michael nudges me on, up the stairs.

We come to a gallery that leads all the way round the area of the entrance hall. We stop at the fourth door. Manfred's office.

'Did you know he was a clarinettist before the war?' Manfred says.

'Who?'

'Wäspli . . .'

'What?'

'Your adjutant, for Christ's sake!'

– – –

Wäspli expels air from his nose. His mouth is gagged.

Blood trickles from his ear. He tosses back his head as Manfred opens the door and enters.

A woman is seated in the room too, a nurse, dressed in white.

'What's going on?' I demand to know, striding up to Wäspli.

Manfred grabs my shoulder, but I wrench myself away, and immediately both the brothers are upon me, a hand grips my neck, I don't know which of them takes my legs.

'Herr Oberleutnant der Polizei,' says Michael.

'I want to know what the hell is going on here!' I shout into the room.

'Put him down,' says Manfred. He has seated himself at the desk, a toothpick of bone protruding from his mouth.

I twist myself free of the Schwabenland brothers, am immediately in his face. Manfred holds up his hand and I halt in mid-movement.

'The Führer says, as you know, that conscience is a Jewish invention . . . one must be strong in order not to attend to its voice. But this little *shit* here . . .'

He nods towards Wäspli.

'This little *shit* almost got away with it. Which is why I find it difficult to believe it was his own idea. Rather clever, actually, albeit simple . . .'

'What are you talking about, Manfred? What *is* this?'

'Do you know Dr Elswanger?'

'From the RKFDV?'

'That's right. The Reich's Commission for the Strengthening of the German People, nothing wrong with that, but the Fourth

101

Office is one of the Reichsführer-SS's less fortunate ideas if you ask me, sending a bunch of old ditherers in here with their skull-measuring calipers and vapid theories, separating the genuine from the false . . .'

'An important job, I'd say . . .' I mumble, sensing that Manfred's awaiting a response.

'But Elswanger! That fat old fool, myopic as a mole and pushing eighty, you should see the way his hands shake. When I put it to him, all he could do was shuffle his papers and drop his glasses on the table. *Crack!* They broke in two! A truckload of Israelites and half-castes could wander past him and he'd still be engrossed in the Aryan convolutions of an auditory canal!'

'Manfred.'

'Yes?'

'What are you on about? You drag my adjutant over here, it's *not* your jurisdiction!'

'Jurisdiction! All their parlour games and commissariats and circulars. It all boils down to one thing.'

'Which is?'

'The SS calls the shots, and here that means me! I must say, though, that I have learned a great deal from you, Heinrich. The methodical approach . . .'

He steps over to Wäspli, stands beside him, slightly to his rear, his blind spot, grabs his hair and yanks his head back.

'This bastard was sending your little girl to Lebensborn . . .'

'Lebensborn?'

'He went to the dressing station and picked out a dead *Volksdeutsche*, one Paul Steiger, Waffen-SS, filched his papers and discovered Steiger had a daughter the same age as your little girl . . .'

'She's *not* my little girl . . .'

'So you keep saying. But anyway, a girl who died a month ago, in some miscalculated bombing. He switches the documents and hey presto she's no longer a Belorussian, no longer a partisan accomplice, no longer a *problem*, but an orphan girl, daughter of a slain *Volksdeutsche*. A German, Heinrich! Ready to be brought up a National Socialist at Lebensborn. Do you know what that is?'

'Tell me.'

'It's despicable, that's what. Mixing of the races. It's . . . He even taught her to sing a few snatches of 'Tannenbaum', and her new name, Sophie . . . quite pretty, isn't it? And our Dr Elswanger in Minsk bought it. She'd be on her way to Germany if it hadn't been for . . . this lady here.'

Manfred turns to the woman seated by the window, who has been silent ever since we entered the room. She must be about forty, dark grizzled hair pulled back tight in a bun – one of the bony sisters of Lebensborn. She nods appreciatively.

'Yes,' she says. 'There was nothing wrong with her papers, but as soon as I was on my own with her it was obvious the story didn't stand up.'

'So what do you say?' Manfred says, looking at me.

'I don't believe it!'

'Very well,' he replies after a moment. Then to the woman, who gets to her feet:

'Would you, Ingeborg?'

Ingeborg leaves the room. We stand there for a second. I step towards Wäspli.

'Don't you say a word to him!' Michael yells in my face.

– – –

103

Ingeborg comes back in with Etke. The girl is wearing a red and white checked dress, white socks and black patent shoes. Who plaited her hair? Who pinned the plaits up above her ears? Have they got Masja as well?

'Dr Elswanger may perhaps be forgiven . . .' says Manfred.

He steps up to Etke, smiles at her, draws an index finger across her throat and chin, pats her cheek. He produces a bar of chocolate from the jacket of his uniform and proceeds to open it. The wrapper rustles. All the time he looks at me. He breaks off a square.

'Well, now that we're all here,' he says, 'what would you suggest we do about the situation?'

'I don't know.'

'You don't know?'

'No.'

'And you're a policeman . . .'

'Yes.'

'Not even if we're dealing with, what do you people call it, aggravating circumstances? Forgery, insubordination, miscegenation.'

I say nothing. Manfred gestures towards Wäspli.

'Should we let your friend off lightly? A penal unit, a spot of minesweeping, perhaps? Or should we put him through a court martial, cause problems for his family? What do you say? Lenience or punishment?'

Silence.

'I wonder who made those pretty plaits,' Manfred says. He smoothes his hand over Etke's little head.

'Lenience,' I say, rather too hastily. 'What do we do so he can be let off?'

Manfred steps up to me, cups his hand around my ear and whispers. At first I don't understand what he is saying, but then the blood drains from my head.

'I can't,' I say.

He leans forward and whispers again:

'Must your little Masja die too? Must she? Must they *all* die?'

– – –

It is raining now.

The beam of the headlights illuminates the grave.

Wäspli is standing at its edge, in mud-spattered boots, face pale.

Michael is behind him, holding his head tightly. He says:

'Close your eyes and I'll cut off your eyelids!'

Wäspli trembles in the morning chill.

Manfred approaches with Etke, his hand on her shoulder. She sees the grave and will go no further. He takes her by the arm and flings her forward along the path. She cries out, stumbles. Her dress is covered in mud.

Manfred hauls her to her feet, shoves her on to the edge of the grave.

She is crying.

The pit is full of lime. The corpses, though, are visible among the green-white chunks.

Manfred removes his PPK from its holster, racks the slide and releases, checks to make sure a cartridge is now seated in the chamber.

He hands the firearm to me.

'Now,' he says. 'Do it.'

She whimpers.

I put the muzzle to her neck. I can feel her trembling through the barrel.

I look away as I fire. The pistol recoils in my hand.

A thud as she lands in the grave.

– – –

Afterwards.

Manfred puts his hand around my neck, his face up close.

'Was it your first time? It was, wasn't it? Your first time . . .'

I have never seen such tenderness in his eyes. He gives my shoulders a squeeze and walks away down the path.

I see him toss something away. I follow him and pick it up.

It is a crumpled piece of paper, already moist with rain.

I see my signature on the document Wäspli gave me before I left for Minsk.

He tried to copy my hand. Destination: *Lebensborn*.

When I retun to the cars I see Masja waiting. She shivers in the cold.

Manfred must have had her with him. I take her by the hand and lead her away.

She will not look at me.

Truth is consistent.

GOGA

Questions

The administrative offices of the
Judenrat, Sjtjutjyn ghetto.

The last of the Zaludok Jews ended up here after the massacre
in '42. We are looking for anyone who knows Tulabajev's friend.
A homosexual deported to the Gulag between '39 and '41.
A Jew from Zaludok. Aka: Goga.

We need a real name, a photograph, a description. If anyone
knows, they are here.

The man in front of us looks down at the floor: he holds his
hands clasped before him, the cap with the coloured ribbon
between his fingers, the armband on his right arm, Jewish panto
police, a traitor to his own kind, a bastard, a slave himself.

There is a hole in his shoe.

We are: Manfred (smoking), Michael and Hans, the
Schwabenland brothers, me, Semjon and some Hiwis (clustered
together in a corner, rolling shoulders, loosening muscles, chat-
ting). Manfred has just yelled at the guy, now he smokes a

cigarette and has calmed down, he takes a handkerchief from his breast pocket, dabs his brow and the corners of his mouth.

'I don't know . . .' says the Jew. 'I don't know, Herr Hauptsturmführer . . .'

Manfred gives Michael a nod, Michael steps up close to the Jew and proceeds to scream in his face, his voice breaks, he waves his hand and steps back. He tries again, but his voice is gone. He laughs, and croaks a *Los!* to the Hiwis, who at first fail to catch the order. Then the tallest of them steps forward from within the group: it is Semjon, he pulls a short studded belt from the pocket of his uniform, it looks like a bootstrap. He wraps it around his knuckles and tightens the buckle with his free hand. He goes up to the Jew and says something to him.

The Jew looks up at the same instant the blow is delivered.

He drops his cap.

'Pick it up,' says Manfred, and inhales smoke deep into his lungs.

The Jew bends down to pick up the cap, Semjon places his boot against the man's hip and propels him backwards against the desk.

'Hey,' says Manfred. 'I told you to *pick it up.*'

The Jew tries again, Semjon snatches up the cap and tosses it to one of the other Hiwis. The Jew looks across at Manfred, who nods. He moves forward to retrieve it. The Hiwi holds it out in front of him, yanks it away as the man reaches out, then steps forward and punches him, a sudden, snapping jab to the jaw. *That's right*, says the Hiwi, and strikes again, his fist an abrupt blur. *That's right!*

Another man slaps the Jew hard in the face, takes the cap and holds it above his head. Again, the Jew attempts to retrieve it, again he is struck, jostled, manhandled. A lashing of fists, then a punch delivered deep to the small of his back.

He is sweating, and bleeding.

Manfred gets to his feet, steps up to him, holds up his chin and yells into his face:

'I want everyone from Zaludok at the hospital in Lida by 14:00. Can I trust you to find every last one of them?'

'Yes,' says the Jew.

Manfred wipes the blood and spit from his fingers on the Jew's sleeve.

– – –

Back at Lida, the SS hospital,
main entrance, 13:59.

A single truck. A Feldwebel jumps down from the cab and goes round to the back of the vehicle, unpins the tailgate and lets it drop with a clatter. He barks a command and the Jews climb out: suitcases, clothes, battered hats. They think they are being evacuated. The Hiwis come forward, snatch the luggage from their hands, jabbing with their rifle butts. They line them up, a dissipated flock, always the same expressions. I think to myself the Jew will be remembered for this: dullness before death, dying with a shrug, a quiver of the lip, a quiet *Elohim Yisrael*.

Manfred looks at his watch and gives me a nod.

'14:03, not bad.'

I study the line-up. Twenty-two individuals. What is left of Zaludok's Jewish population. In 1942 there were two thousand of them. Before the day is over there will be none.

It is stiflingly hot.

111

They will be asked the same question: names of Jews deported to the Gulag between 1939 and 1941.

Manfred says:

'Do you want to do the interrogating?'

'No,' I say.

— — —

The hospital basement, 15:12.

I rinse my face with cold water from a bowl placed on a trolley in the corridor. Semjon comes in with a boy, seven or eight years old, the last of the Swiderskis. Semjon steers him into the room with a hand on his shoulder, speaks to him softly, nudges the door back with his foot. The boy sees something at the other end of the room, outside my field of vision. He looks at me; his mouth opens slowly. He begins to scream.

The door shuts with a click.

— — —

The hospital basement, 15:34.

Semjon opens the door with his elbow. He has the naked boy in his arms. The white corpse is perforated by large, dark holes. He goes over to a rubbish container, blocks the wheel with a foot and dumps the body inside.

Manfred pokes his head round the door.

'Come on,' he says. 'Get a move on.'

— — —

He is lying on the steel bed, the springs of the bare frame are knives in his back, buttocks, hips, lower arms – a wash of blood beneath him. White tiles, creaking springs. The Ukrainian has returned from the table by the sink, he needed to get something, pliers perhaps, and now his knee is embedded in the man's chest, he waves the instrument about in his right hand, the Jew's mouth is no longer a mouth, his head is no longer a head, he is inside his own death, screaming, whispering, sobbing, gurgling, wailing: *Bliznez, bliznez, bliznez!* The Ukrainian jabs at his throat and, as though at the clap of a hand, the Jew succumbs.

The Ukrainian has severed his windpipe.

What he fetched from the table was a pair of poultry shears.

Only the echo of the lungs can be heard now, a low hum from the depths of a soul.

Then silence.

I remove my spectacles, take a handkerchief from my jacket pocket and wipe some mist from the lenses.

My ears are ringing.

'What did he say?' Manfred asks. He has risen from his chair in the corner.

The interpreter turns to the Ukrainian, who has climbed down from the bed, a sheen of perspiration upon his skin, and now puts down the shears on the table with a clatter. He is wearing uniform trousers, his chest bare, his head is rectangular and Slavic: all jaw and no brow. He exchanges a few sentences with the interpreter, then stands with his back to us as he arranges his instruments on the cloth, rolls them up and ties a knot.

113

'He said he saw him picked out three months ago. His twin,' says the interpreter.

'Whose twin?'

'Bronstejns'. They were identical.'

'Our man's name is Bronstejn?'

'Bronstejns. With an s. One of the Bronstejns brothers came to Vorkuta in '39. The other stayed in Zaludok and got special treatment in Sjtjutjyn this spring.'

'Does he have any other names, besides Bronstejns?'

'He didn't say.'

'Goga . . . did he mention that name? Goga?'

'No. But he did say something else.'

'Yes?' says Manfred.

'He didn't look like a Jew. His eyes were blue. The Bronstejns brothers have blue eyes.'

– – –

Shortly afterwards in Manfred's office
on the first floor, where Wäspli
sat gagged the night before.

Manfred is on the phone.

He gesticulates to me, writing in the air, points and nods.

'That's it, Bronstejns with an s. No, I don't know. Bronstejn, perhaps. About three months ago.'

I take my fountain pen from my inside pocket. He snatches it from my hand, twists off the cap with his teeth and writes.

'Yes, got it. Thanks.'

He puts down the receiver.

'Bloody hell,' he says. 'One of the heavyweights, he said.'

'Heavyweights?' I pick up the note:

Elias Bronstejns, Sjtjutjyn, behind kolkhoz dairy. Grave IV, at least 1500. Inquire R-F Müller.

Manfred stands with his back to me over by the sideboard. When he turns round he has a bottle of the Hungarian cognac and two glasses in his hands.

'I really couldn't be bothered making that long trip again,' he says with a sigh.

He flops down in his chair and fills both glasses with the amber liquid, without asking if I want any.

'Join me?'

At that same moment it begins to rain.

'What have you done with Wäspli?' I ask.

He knocks back the second glass.

'Peculiar thing about you, Heinrich,' he says. 'You're soft. But you're not soft enough . . .'

'What?'

'You're malleable. Like clay.'

'Like clay?'

'Yes, clay. Soon you'll be like me.'

— — —

The rain has stopped.

The soil of the plain. I pick up a clod, crumble it between my fingers. It is dark, porous.

It fertilises itself, they say.

We are back in Sjtjutjyn, some fifty metres behind the charred remains of the Kolkhoz Vorosjilov's dairy, Grave IV, Rottenführer Müller in charge of the excavation.

Goga's twin is buried here among the thistles and rusting oil drums, the discarded caterpillar tracks.

A Jewish woman from the truck stands next to Manfred.

Her movements are stiff and silent.

The corpses in the grave are blackened and fusty. They lie top to tail and seem oddly jointless, already withered, amalgamated, without shape of their own.

Manfred is holding a handkerchief to his mouth. The Rottenführer is drinking schnapps and shouting at the Jews in the grave. I'm smoking. Piles of bodies next to the pit. Manfred swears, but Bronstejns is here somewhere, I checked the ghetto archive when I went for cigarettes.

Suddenly the woman stiffens, and nods. We have reached some four metres down, approximately the middle of the pit, about ten or twelve metres from where I stand.

She points down. A male body: jacket, trousers, one shoe missing. Manfred nods to one of the Trawnikis, who shouts out a command.

Two Jewish labourers cross the pit, recover the body. Its head bumps over the ground.

Manfred roars, they nod, making hectic, jerking movements, a hand underneath the neck as support.

I sit on my haunches.

The man's head is rectangular, the skin dark brown, low hairline. Exit wound at the right cheek. The bullet has splintered the bone; the upper lip and the wing of the nose are gone. He must have lifted his head as the shot was fired.

The eyes are colourless and sunken.

The face is unrecognisable.

– – –

A black liquid runs from the throat as one of the Jewish labourers separates the head from the body with a spade and allows the corpse to slide back into the pit. It flops into place next to the woman from before, a shoulder upon her neck.

'What now?' I ask. 'That face is no good for identification.'

'Come on,' says Manfred. 'I know someone who can help us.'

Taxidermy

'The specimen is no good, it's ruined,' he says in his Jewish German.

Davaj Manfred says, not good enough, and nods to Semjon, who strikes the man hard with the flat of his hand. The Jew recovers his spectacles and straightens up, head bowed and turned to the side. His hand trembles as he reinserts the bloodied dentures.

Manfred says something I fail to catch to Semjon, who goes and stands by the door.

I sit down in the far corner. Manfred has taken over the investigation – I just follow along. It was he who found the Jew in the hospital laboratories and drove us out here, to his workshop in a village bordered by wilderness, close to the puszcza. Now the area is cleansed of Jews, *Judenrein*, and is partisan country, but Manfred has us well protected: there must be a hundred and fifty men outside.

The Jew is back at his workbench and has begun to unpack the parcel; the newspaper is soaked from the ice and the dark oozing liquid that seeps from the head. I sense the stench that is suppressed by the coldness of the ice. In a moment it will fill the room.

He goes over to a glass cabinet; the panes are shattered, items lie scattered inside and on the floor.

His movements are small. Hands busy now, he jabs his bony head abruptly like a hen, now and then he bends down and picks something out of the mess on the floor. Then he is at the lathe, he puts down some bottles filled with liquids, removes the glass bungs and sniffs at the contents. He places a number of items on the worktop: pipette, scalpel, sharpening stone, brushes, gloves, wooden blocks of various sizes, tow, wood wool, wire, scissors.

'Eyes,' he says. 'I need eyes.'

Manfred stands for a second, hesitating and speechless. He goes out through the door, into the sun.

The Jew returns to the head, studies it a while in silence, as though considering his approach. He picks up the scalpel and makes a sweeping incision behind both ears, continues down along the hairline at the nape of the neck, turns his wrist and folds the skin upwards. Gripping firmly with the right hand, adjusting with three fingers of the left, with small, meticulous tugs he draws the scalp from the back of the head: the crown, the upper forehead. He cuts away the ears with measured precision and arrives at the sockets, exposing them, placing an incision at the root of the nose and pulling away the rest of the skin that encloses the skull. Only the mouth remains fixed in place.

He picks up a small folding knife, slits open the lips, removes the entire face and places it down on the worktop.

Then he begins to scrape the flesh from the skull.

When he has finished he fetches a hacksaw. The brain has collapsed inside the cranium. He places a pot of water on the stove. He boils the skull.

I find my matches while he prepares the solutions for the tanning.

He looks up at me as I light an Efka: *Bitte* . . .

Semjon steps forward, ready to strike, but I shake my head, pinch the glowing end from the cigarette and put the unsmoked remainder in my pocket.

'Come on, Semjon,' I say. 'Let's leave him to his work. This could take hours.'

– – –

The sun dazzles me, and for a moment I lose my bearings.

Our column extends several hundred metres along the dirt road and out of the village. The little square with the church and the burnt-out synagogue is jammed with vehicles: our six Sd.Kfz 222s, four lorries, six Kübelwagen and the RSO, a train of horse-drawn carts. The lorries' exhaust fumes are blue, they pollute the hot air with their caustic smell. Troops scurry back and forth and yet there is a slowness about it all, an indolence about the spoils. Two Hiwis pull a cow by its nose from a shed, a Ukrainian holds his hand to the blazed muzzle of a mare, his movements abrupt as the horse nips at the fodder in the palm, foaming at the mouth.

Its flanks steam in the heat.

There are no inhabitants to be seen, but we know the village is not empty.

They are waiting inside, in their houses, just as they did when Steiner was here in '41, when he led their Jewish neighbours into the woods only a kilometre away.

Sonderkommando 1005 is exhuming the bodies now. We saw the whole process on the drive here, the Jewish labourers loading the corpses onto the conveyors, tipping the porous, brittle cadavers into the burning pits. And at the edge of the old graves, shining white bathtubs, a shimmer of hydrochloric acid, H_2O HCl *for the extraction of metals*, the stacks of fusty bones, jawbones, incomplete skulls. Jews toiling, heaving, wrenching at the heads with crowbars and tongs, SS standing about or lounging on the slopes, or supervising the filtering. One of them seated on the stub of a tree at the roadside, a finger prodding at the small lumps of dental gold in his palm. His hand slides back into his pocket as we pass, an exaggerated wave.

The last plunderings, the last traces.

By some stroke of luck, our taxidermist was still alive.

It strikes me, as I cup my hand against the wind to light my unsmoked Etka, that Manfred was here, at this place, in '41, along with Steiner. It was Manfred who saved the Jew then. Of course. He pulled him out of the line after discovering the marvel of his workshop.

Did you feel sentimental all of a sudden, Manfred? Were you thinking of Dr Zeisler?

How many times had we visited Dr Zeisler's basement shop together – with the snipes, plovers and greenshanks we found in the reeds at the mouth of the Elbe or at the Wadden Sea: sanderlings and turnstones, wings entangled in the trap wires? During our birding period in the Untersekunda, we were inseparable; in waders we set our traps and lines, glued to our binoculars in the early mornings in the dunes, noting down the migrations, numbering the nests, counting the eggs, smoking cigarettes, gazing out upon scenery of grey and green.

He was not a doctor at all, but we called him Dr Zeisler because he stuffed and mounted the birds and animals for the *Gymnasium*. Birds were his speciality. He had hundreds of them in drawers, pale and dusty in colour, and we fed him with specimens. He gave me a goldcrest, mounted in a nest with two red, speckled eggs, its faint green feathers a sheen. He had closed the holes in the eggs and painted them over in a slightly paler red.

A perfect still life.

I gave it to Eline. It was the only time I saw her cry.

'*I don't know why I'm crying. Why you make me cry.*'

'*Because it's dead?*'

'*No, because you're cruel . . .*'

I go over to the Kübelwagen, dig out a bottle of plum schnapps and sit down to wait on the footboard. I know Manfred will make us hang around until the Jew has finished.

A black cockerel with a fiery red comb comes running across the square, little clouds of dust kicked up in the air behind it. It stops, and turns its feathered head towards me.

— — —

Manfred eats in silence, broken only by the sound of engines and occasional shouts in the distance, his slobbering as he sucks on a wing or spits out a black feather that has not been plucked.

The light has already grown dim. Soon the dew will fall.

A Zündapp with a sidecar skids along the track, steering its way between horses and troops unwilling to move out of the way. It pulls up in front of us, a Feldwebel extracts himself from the sidecar and takes a glass jar from his leather satchel. He holds the top and bottom between his palms. It is full of eyes.

'From the Central Infirmary,' he says, and hands it to me.

'Are any of them blue?' Manfred asks, wiping his fingers.

'No,' I say. 'They're all green.'

'Idiot!' Manfred yells at the Feldwebel. 'Green!'

He holds two green glass eyes in his hand, shuffles them around in his palm.

— — —

The first of the vehicles pulled away some minutes ago. The outskirts of the village are already in flames, the firing is scattered now, followed by the report of a handgun from inside the workshop. Manfred comes out with a wicker basket in one hand. Semjon glances back through the open door, lights a rag and tosses it inside. The familiar whoosh as the petrol fumes ignite, and moments later the dry timber crackles.

Manfred gets in, pats my cheek and slams the door shut.

'You're daydreaming,' he says. I put the Kübelwagen into gear and pull away into the convoy.

He takes Bronstejns's head from the basket and places it on the dashboard.

'What do you reckon?'

The head is mounted on a wooden board, the holes in the skin covered up with pastel. I tap the forehead with the knuckle of my index finger.

A rustle of wood wool.

The green eyes glisten.

'I'm not sure,' I say.

He offers me a cheroot, I have to ask him to light it for me as I hold it between my teeth.

'A handsome fellow,' he says, turning to Semjon and the two Schwabenland brothers on the back seat, offering the packet. 'Don't you think?'

'He's the spit of Franz,' says Michael after pausing to think.

'Franz Bibermann?' says Hans. 'The grocer on the corner?'

'Yeah. Frogface.'

'You're right!' Hans splutters. 'Frogface! He had a skin problem.'

'I hated him,' says Michael. 'He was a bastard.'

'Franz Bibermann . . .' says Hans. 'Fucking hell!'

Michael takes something from his breast pocket, a small case he passes to Manfred.

'I can't stand to look at him,' he says.

Manfred opens the case and clicks out a pair of round eye-glasses with mirrored lenses. He bends the pliable earpieces around the delicate ears and pushes the glasses into place at the root of the nose, adjusting the angle of the frame.

'There we are . . .' he says.

'I'm feeling a bit off,' I say shortly afterwards.

'There *was* something funny about that chicken, wasn't there?' says Manfred.

The roads

The sun is thick, fat. The landscape swells and seeps away at the edges. I unbutton the jacket of my uniform. I ask Manfred to stop the car. He looks at me, and his mouth cracks into a grin.

'Look at him . . . a true *Norddeutscher* . . .'

I am not laughing.

I am holding my hand up to my mouth. I swallow.

I ask for the binoculars. Michael hands them to me.

I stand up in the vehicle, wind buffeting my face. Dust blows up from the road.

I put the binoculars to my eyes: a shimmering, oscillating section of landscape reels in the heat haze.

My legs buckle. I sit down.

'You're white as a sheet, Heinrich.'

'Yes, Manfred, I am *white as a sheet*. Where are we going?'

'Wait and see.'

'Just answer me, for God's sake!'

He twists round to face me, looks at me in astonishment, his arm hooked around the seat.

'Wait and see, I said . . .'

– – –

SS marschiert in Feindesland
Und singt ein Teufelslied
Ein Schütze steht am Wolgastrand
Und leise summt er mit . . .

SS men march in hostile lands
And sing a devil's song
A steady guard, on the Volga stands
And hums this tune along

'Again! Come on, Heinrich. Don't be so bloody boring.'
  'Again!'
'Well, if we must.'
'That's the spirit!'
Manfred raises his index finger, points at us in turn, me, Hans, Michael, Semjon, then twirls it in the air, conducting:
'One . . . two . . . three!'

SS marschiert in Feindesland
Und singt ein Teufelslied . . .

I take the bottle Michael hands me.

– – –

Navahrudak, we pull up outside Oscar Dirlewanger's house. Former Freikorps man, convicted of pederasty and murder before Hitler took power, now Oberführer with his own battalion, *Sonderbataillon Dirlewanger*, Belorussia's most notorious slayer of partisans, not even Generalkommissar Kube or the Polizeiführer can keep him in check. Himmler waxes lyrical, calls him Heinrich the First's robber king, the Teutonic Cossack, the Slavic campaign of 928 incarnate, buccaneer, marauder, *Landsknecht*. But a bastard murderer is what he is, and I am reeling drunk on schnapps.

Manfred is not here.

I sit in the vehicle, bottle in hand, shivering with cold.

The bottle is plump, fascinating.

It has a cork that pops when I remove it, a partial vacuum inside.

I remove it again. *Pop*.

Pop, once more.

Now with my thumb.

Pop. Or perhaps more of a *pfop*. The equalisation of pressure is not quite as forceful. *Thop?*

I wait. I drink.

Drink and wait.

Thwop.

Like a skull being cracked with a crowbar.

I have a fever. I need to piss.

I pull on the door handle and tumble out of the car.

Michael, who is standing smoking on the other side of the vehicle, comes round to me.

'Ups-a-daisy,' he says, pulling me to my feet. 'Oberleutnant . . .'

'Where's Manfred?' I ask. 'Where the *hell* is he?'

I jab a finger towards Dirlewanger's house, the fine cast-iron gate, the driveway and the wide steps leading up to the main door of the yellow-washed residence. There is an espalier of red roses. I jab at that too.

'When did he go in? What time is it anyway?'

I pull up my shirtsleeve and stare at my watch, but the hands are a blur.

'It's been *hours* . . .'

127

'We need Dirlewanger on our side,' says Michael, and thrusts out his lower lip, turning down the corners of his mouth. 'Without Dirlewanger we can forget all about it.'

'About what?'

'Wait and see . . .'

'I'm going in to get him.'

'No,' he says, then more softly: 'Don't.'

I stand for a minute, then offer him the bottle. He wipes his mouth on the sleeve of his uniform, twirls his thumb around the lip, sticks it inside and pulls it out, that sound again, and raises the bottle to his mouth. Saliva bubbles on his lips, he takes a good swig.

'*Erst ploppt's, dann schmeckt's* . . . first the pop, then the taste.'

'What?'

'The one with the stopper. You know . . .'

'No, I don't. What?'

'The bock beer, Schwaben Bräu . . .'

I swipe the bottle from his hand and drink again. I watch him as I swallow, his ruddy face, the mealy eyes, mealy, benevolent eyes, transformed now, welling with sentiment. He prods my chest.

'*Du* . . .' he says.

'What?'

'It can get to you, all this, can't it?'

'How do you mean?'

He is breathing heavily in my face. His right fist is on my shoulder.

'Like having a great big hole knocked into you, and it's all . . .'

'All what?' I say. '*What?*'

'Like all it takes is something to prick a hole . . . for it all to rush out through your arse, *whoosh* . . .'

'Whoosh?'

'Yeah. Everything we are . . . Our, whatever it's called . . . our soul,' he says, and swivels away on his heel, sober at once. 'I think about that a lot.'

– – –

I leave him to ponder on his lapse, and press the bottle into his open hand. His mouth is open too, but he stays put as I go through the gate to Dirlewanger.

Once on the property, I am struck by uncertainty.

The neatly raked driveway up the house, the gravel, the roses.

It seems so empty.

At once I feel scared. Drunk-scared.

I walk past the house, following a new path, and come to an eight-sided gazebo. A man is standing there in striped prison uniform as I come round the side, a *Mütze* on his head. He is quite as startled as I am, stares, then realises his mistake.

I bark at him:

'*Mütze ab!*'

He stumbles and falls, is chained like a dog to a ring in the ground. He gets to his feet again, picks up the cap, stands with it clasped in his hands.

'Do you speak German?' I ask.

'*Ja, Herr . . .*'

He looks down at his feet.

'I'm looking for the Oberführer,' I say.

'The zoo . . . Perhaps he is in the zoo,' he says, in whatever accent it is – Yiddish, Dutch – are there Dutch Jews here too?

He points to the other side of some greenhouses in the extensive gardens.

— — —

I follow the path, entering a system of pens and small sheds. There are goats, cats, bales of straw. At first I fail to realise that what I see is a woman seated on a stool in a small pen, in front of a red playhouse. Her head is shaven, a shadow of red hair about the scalp, ashen skin, her nails bitten down. She is bottle-feeding a fox, a scrawny animal with wretched skin, it too red. It has scratched itself to the bone, down the length of the spine to its hairless brush. The bottle is deep inside its mouth, milk seeping from behind its black gums – it is mad with hunger, and she herself has all but wasted away in her striped jacket. Now she lifts her head, I can see her skull beneath her skin, her small brown teeth, and yet she smiles, a slight blush that departs immediately from her face, but remains on her lips, a glow as though of consumption. At this moment they are as one: the scabby beast and her emaciated, angular frame. The fox turns its long head towards me, looks at me for a second with black, malicious eyes. *They are no longer afraid of us*, I think, and it twists free of the young woman's grasp to slink away, its paws hardly touching the ground. She looks right through me.

Am I invisible now?

— — —

And then we are interrupted.

He has come running from the sheds at the bottom of this pitiable menagerie – furious, a red-blistered SS-Schütze. In his hand is a whip, Dirlewanger's insignia on his collar patches, the crossed rifles with the stick grenade. He grabs her by the scruff

130

of the neck, lifts her up in a single movement and flings her to the ground, lashes her shoulder with the knout. I watch as he works himself into a lather: she face down, hands at her head, he screaming and yelling. Presently he ceases, turns his ruddy face towards me, his mouth foaming. He drags the sleeve of his uniform across his brow and pants for breath.

'Was she bothering you?'

'Not at all.'

'Bloody Jewish whores. They . . .'

'Oberleutnant der Polizei Hoffmann,' I say, cutting him off. 'I'm looking for Oberführer Dirlewanger.'

'What?'

'Yes, Oscar Dirlewanger . . .'

It is as if he only wakes up now. What is the matter with him? I ask why they have a zoo here, what the idea is. I look into his eyes as I speak. Why the performance? Then it clicks: he is protecting her, he allowed her to lie on her stomach, to lessen the injuries, his punishment was half-hearted, more bluster than beating. He is involved with her, *Rassenschande*, and so has to be at her all the time, ranting and railing, keeping her on a short leash, making sure no one gets close.

So no one kills her.

Does he love her? Is she pregnant with his child?

'It's satisfying,' he says.

'What is?'

'To see a young fledgling with only one leg grow strong, when you've seen it fallen out of the nest. Dirlewanger's right about that. There's something soothing about it. Watching something grow . . .'

Should I report him? Investigate? He has done me no wrong, he is in love. A little, amorous heart. Am I to break it?

131

'Where do you find them, these animals?'

'On the hare hunts . . . it's like when you throw dynamite in a stream . . . they're all just lying there, the birds, unconscious from the blasts, you can go and pick them up . . .'

Should I? Yes or no? Strictly speaking it would be misconduct *not* to investigate the matter, not to *report* it. Dirlewanger himself has had charges brought against him by the SS Court for some mess or other in Poland, a Jewish girl. Was it Kraków?

'What did you say your name was?' I ask him.

'Klaus. Klaus Maier.'

'Hello, Klaus Maier.'

– – –

I walk down a path that leads me between two small henhouses, a cat leaps across in front of me, there are goats in the darkness of one of the structures, hens clucking, pecking at a pile of grain. I look for children, but there are none. Instead I see another Schütze scooping grain into a trough a little further on.

'Where's Dirlewanger?'

'Who wants to know?' he says, looking me up and down.

This one too is well-fed; he looks after his own, Dirlewanger.

I tell him who I am. *Apologies, apologies* . . . He drops his scoop. *Follow me.*

We walk on past some garages, following a white wall, the ground falling away, an orchard full of apple trees.

'Over there,' he says, pointing.

Manfred is facing away further down the slope. Dirlewanger stands with Bronstejns's head under his arm, looking up at him. Manfred gesticulates, making short, fiery movements. Dirlewanger smiles and hands him back the head, then walks off in the opposite direction, down the slope.

132

'What's going on?' I ask as Manfred returns.

'What are you doing here?' he says.

'Just answer me.'

He looks at me as though I have said nothing.

'We *have* to be in! We have to!'

I grip his shoulders and shake him.

'Manfred, what the hell are you on about?'

He shoves me away, a flat hand against my chest, I stagger back and fall.

'You're drunk . . .'

'So what?'

'It'll be a hare hunt like no other. Starting tomorrow. The area around Belize. Operation Hermann.'

'An anti-partisan operation?' I ask.

'Yes. Goga's a partisan, isn't he? He must be in there somewhere, in the woods, yes? For God's sake, Heinrich!'

He reaches out a hand and pulls me to my feet.

'You're going to have to convince Bach-Zelewski . . . that's *your* job! We bypass Oscar and go straight to the top!'

'Bach-Zewelski? The Polizeiführer? What makes you think he'll see us?'

'He's in Ivenets. Come on.'

Hare hunt

Ivenets, a couple of hours east of
Lida. The square in front of the little
matchstick house of a town hall.

We wait to be admitted and present our case. Engines idling, more than two hundred vehicles split according to battle units, some 8,800 men, all of them under Curt von Gottberg's command: Kampfgruppe Gottberg. Even Höherer Polizeiführer Bach-Zelewski, the most powerful man in the East regions, is here. They study their topographical maps and finalise Operation Hermann's remaining details with the commanders of SS-Polizei-Regimenter 2 and 31, 1. SS-Infanterie-Brigade, the Latvians and the two Ukrainian SchuMa battalions, Dirlewanger's Sonderbataillon.

Here in the sun Manfred wanders restlessly about with his hatbox. I sit on my briefcase with the file documents on Goga Bronstejns.

'Are you ready?' Manfred asks.

'Yes, I'm ready.'

'Why is it taking so long?'

'I don't know, Manfred.'

Operation Hermann, commencement tomorrow, 13 July. The Naliboki forests are to be hemmed in from the north, west and south, a triangle from Ivenets here to the fortified villages of Naliboki and Rubesjevitj; according to the SD the area contains the greatest concentration of partisans in the whole of Belorussia. The four phases of the anti-partisan strategy: (1) marching up and forming the cauldron; (2) tightening the cauldron, definition of the battle area; (3) clearing the cauldron, the last concentric attack; (4) mopping up. Problem: the Naliboki forests are not woodland, but puszcza – swamp, primeval land, wilderness, hills, underground bunkers, beavers and mosquitoes. And in the midst of it all the Neman river that keeps all of it wet and impenetrable and is the reason we cannot maintain Belorussia, a wetland of fetid yellow water punctuated only by occasional mounds, fortified Stützpunkte, guarded roads, secured railway lines, bridges, telephone lines, but all of it corroding and crumbling, and constantly bursting into forest.

Bach-Zelewski's goal: to eliminate the partisan disorder in the Naliboki forests: Poles, Jews and Russians. Bach-Zelewski's subsidiary goal: to secure provisions and slaves for the Reich. Manfred's goal: to find Goga, perhaps to make an impression on Bach-Zelewski. My job: to convince Bach-Zelewski that the three goals can be combined.

'It's like the Greek exam in the Obersekunda,' says Manfred. '*Akylos* and *balanos* in the *Odyssey*. Which is acorn and which is beech mast? It's a lottery!'

'Akylos is *acorn*—'

'Oh, shut up, Heinrich! Do you think we'll get in?'

'I don't know, Manfred.'

'Do I look nervous?'

'Yes.'

'Then give me a cigarette!'

At Navahrudak Manfred had the head of Goga's twin photographed in a dusty studio from the turn of the century by a doddering, obsequious old man with a sharply pointed moustache, left arm raised above the camera from under the black cloth. The mounted head was positioned on a Doric column of gypsum, some bulrushes in an elephant's foot next to it, captured in a magnesium flash, a phosphorescent explosion of light. Manfred had thirty copies made.

The head is in its hatbox made of tin. The box has a metal handle, and Manfred keeps lifting the lid.

He does so now, just as an adjutant appears on the step and beckons us in.

— — —

'You've got *two* minutes,' says the adjutant before opening the door and showing us in to the staff meeting. He spreads a pair of fingers in the air: two.

The room is dim, I recognise Curt von Gottberg, operational commander, at the large chart table in the middle of the room, while others are unfamiliar to me. Dirlewanger glances up at us with no sign of recognition, then points a finger at the map, draws a line. Gottberg nods.

Bach-Zelewski must be the big man with his hands behind his back over by the window, surveying the square outside.

'HSS-PF Bach-Zelewski . . .' Manfred begins.

'Who addresses me, Curt?'

The man at the window turns slightly towards Gottberg at the table, and now I recognise Bach-Zelewski from the newsreels: hair tightly cropped to the temples, the round glasses, the soft folds of his neck, the looseness of his face. He narrows his eyes myopically.

Manfred clears his throat and steps towards him:

'Hauptsturmführer Schlosser . . .'

'DO NOT ADDRESS ME!' Bach-Zelewski bellows.

Manfred stops as abruptly as if he had received a slap in the face.

Gottberg lifts his head slowly.

'Curt,' Bach-Zelewski continues. 'Who gave him permission to speak?'

'He's one of Steiner's boys,' says Gottberg. 'He wants a command for Operation Hermann.'

'A dick-licker looking for a new protector?'

'I don't know about that,' Gottberg goes on. 'But he thinks Hubert's killer is out there in the forests.'

'Aha . . . Hubert, indeed,' says Bach-Zelewski. 'And what's he got in the hatbox? Evidence?'

He has yet to look at us.

'Tell him to show us what he's got in his box,' says Bach-Zelewski. His words trail off into sedate chomping.

'May I?' Manfred says, an inquiring nod towards Gottberg, who holds out his hand obligingly.

Manfred steps up to the table, opens the box and lifts out the head with both hands.

'This is what he looks like,' he says. 'This is his twin brother, Elias. Our perpetrator goes under the name of Goga. Goga Bronstejns. Bronstejns with an s.'

No one speaks. Dirlewanger stares stiffly at the head, as though bored.

'Ha!' After a pause, Bach-Zelewski bursts out. 'Such tenacity, Curt! What did you say your name was?'

'Hauptsturmführer Schlosser. Manfred Schlosser, Herr Polizeiführer.'

'Erich. Call me Erich. Curt, this is just the sort of man we need. What do you say, Oscar?'

Dirlewanger remains silent. He takes his cigarettes from his breast pocket, places one in his drawn mouth, and strikes a match on the heel of his boot.

'Hubert,' says Bach-Zelewski, now at the table, wagging a finger at the mounted head of the Bronstejns twin. 'I knew Hubert in the old days. And his lovely Gisela! Why on earth would this fellow here . . . or rather his twin, ha! . . . why do you think he would do a thing like that?'

'I have brought a crime investigator with me.'

Manfred nods at me, I step forward with my briefcase.

'Heinrich Hoffmann, Oberleutnant der Polizei, from Kripo, Hamburg,' he goes on. 'He found him. Meticulous police work. It all began with a little girl who witnessed the murder and saw some tattoos . . .'

Bach-Zelewski sits down, scraping the chair loudly as he draws himself in to the table.

'Fritz, some more of that delicious cake!' he thunders, then stabs a finger towards me. 'And you're going to tell me a story . . .'

Almost simultaneously, a young SS-Schütze enters carrying a tall, marzipan-covered gateau on a silver plate. The cake is topped with glazed raspberries.

I clear my throat and begin.

– – –

They sent me out of the room after I had delivered my report. Manfred remained, bent over the maps as the door closed behind me, Gottberg standing with a plate in his hand, Bach-Zelewski at the telephone, already relaying his new fairy tale: *The Little Jew with the Strange Tattoos.*

I am sitting in the shade on the square when they come out, Bach-Zelewski first down the steps, smoking a cigarette. Then Gottberg and Dirlewanger. Manfred beams like a little sun at the rear.

They gave him four companies, 8. SS-Kavallerie-Division, carte blanche, and a slice of the southern sector – starting point Ivenets.

The photographs of Elias Bronstejns are handed out to the company commanders of all regiments. To make sure no one shoots Goga by mistake.

– – –

The next day at 09:00 the cordon is in place and we enter the forests.

Manfred is on horseback and is photographed for the *Wochenschau*. He has laid his hands on a decorated Cossack saddle and mounted the hatbox with the head inside it on the horn.

He holds a short leather whip in his right hand.

Michael is behind the wheel of the Kübelwagen. I sit in the back and stare at his ears.

Semjon and Hans sit with their weapons at the ready.

Manfred sweeps out his arm and barks *Forward!* for the sake of the cameras. We descend into the landscape and are gone.

– – –

The following morning, a gravel track.

In the hollow north-east of our sector, we reach a sign bearing the name of a village: Dory. Low fencing, the flames are splinters in the dazzling sunlight, but we can feel the heat as far away as this. The soldiers, Dirlewanger's Sonderbataillon, the left flank, are flickering shadow puppets; they have dragged furniture, goods and chattels out in front of the crackling church, the haze reaches fifty metres into the air. Someone has put a record on the gramophone – a march at full volume. They lounge around in armchairs, weapons cradled.

The animals have been herded into a pen to await collection.

The local inhabitants are nowhere to be seen.

Timpani and snare drums.

A ponderous creaking from inside the church.

'Where death is, I am not,' says Manfred. 'Where I am, death is not.'

'The Bible,' says Michael. 'Isn't it?'

'Right,' says Hans. 'Jehovah himself.'

'It's Epicurus,' I say.

'Epi-who?' says Hans.

'Epi*curus*,' says Manfred, and flashes me a smile. 'A Greek. You wouldn't know him.'

A couple of hours later we run into a police regiment on our right flank, and phase one is complete: *Marching up and forming the cauldron.*

– – –

The same evening, in the forest.

Our Kübelwagen is stuck.

The rear wheels kick up silt and gravel, while four Hiwis shove from behind. Michael, his head turned, yells. Manfred has dismounted, we stand smoking, staring out at the endless puszcza, its ceaseless undulation, soaked in mud, ravaged by creeping insects, mosquitoes – but as yet no partisans.

'What's kok-saghyz?' he says. 'Do you know?'

'Kok-what?'

'Kok-saghyz . . . look.'

He produces a crumpled piece of paper from the jacket of his uniform and hands it to me. I unfold it. Where did he get this? Der Reichsführer-SS, Order of the Day No. 160/43/10.7.43. Addressee: Bach-Zelewski, cc. Gottberg. Directly from Himmler.

I stare at him.

'What? Go on, read . . .'

```
'"1. The Führer has decided that the partisan-infested
areas of northern Ukraine and central Russia are to be
evacuated of their entire population. 2. The entire able-
bodied male population will be . . . "'
```

'Not that,' he says, snatching the document from my hand and finding the passage in question with his finger. 'Here . . .'

```
'"5. The areas evacuated of their population are to be
planted, in part, with Kok-saghyz . . . The children's camps
are to be located at the border of these areas, so that the
children will be available as manpower for the cultivation
of Kok-saghyz and for agriculture. "'
```

'Kok-saghyz. What the *hell* is kok-saghyz?'

'Kok-saghyz?'

'Kok-saghyz.'

'Kok-saghyz!'

'The final solution to Jewish Commumism. Kok-saghyz . . .'

'Heil kok-saghyz!'

'Hallowed be Thy name . . .'

'Manfred,' I say seriously. '*Evacuated of their entire population*. All this? Does the Reichsführer know what he's saying?'

'Of course. Once we find them. And all the outlying villages to boot.'

— — —

Michael is the one who makes the discovery, on the morning of the third day.

The hole is no more than a couple of centimetres in diameter, half concealed by scrub at a sandy bank. He stands with one leg bent at the knee, foot buried in the silt, the other in the stream, his whole body aslant. He begins to scoop at the hole, and the sand gives way. It is an air-hole. I stand and stare.

'I've found a tunnel!' he shouts out, and men come running. Manfred comes too, cigarette in hand.

'Smoke grenade,' he barks.

He looks at me, elated.

'The bastards are building tunnels. There could be exit holes all over the place.'

'Like when we used to hunt foxes back home,' says Michael. 'Do you remember that, Hans?'

'Mm,' says Hans. 'The crucial thing is locating exits and digging out the lair. But always make sure you've found all the holes first.'

A young Sturmmann appears.

'What colour smoke have we got?' Manfred asks. The Sturmmann scurries back to the lorries, then comes staggering back with a heavy box.

Manfred opens it, cigarette in mouth.

'Purple, yellow, blue . . . what do you think, Heinrich?'

'I don't care,' I say.

'Oh, come on . . . play along . . .'

'Well, if you insist . . . purple.'

'Excellent.'

Manfred picks a long, bulbous grenade from the box, takes the rifle from Hans and fixes the grenade to the muzzle, thrusts the end into the hole and fires. He repeats the procedure twice. We hear the dull thuds of the exploding grenades inside the tunnel system.

He gathers a company, spreads them out in the forest. We wait.

After a while the cries go up:

'Here!'

'And here!'

Purple smoke seeps up into the air in six different places. No, seven. The last plume is perhaps two hundred metres away.

– – –

They have placed explosive charges and incendiary bombs at all exits, as well as within the tunnels. When the bombs go off we see the ground lift and shudder, but the tunnel itself retains its upper boundary, the explosion goes inwards and down. The sudden change in pressure leaves me deafened for a moment.

Peasant villagers, press-ganged, begin to dig, from the periphery towards the middle. After an hour we encounter the first human remains. The peasants lay them out in the clearing, and the hours pass.

Manfred hovers, trying to make head and tail of things. I can see his lips moving. He is counting.

Michael comes waddling over on his short legs.

'Come on, we've found some intact.'

– – –

As we stand at the edge of the crater, which is some five or six metres deep, we see them at the bottom. Presumably perished in the blast. There are three, clinging to each other.

A Hiwi in the crater attaches ropes to them, so they can be winched up and placed in the grass. Two elderly women and a boy, ten or twelve years old. Manfred crouches down and puts two fingers to the boy's neck.

'He's alive!'

He drags him to his feet, slaps him hard in the face, twice. It is as if the boy is drugged, in another world entirely.

He stands and sways, eyes closed. Manfred yells in his face.

Michael takes over, pulls out his P38, raises his outstretched arm towards the boy.

'No, for Christ's sake!' says Manfred and pushes his arm away. '*Not like that . . .*'

Michael blinks, his eyes like a pig's.

'How, then?'

'I don't know yet.'

– – –

I have lost my bearings. We skitter through mud, up and down.

The boy sits between Michael and Hans.

A bottle is passed around.

The machine gunner pulls back the charging handle, disengages the safety catch and swivels his body to the left. The vehicle lurches as he discharges a round into the forest.

Manfred pokes his head through the window, steering with one hand so the vehicle swerves. He straightens up, and yells at the top of his lungs:

'Heil Hitler!'

The machine gunner turns again, lets off another round. I hear the shots against the trees, the bark ripped from the trunks.

We each of us drink from the bottle once more, I hand it to the Schütze.

We screech:

'Heeiiiil Hitleeeeeer!'

— — —

Manfred is on the roof, while the machine gunner holds on to his legs. He is pissing.

He hurls the bottle into the trees with his other hand.

'Steiner . . . you old Nazi *bastard*! *I love you!* Prost!'

He climbs down again.

I can see he has been crying.

'He taught me *everything*, Heinrich,' he says, and splays out his hand in front of me.

On the index finger is a large gold signet ring bearing the Runic insignia of the SS.

'Hubert gave this to me. Twenty-four carat. Studded with diamonds. Don't you find it . . . vulgar?'

He wipes his eyes, sniggers, and is at once transformed. He begins to turn the ring with his thumb.

'I didn't want to wear it then . . . but now . . .'

Michael puts his hand on Manfred's shoulder, but he shoves him away. He looks at me.

'Heinrich?'

'What?'

'I know how he's going to die now . . . Goga.'

Belorussian Black Pied

Kolkhoz 31

Manfred handed over command and our small party left the forest, driving back towards Lida. We stopped here, where we have been waiting for three quarters of an hour, engines idling. Manfred is inside. He went in through the gate with Hans and Michael and some Lithuanian SS. The low concrete buildings of the collective, tin roofs matt in the sunlight, are cluttered with corroding machinery, the kolkhoz abandoned, plundered to its foundations two years ago, livestock confiscated, peasants driven out, the party chairman dragged off with a rope around his neck and strung up in the grain silo. His boots disappeared while no one was looking, I found them on a nine-year-old boy in Lida a week later: white matchsticks in great, black, shiny commissar boots. Now Manfred has got wind of some kind of pig breeding station that has been established here, Institut für Landwirtschaft, Göring's Four Year Plan, or Kube's colonists perhaps, together with the university at Munich – crossing north German breeds with inferior Russian ones. Long-eared Irkutsk with Hanoverian; the one with the long hams and the small ears; the Danish Landrace with its extra rib crossed with the Tsivilsk, a short-snouted Soviet breed with spots and thirteen pairs of teats. Something like that. But this is a forbidden zone: I have no idea what they do inside, the sun is out and for a moment I find it all so delightful – this yellow-green haze, the quiet rustle of the birch leaves – they could be making *monsters* for all I care, I'm really not bothered about any of it: this place smells of hay and earth, and that's enough for me. I pull the last-but-one of my Efkas from the packet and light up, and then I see Manfred weaving an RSO towards him. It reverses into the yard on its caterpillar tracks and the Lithuanians hitch up a livestock trailer.

Michael is standing over there with the boy from the forest, holding him by the shoulders.

'Come on, Heinrich,' Manfred shouts, and thumps Michael on the back. 'Come *on*, for goodness' sake!'

– – –

There is a passage running from the pigsty into a system of pens, the smallest some five by five metres. This is where Manfred leaves me, two hands on my shoulders: *wait here . . .*

The earth in the pen has been rooted up – trotter marks everywhere, cloven hooves stamped in the mud.

Manfred lights a cigarette.

He opens his eyes wide:

'Piggies!'

– – –

The boy's head has been shaved.

He looks down at the ground and shows no reaction to the Lithuanian yelling at him.

The Lithuanian goes up and punches him in the face. The boy staggers backwards and looks up inquiringly. The Lithuanian yells some more.

The boy moves his lips in an echo, unable to understand.

The Lithuanian lifts the butt of his rifle.

'He's deaf, for God's sake, *Bulbis*,' Manfred calls out, laughing, and puts his hands to his ears. 'Deaf! He can't hear anything! Hello!'

The Lithuanian smiles, embarrassed, then turns back to the boy, holds his hands up in front of him, joins them together, flutters his fingers down as he draws them apart, a mime concluded by his hands tossing something over his shoulder.

The boy is perplexed. He stands open-mouthed, watching the man's hands.

The Lithuanian exaggerates his movements, the tip of his tongue protruding from his lips in concentration, but to no avail.

Manfred laughs.

Then he shouts:

'Come on, get on with it!'

The Lithuanian removes his belt and pulls down his pants, nodding to the boy. Now he understands.

Everything off?

With each item of clothing the boy removes he glances up.

This too?

That too.

And there he stands, in underpants and boots, body crooked and deformed from malnutrition, his navel a tight knot.

Boots as well?

Boots as well.

The boy hesitates, shuffles his feet, and gazes back at the ground. He does not remove his boots.

The Lithuanian steps forward and knocks him down, pulls the boots from his feet and tosses them on the dungheap. The boy gets up and stares at his boots.

He bends down and takes off his underpants.

The Lithuanian doesn't waste any time.

He snatches him up, one arm between his legs, the other under his chest, throwing him into the pen.

Manfred howls with laughter. Hans and Michael join in.

Someone produces a hip flask and offers it around.

The boy is covered in mud, he stands quite still, eyes on the ground.

Then he lifts his gaze and smiles awkwardly.

He cannot yet hear the screaming hogs in the sty, though they batter at the door. Nor can he hear the Lithuanian who climbs the fence and kicks the pin from the hasp.

– – –

One of the boars, black with a white spot on its right ear, charges immediately, rams the boy at the hip, butting him with the side of its head.

The boy is sent flying. He scrambles to his feet, struggling to find purchase. The boar is upon him, raging, battering the small of his back with its head, tossing him around the pen – the boy flails, upended.

He has hurt his head; his face is in the mud.

He is very still.

The boar gores at him now with its snout, snorting and grunting. The boy lifts his head; the boar recoils, four, five metres, then returns, snout to the mud, flipping him over with a toss of its head.

The boy's mouth is full of earth.

Michael goes up and pokes at him with a stick, thrusts out his lower lip, shrugs.

'Dead,' he shouts.

'What, already?' says Hans.

The second boar has been passive – this one is smaller, mottled pink and black, with white ears. An aperture in its flank is held open by a surgically inserted metal collar with a glass peephole, exposing the guts that churn inside. Pus seeps from the wound. It trots over nimbly, skipping across the mudbath, stretching its great curved head out, nostrils moist and flaring, and issues a grunt from its pink jaws.

Its tongue is between the boy's lips now, trailing saliva across the mouth of the corpse.

The other discharges a hard jet of piss into the mud.

The smaller one is the first to bite.

To begin with they do not penetrate, but toss and flail their heads.

After a moment they rip and tear.

Manfred grips my jaw, clasps my head tight in his hands.

'Look, Heinrich, *look* . . .'

I see the slop turn inside, through the glass: the boy's flesh devoured, ingested into the intestines, the stomach.

'There we are,' he says. 'Just like that.'

He lets go, and I twist away.

'Only it ought to be slower,' he says. 'Much slower.'

– – –

The water is sweet and cool; I scoop it up in my hand and drink, splash my neck, dip my head into the bucket, rub my scalp, and groan.

Michael and Hans laughed. I couldn't keep it in. But I made eye contact with Manfred, my hands on my knees. The look in his eye was hard as stone.

I straightened up, and teetered over to the well without looking back. I feel better now.

'It's an instinctive reaction, that's all,' says Manfred, and squeezes my neck. 'It's because we're animals. And animals don't like to see other beasts suffer.'

'I can't go on with this, Manfred,' I say. 'Why am I even here? My part of the job is done . . .'

'Rubbish,' he says. 'It's like when you see someone yawn, you yawn too. It's nothing to be ashamed of.'

I wrench myself away.

'I want nothing more to do with this, Manfred . . . This isn't police work, it's a slaughterhouse . . .'

'But you *must*, Heinrich. You have to be with us for the hunt . . .'

I am about to reply, but pause as he puts an index finger to his lips.

'I'm not SS,' I tell him, staring him in the eye, refusing to look away. 'I shall write to my superiors, ask to be taken off the—'

I am not fast enough to duck.

His first punch hits me above the eye.

The second is on the mouth.

Searing pain from the signet ring.

– – –

151

I am sitting on a tree stub, gazing out across the river behind the kolkhoz. Blood seeps from my mouth if I ease up the pressure on the cloth. Manfred has put some boys to work cutting down willow, the switches are piled up high, one of the boys strips off the bark with a knife and tosses them onto the pile. They are hardly more than ten or twelve years old, the five of them, part of the entourage of flotsam and jetsam that surfaces wherever we go: remnants of families; barefoot children with runny noses; the elderly; the crippled; mad people with filthy, slobbering mouths. One of them has mounted a flag on a stick, a hammer and sickle defaced by the words SMERT SUKAM, *death to the whores*. He waves it about, jabbering away, showing off the tattoo on his stomach, four onion-shaped cupolas and a saltire, Andreaskreuz. They emerge from the undergrowth, from the low houses, to see if there might be some crumbs for them, a few kopeks or Reichsmark, a hunk of bread, a bag of salt.

Manfred inspects their work.

He comes towards me.

He is holding something in his hand; it looks like the lid of a wicker laundry basket. He holds his other hand behind his back.

'Lovely, isn't it?' he says, and produces a wooden sword and a three-pronged trident carved from a forked branch. 'And look here. A gladius and a fascina, and a what's it called . . .'

'Parma,' I say with a nod towards the woven shield.

'A parma, that's it. You were always so *clever*, Heinrich. What was the name of them now, the Thracians, and the ones with the tridents and those nets . . .'

'Retiarii . . .'

'That's it!' Manfred exclaims, and thumps me on the back. '*In my nostrils, the scent of mortal blood doth laugh me welcome* . . . Aeschylus, wasn't it? They knew a thing or two, the Ancient Greeks.'

He puts his hands on my shoulders and turns me around, narrows his eyes.

'Let me have a look at you,' he says.

'It's nothing.'

'Open your mouth . . .'

He grips my hand and pulls away the cloth. I feel the blood as it begins to leak from my lower jaw.

'That needs cleaning up,' he says, and whistles for a Sanitäter.

– – –

Later, still at the river.

Manfred stands with his legs apart, his piss thick and lazy.

The Sanitäter picked the remains of a lower incisor from my jaw with a pair of tongs and injected a shot of morphine directly into the wound.

'I'm sorry,' Manfred says. 'I don't know what got into me. It was . . . I can't explain it.'

'A reflex?'

'Yes, a reflex. Exactly.'

He hitches up his trousers, buttons the fly and turns back round, fishes his Efkas from his breast pocket and comes towards me. Cigarettes protrude from the packet. I take two, poking one between Manfred's lips.

'Can you forgive me?' he says.

'Yes,' I say. 'If you throw that bloody ring away.'

He stiffens for a second, then steps back. He twists the ring from his finger, weighs the heavy gold in his palm, gazing at the matted surface of the metal, the sparkle of the gemstones.

'Twenty-four carat. Studded with diamonds. Have you any idea how much this is worth?'

He looks me straight in the eye.

'No.'

He hurls it into the river.

'Happy now?'

We stand for a while, smoking, staring at the warm, green water amid a hum of insects.

'We pick things up, don't we?' Manfred says after a while. 'A picture, a fragment of conversation, something that makes an impression. Sometimes I find it odd that we should be the ones who will remember them. That they should only live on in our memories.'

'Who?'

'The Jews.'

He smiles and spits a shred of tobacco from his tongue.

'Like the other day: Michael's always so clumsy, so I shouted at him. Do you know what I said?'

'No, what?'

'*Klutz!*'

'Klutz?'

'Yes, it just came out . . . *klutz!*'

He turns his head towards me, and laughs.

'*Mentsh* . . . never forget to stay a *mentsh* . . . otherwise we're nothing but *mumkhes*, are we? *Mumkhes* from *Daytshland*.'

'What?'

154

'*Experts from Deutschland . . .*'
'Manfred . . .'
'What?'
'I will go back with you. But on one condition.'
'Yes?'
'I don't want to kill any more.'

In the death zone

Manfred lets me sit in the command vehicle when we return to the forests for the second phase of Operation Hermann: *Tightening the cauldron, definition of the battle area.* From the vehicle I see Stukas diving in a howling swarm, then, on the pull-up, a fierce series of explosions.

They emerge from the forests, drawing livestock. Cows, horses, goats, small home-made cages containing birds and frogs. A Ukrainian from the SchuMa battalion cradles a hedgehog in his arms, he has mixed some powdered milk in a cup, a small darting tongue.

The lines of human slaves, joined together at the neck by nooses, swaying.

Inner Congo.

Manfred dictates the report of the day to me.

He gives me the figures and the words: blood sacrifice, bandit, loot.

— — —

Daily dispatch, Transcript
Telegraph. 16 July 1943

From: Hstf. Schlosser, SS-Kavallerie 2

Re. Operation Hermann, south-west sector

Operation commenced 10:00 hrs.

Cordon positioned, coordinates 54°1'N, 26°19'Ø.

Shock troops formed 1/2/40.

Total force:

SS-Kavallerie 2/4/75

SchuMa 3/6/130

Orpo 1/21

Lith. Hiwi 3/7/139

Armament:

2 anti-tank guns

1 anti-aircraft

24 Mg 42

Transport:

3 lorries

1 self-propelled gun

3 Kübelwagen

2 Sd.Kfz: 1 233, 1 250/command vehicle

324 horses

Losses, ours: 1 slightly injured (Orpo). Neutralised
2 bunkers. Incinerated 3 abandoned camps, fortified. 988
bandits killed, incl. 251 Jewish. Loot: 1 German carbine
model 98, 6 pistols, ammunition, 40 wooden mines.

128 men, 73 women, 19 children deported to the Reich.

120 horses, 21 cows, 214 goats sent to Ivenets.

Hauptsturmführer Manfred Schlosser

Hereby attested,

Oberleutnant der Polizei, Heinrich Hoffmann.

— — —

At the campfire, evening, under
a bright summer sky.

It's the fifth day of the operation.

Everything squelches with moisture here, the damp darkness of the trees, the fat grass. Mud prevails.

Manfred has mounted his boots on two sticks angled over the fire, as though he were roasting sausages.

He is reclined, making dog ears in my copy of Jünger's *The Adventurous Heart*. He hums a popular tune, moistens his finger and turns down the corner of another page.

'Manfred?'

'Mmm . . .?'

'We found six pistols and one carbine, how does that match up with 988 partisans?'

'Bandits . . . they're called bandits. Himmler's decree, as of today.'

'Bandits, then. It doesn't make sense.'

'You wrote it down yourself.'

'But it's a lie, Manfred, for Christ's sake. And stop ruining my book.'

He props himself up on his elbow.

'It's quite simple, Heinrich. Once they're dead, they can't ever *become* bandits, can they?'

'It's not funny, Manfred.'

'No, you're right. It's not.'

He puts down the book, gets to his feet and turns his boots.

'It's all politics,' he says. 'Sometimes I think we do it all the wrong way.'

'How do you mean?'

'By separating words and reality. "Special treatment", "liquidation", "cleansing", "*Judenfrei*". It's all killing, Heinrich. I mean we're not cleaning ladies or functionaries, are we, for Chrissake? We're not just giving the Jews a clean, like they were some bloody germ. We plunder them, we take everything they own, whip the shit out of them, we strip them naked and put bullets through their brains while their children are watching . . . the prayers, fear, all that trembling before death . . . Elohim Yisrael . . .'

'Manfred, stop—'

'No Heinrich, you stop. For once, just shut up. It's what we do . . . it's what we do, for God's sake. We burn down a village, but what we have to say is we killed twelve hundred partisans. Sorry, bandits! Bandits and *evacuation* . . . one sounds like a boy's adventure story, the other's a bodily function . . . Winnetou and castor oil!'

'Not so loud, Manfred . . .'

'Why, are you scared? Are you actually scared?'

'Of ending up in the basement, yes.'

Manfred considers me for a moment, disappointed, wounded.

'It's Himmler,' he says quietly. 'That *cretin*.'

'What?' I say, astonished.

'He came out with us in October '41, near Minsk. He wanted to see an operation; Steiner had kept some Jews for him. He stood on the edge of the pit, much too close to the edge, only no one had the guts to tell him. You should have seen the man! He couldn't stomach it – spewed up and fainted . . . And now he wants to gloss things over, so they can all sit nice and cosy at home and think it's being done in an orderly fashion. As if killing can be detached – gas chambers and Zyklon B . . . as if it's a science . . . How sentimental, how *stupid* . . . As if fucking categories are going to help us . . .'

'Carl Schmitt says our whole identity rests on having an enemy . . . which is a category of sorts . . .'

'Exactly! But why can't we just *say* it, like Jünger here. We've overstepped a boundary, where everyone is equal. This—'

He rises, gesticulating.

'This is a new *world* . . . to kill is to strike down into that new world, a virgin land . . .'

'So when you sent the boy in to the pigs you created a new world?'

'Yes! Truth is—'

'. . . consistent. So you said. But it's grotesque and cruel . . .'

'Who says so?'

'I do!'

'You? What about your beloved Romans? They celebrated killing, dressed it up, made an occasion of it, but you think you can take their marble statues and splendid poetry – oh, Cicero, the Capitol – and forget all about the violence. *That*'s grotesque, Heinrich.'

'You killed a boy, for Christ's sake!'

'Yes. And that's exactly what Steiner taught me. Consistency. To stick it out and remain *decent*. The community . . .'

He lifts his sleeve to his eyes, and for a brief moment he seems infinitely small and frail as he stands there in the hum of night, rocking on his bare feet.

'Do you even know what it means?' he continues. 'Community; love?'

'That's just a lie, too,' I say, but he throws up his arms. 'A malicious lie.'

'So what is it you want, Heinrich?'

He sits down and puts his boots back on. His foot slips inside the thick leather, making a moist suction sound.

'Would you rather be on your own?'

– – –

160

Later, when I wake up, it is still night.

Manfred is gone, his sleeping bag with him.

I sit up. His saddlebags are gone too. And the hatbox.

I wriggle out of my sleeping bag, draw back the canvas.

The other tents have been dismantled.

The fires have gone out. Where are the guards?

Vehicle tracks.

At once I am wide awake. I take my PPK from the holster and crawl out.

'Is anyone there?'

Nocturnal noises are my only reply; the wind in the tall firs.

There is no one here, not a single person.

Only darkness and stars, and a little further away, a babbling brook.

My pulse races at the snap of a branch.

'Where the hell is everyone?'

A swish, a crack, the thin slit of a spade.

Behind me, in the low birch trees, back in the scrubland.

I am there in a second.

Just some tins left behind, half dug into the earth, and the remains of preserved fruit.

A shadow. I swivel and shoot.

The bullet whistles through the bushes.

I sprint after it, branches whipping into my face, PPK, right to left.

– – –

I pull up.

Nothing but leaves; they flutter in the darkness.

No. There *is* someone there. A sudden movement, and I shoot again.

Hindquarters in the air, a kick of the legs.

Shots, bark ripping; the flash of the muzzle.

The white rump patch is gone in a rustle of undergrowth.

A deer. It was just a deer, eating the fruit from the tins.

I click out the magazine. One cartridge left.

I am alone in the forest.

– – –

I return to the tent in the diffuse light of dawn, a pale illuminating haze.

I bend down to pull up the tent pegs and hear the sound again.

There is someone, down at the stream now. I straighten up and go slowly down the slope.

The sound increases, becomes more distinct: a knocking noise, a clatter of stones, splashing.

It's coming from behind the rocks, where the stream turns, a few metres below me.

Someone is sitting there with their back to me.

It looks like a child, in a coat that is far too big.

A boy. Washing something in the stream, with hectic movements.

Something red seeps into the water, lumps of something.

I still cannot see his face, but I can see his hands quite clearly now, his fingers buried in something bloody, shreds of skin, flesh.

He turns his head and looks at me.

He has no mouth, no lips.

I can see straight to his bones, the three rows of teeth in his gums.

'Do you want the treatment too?' he asks.

I turn and run the instant he raises himself up to his full height.

'YES, YOU *DO!*'

– – –

'Where the hell have you been? You've been gone for three hours!' Manfred bellows on my return, already on horseback. 'Another minute and we'd have left without you.'

'That person . . . didn't you see him? Down by the stream?' I stutter, reeling round to see the tents packed up. The horses are being saddled, the campfires have all been extinguished. A lorry rumbles away down the slope.

'Who?'

'There was a boy, with three rows of teeth. He had no . . . face.'

Manfred swivels his head away, tugs on the rein and the horse turns.

'What are you talking about . . . Anyway, it's a good thing you're back,' he says, and smacks the horse with the crop. Its flank tenses as it sets off at a gallop down the hill.

– – –

The seventh day, at the campfire.

Manfred is still reading *The Adventurous Heart*, though not nearly as absorbed as before, no longer turning down page corners but scratching himself, farting, getting up to stretch his legs.

'That boy you were on about,' he says.

'Yes. What about him?'

'I think we got him. Was he wearing an oversized coat?'

'Yes, he was.'

'Michael chased him down on his horse, like a pheasant, and shot him. And you were right. He had three rows of teeth, I checked. Baby teeth at the front, then the adult ones, and behind them an extra row of sharp little needles. He looked like a bloody shark, the little fellow. Only he wasn't a child at all, he was ancient. Oh, and by the way, the Führer thinks they're Finnish.'

'What?'

'That *rus* is the Finnish word for *Swedes* . . . So the Belorussians are Swedes. Or was it the other way round – the Swedish word for Finns – I've forgotten.'

'Why shouldn't they just be Belorussians?'

'Don't ask me. Something about the shape of their heads, apparently. They're not like the Slavs at all. It may be one of his more peculiar theories.'

'But we've got nothing against Swedes or Finns, have we?'

'Not as far as I know.'

'Then why are we killing their Belorussian kin?'

'I don't know, quibbler! You're no better than Jünger here.'

He snaps the book shut, flashes me a malicious look and tosses it onto the fire.

'What are you doing?' I shout, and leap to my feet.

I reach into the flames to rescue the already soot-covered volume and drop it in the grass.

'What the hell was that for?'

Manfred is on his feet too, his fists held up, tossing his head, quick shadow punches in the summer night.

'Do you want to fight about it? Come on, then! Take that . . . and *that* . . . you little liar . . .'

'Stop it . . .'

'All those little poems to my sister . . . *How much he says who utters night, for from this word deep grief and meaning pour, like heavy honey from the honeycomb* . . . How profound. How priceless!'

'Have you been through my things?'

'You left me no choice. Clearly you can't be trusted . . .'

He ducks and weaves, feigns a step to his left and delivers an uppercut into the air.

'Come on!'

'I can't be bothered . . .'

'I've even thought up a whole new aesthetic, specially for spineless drips like yourself.'

He relaxes, extends his hand.

'Come on, shake . . .'

I step forward and put my hand out. He hits me.

'That's it! That's the way.'

I stagger back, clutching my cheek.

'A slap in the face, is that it? How original.'

'Yes. But it's the principle, isn't it? What does a hand mean? Nothing in itself, am I right? How do you know if it's going to be a handshake or a slap in the face?'

'The context . . .'

'Context? It's to do with being scared of what you don't understand, that's all. There *is* no context here. The peasant you just gave a Reichsmark, whose daughter you just patted on the head, will twist a butcher's knife in your stomach the very next second . . . We find a freak in the forest with no face and three rows of teeth. A boy or an old man? We've got no language for this.'

'So what's this new aesthetic of yours?'

'It won't be a refuge, Heinrich. What I want is an aesthetic of the *uncertain*. Sounds good, don't you think? You're not to know if it's for fun or for real, if I'm coming to kill you or not. It'll be hysterical! Come to think of it, an aesthetic of hysteria might be better, what do you reckon?'

'I wouldn't know . . .'

'Things turn in an instant, you can never know for sure, all you can do is laugh in terror. Think of it as Nietzsche and Munchausen rolled into one! And lots more besides! I even know what to call it now!'

'What? What will you call it?'

'Manfredism . . .'

'Manfredism?'

'Precisely. You'll love it . . .'

– – –

Day nine, campfire.

We found Semjon the Hiwi with his head twisted down in the mud this morning, the back of his skull and the right side of his jaw gone. Grenade, accidental. I ought to feel something. His tall body slopped in the mire. In the daily report I put it down to bandit fire and wrote Losses, ours: 1 fallen (Hiwi), attested the signature and sent it off by telegraph. He saved my life, he smoked my cigarettes, he killed a child with his bare hands.

We are having rabbit.

Manfred attends to the wants of nature. I hear him in the bushes, emptying his bowels with a groan as the animal drips its innards onto the flame. It has become a routine, the two of us alone at the fire, the hum of the camp, the chatter, the foul-smelling men, the snorting, recalcitrant beasts about us, alcohol and gun oil, the towing and heaving and shoving, the orders and counter-orders, the roaring engines, the cries and shouts, and sudden, deathly sleep. Now there is only Manfred's business and the low-voiced talk of the guards, an abrupt round delivered into the wilderness by a machine gunner, a spotlight sweeping the landscape, the waver of forest in its artificial light.

Manfred skinned the rabbit and rubbed honey into its flesh. '*Tomorrow's the day,*' he said. '*And you've not eaten in two . . .*'

I turn the skewer, the tight, glazed body above the flame, the melting, rodent-like head.

I am beyond hunger, exhausted and sleepless.

Tomorrow the third phase commences: *Clearing the cauldron, the last concentric attack.*

I see no cauldron, only trees and darkness, trees and light.

I try to think of Eline, and close my eyes.

After a short while I open them again.

I take *The Adventurous Heart* from my inside pocket, the book I saved from the flames two days before. It is singed and reeks of smoke. Manfred has vandalised it with all his underlining, his exclamation marks and symbols that look like stenography, code or just helpless doodles, diagrams, little drawings of what, animals? One passage, *Terror*, is almost obliterated by his hand.

I read the final lines through his pencilled ornamentation:

> Do you have any idea what goes on in
> this space that we will perhaps some
> day plunge through, the space that
> extends between the recognition of the
> downfall and the downfall itself?

Manfred has drawn an ugly triangle in the margin and written some figures at each angle. I turn the book in my hand, and now I see they are coordinates. I know them already. It is the triangle of Naliboki, Ivenets, Rubesjevitj. Operation Hermann.

It is here, in this space.

Now I hear him come creeping up behind me.

'*Psst* . . .'

'Manfred,' I say, and hold the book up in my hand, turning my head to face him. 'What is this *shit* . . .?' But there is no one there. I am on my feet in an instant, in the midst of empty night.

'Manfred?'

'*Psst* . . .'

I turn towards the source, gripped by sudden panic, but in the darkness there is only the rush of wind in the trees, the pulsating glow of embers, the meagre little corpse on its rotating skewer.

I listen. Not a sound.

I bend down to pick up my pistol and stare into the vacancy of the rabbit head.

The fire snaps and sizzles as the animal is dislodged, the head coming to rest diagonally against the skewer.

'*Psst* . . .'

'What do you want?' I say, taking my cigarettes from my breast pocket, pursing my lips as I light up. 'What is it, bunny . . .? Something bothering you?'

'*Psst . . .*'

Spitting fat as the belly opens, discharging its juices.

'*Psst . . .*'

– – –

I wake up in the night, Manfred clinging to me from behind.

I try to extricate myself without waking him, but with each movement his arms and legs clamp tighter around my body.

'Manfred, you're strangling me . . .'

He fails to respond, his knee is in the small of my back, his chin dug against my shoulder blade.

I manage to get an arm free and begin to prise his fingers apart, but his joints are locked and cold, his nails blue.

'Manfred, what's the matter with you?'

I arch my back and try to push him away but end up rolling over, still in his grip, his face in mine.

I cannot hear him breathing.

'Manfred, for crying out loud!'

His jaw opens, but no sound emerges.

'Wake up!'

And then he opens his eyes.

His pupils are wide and stiff, a film of grey-blue.

– – –

I am inside his eye.

– – –

At first there is nothing, then I hear the clicking sound from the innermost darkness.

I glimpse something black, a hand with rings on its fingers, a neck. A woman, facing away, in a black velvet dress with puffed sleeves.

She lifts up her hem, and is wearing patent leather shoes.
They click against the floor, her movements pick up speed.
Is she tap-dancing?
She waves to me, turning her head slightly towards me.
She is Zarah Leander in *Die grosse Liebe*.
Now she is singing:

> *Ich weiss, es wird einmal ein Wunder geschehen*
> *und dann werden tausend Märchen war.*
> *Ich weiss, so schnell kann keine Liebe vergehen,*
> *Die so gross ist und so wunderbar.*

> *I know one day a miracle will happen*
> *And a thousand dreams will come true,*
> *I know love cannot be so fleeting,*
> *That was so fine and wonderful.*

Phase 3: The concentric attack

Early morning, day ten.

Manfred sits on his haunches beside my head, face daubed black and green.

'Wake up . . .' he says when I fail to respond.

'Put this on your face,' he says, handing me a tin.

I wriggle out of the sleeping bag and take it from his hand. It is shoe polish, black.

'What am I supposed to do with this?'

'We've run out of green,' he says, and backs his way out of the tent. 'Sorry.'

There is a net over his helmet, stuffed with straw and leaves.

'There'll be a lot of traffic over the radio today. Can you manage?'

'I think so.'

'Can you manage or *not*?'

'Yes.'

'And you've got the signal codes?'

'Yes.'

'The overview of all the units? The map?'

'Yes.'

'Yes, what? Overview or map?'

'I *have* done this before, Manfred.'

'What then?'

'Yes. Overview *and* map.'

– – –

'They ran out of green,' I tell the wireless operator and the driver as I climb into the already moving command vehicle.

They are tense and say nothing in reply. I sit myself down and look out over the sloping terrain, woodland and scrub here, the clatter of armoured caterpillar vehicles in the mud. The forest around us is alive, waves of camouflaged troops, black and green, proceeding through the landscape, silent and effective. Only the noise of the vehicles indicates our presence. Manfred comes up alongside and puts his hand on the steel plating.

'It's actually all rather beautiful, don't you think?' he says.

'Yes,' I say, and lean back into my seat when I accidentally place my hand on his.

I unfold the map: everything was photographed from the air yesterday and the day before, we have assigned coordinates to all the landmarks. The starting positions of the various units are dotted about the complex of low ridges, dales and primeval forest that wreathes *the tightened cauldron*, the one place we have yet to enter, an area of some four or five square kilometres, edged on two sides by lakes and swamp in which our vehicles cannot operate, but which offers a free field of fire to the squadron of Stukas and Heinkels constantly buzzing over our heads, trails of roaring white in the sky. If there are large partisan groups operating here, not just frightened Jews and expelled peasants, they will have to get past either us or Dirlewanger who is somewhat north-east of here in a funnel slightly more than two kilometres in width.

We are to lead the attack.

At 05:50 we pull in among some trees, sheltered by an incline so as not to attract enemy fire to the heavy antenna that is like a bedstead on the body of the vehicle. At our rear, medical assistants rig up a dressing station and a big green tent. In front of us lies first the ridge, then a wide clearing. After that, in the dark of the forest, the combat zone.

A moment later the Stukas begin the attack, turning in formation and diving.

The air shudders as the bombs explode.

Once they have passed, everything is still, except for the plumes of smoke from the strike.

'Second company move forward on right flank,' Manfred instructs the operator. 'Up to the clearing, five hundred metres. Third in from the left.'

The concentric attack on the cauldron is under way.

– – –

It is raining.

Manfred has climbed the hill in front of us to get a better view.

The driver pulled the tarp over the vehicle and fastened it to the antenna half an hour ago, the rain keeps on and I keep punching the tarp to get rid of the accumulated water.

I can see only a thin sliver of sky, the top of the bushes and grass on the hill.

Now and then Manfred enters my field of vision with his binoculars.

Three units are in action, two bands of shock troops proceeding with three or four hundred metres between them over the hills, below them a broad line of skirmishers to pick up the fugitives if any should slip past the first two lines.

Enemy contact just after seven o'clock.

Voices, frantic, from the front, the stutter of MGs, slow Russian sub-machine guns, minutes of transmission.

Then silence, more shots, more calls, smoke grenades pumped into what turns out to be an empty underground bunker between ten and eleven o'clock. Silence again.

For some time now reports have merely noted positions. I mark them down in red pencil on the map.

I punch the tarp.

Manfred pokes his head inside.

'Why is nothing happening? Where the fuck are they?'

– – –

Half an hour later we are sitting around in rain capes eating boiled corn from the primus stove. It is still raining, the clouds are up close.

Manfred has the hatbox between his legs.

The heat is insufferable.

'Do you think he's in there? Goga?' he says, attending to his teeth with a toothpick. 'Or is it all just a figment?'

'What do you mean?'

'This. How we got here. The logic of it: the cockerel tattoo, Vorkuta, shibboleth, the twin from Zaludok, Goga. Is it just an idiotic joke?'

'I don't know. Perhaps. But who would be the idiot then?'

He swallows his food, licks his fingers. He unclasps the lid of the hatbox and lifts out the head, holds it out towards me in both hands.

'Maybe *he* is.'

Elias Bronstejns's green glass eyes stare out at me.

His low hairline, his oblong face.

The mouth is sewn together inside, the thread drawn out through the thick lips.

'What if it wasn't even him? What if it was just some maniac out of the blue?'

'What then?'

'In that case . . .' he says, folding down the seat on the side of the vehicle and placing the head upon it. 'In that case we're making fools of ourselves . . .'

The radio crackles.

'*Faust 1 to Hermann 2. We've located another bunker.*'

'Hermann 2 here. State position . . .' says the operator.

'*A couple of hundred metres south of Hill 11. We've found two exits . . .*'

I note down the position.

'*We've run out of smoke grenades. Do you want us to send some men in or blow it up?*'

'Send some men in,' Manfred says over my shoulder.

'*Understood . . .*'

A few minutes later.

'*Faust 1 to Hermann 2.*'

'Hermann 2. Go ahead.'

'*It's a maze down here, we can't find the exits . . . do you want us to carry on or wait for smoke grenades?*'

'Any sign of the enemy?'

'*Not yet, but we've found ammunition and supplies . . .*'

'Carry on,' Manfred barks.

'*Hang on a second . . .*'

Manfred takes charge of the receiver.

'Hello? This is Hermann 2,' he barks again.

All we hear is interference, then transmission again:

Gunfire. German weapons, by the sounds of it.

'*We're under heavy fire. The place is alive . . .*'

A dull explosion. Silence.

Manfred looks at me.

'Get hold of Company 3, they're further up the hill, aren't they?'

I check the last report.

'Yes.'

'Hermann 2 to Georg 2. Georg 2, are you there?'

'*Georg 2 receiving.*'

'What's going on?'

'*I can't see a thing, it's heavy up here.*'

'Any estimate on the number of partisans?'

'*At least two hundred. They've got mortar, MGs.*'

'Any contact with Company 1?'

'*They're coming out of the ground!*'

Silence.

Transmission:

'*Faust 1 to Hermann 2.*' The company midway up the hill.

'*They've broken through . . .*'

'Where? How many?'

'*We've got six wounded and one dead.*'

'How many got through?'

The soldier confers with someone in the background, we hear shouts, explosions.

'*Twenty, thirty, at least . . . They're heading down . . .*'

'Where to?'

'*Straight towards you.*'

Manfred looks at me again.

'Who have we got here?'

'Orpos, one Hiwi platoon, one SS-Kavallerie platoon.'

'Form a firing line!' Manfred shouts at the operator. 'Get the MGs ready!'

'*Faust 2, form a firing line, enemy headed your way,*' says the operator.

'*Faust 2 receiving. We can't see anything.*'

'They should be with you in a couple of minutes, about twenty or thirty of them.'

Manfred raps his knuckles on the driver's helmet.

'Drive up the hill and cover from there. I'm going in.'

He jumps out and the vehicle sets off.

Once we come out of the trees and climb up onto the ridge we hear explosions about a kilometre further on into the fog, towards the massif, but all we can see is the forest fringe and the clearing ahead of us.

Manfred rides past, carries on down the other side towards the clearing.

Ten Hiwis run on behind.

They vanish into the trees some five hundred metres further on.

The rain pours.

The gunner pulls back the charging handle.

All quiet again.

– – –

I sweep the line of trees below with my binoculars, but spot nothing.

It is five minutes since Manfred headed off. The gunner is right beside me, his eyes fixed on the forest, finger on the MG's trigger. I have seen him before, when we found Steiner at Belize, the retard who shot at the dogs.

A volley of machine-gun fire to our right, I sweep the binoculars, but the forest is a shimmering haze. Another burst, more explosions, cries, and then a Hiwi emerges from the trees, running towards us, carbine in hand. His body contorts as he is hit by fire from behind, from among the trees.

'Are you ready?' I say to the gunner.

I knock on his helmet and point.

I direct the binoculars to where the Hiwi emerged. More shots are fired within.

A man comes out from the trees wearing a jacket and cap, gets down on his haunches, glances about, twists round and gestures into the forest. In his hand is a Soviet sub-machine gun, the drum magazine below the barrel. Four men appear at his rear, with carbines and rucksacks.

They hesitate for a moment before moving out into the clearing and starting to run straight at us.

We wait until all five are properly in the open before opening fire.

The MG stutters at the gunner's shoulder, spent cartridges clattering to the floor.

'Fuck you!' he yells.

We give them an extra burst for good measure once they are down.

'Fucking cunts, fuck you!' he yells again.

'That's enough,' I tell him, but my head too is seething with excitement.

'*Did you get them?*'

Manfred's voice on the receiver.

'Yes.'

'*Good. We'll mop up here, I'll get back to you later.*'

'Any sign of Goga?' I ask.

'*No. Sending back wounded.*'

The gunner turns the MG towards the trees again, snaps back the charging handle.

'They're ours, for Chrissake!' I shout.

Two medical assistants emerge, a stretcher between them.

A moment later two more, then two more still.

A hail of shots from the trees.

– – –

A few minutes later.

The first two stretchers have passed through to the dressing station behind us.

The third pair of medical assistants are halfway up the hill when a burst of fire rings out, the one at the rear is hit in the back and falls. The wounded SS-Sturmmann is turned out of the stretcher with a cry.

The radio crackles.

'*Heinrich!*' Manfred barks.

I am already out of the vehicle, sliding down the slope, feet first.

The Sturmmann has lost a leg at the knee, he is on his side, screaming, a jagged stump poking in the air.

The dead medic lies with his head in the grass. The other administers morphine to the wounded soldier, tightens the tourniquet, the gauze gripped between his teeth. Water sprays

179

up from the earth around us as another burst of machine-gun fire rips through the air. We bundle the Sturmmann back onto the stretcher. Another staggered round of bullets thuds into the corpse, sending plumes of water from the saturated soil. I grip the rear handles and make eye contact with the man at the front end.

His face is oblong, daubed black. Blue eyes.

'Ready,' I say. He turns and takes hold.

Bullets whistle as we struggle back up the hill.

The man on the stretcher is unconscious.

– – –

When we get to the top they stop firing.

Three soldiers on horseback come galloping out of the undergrowth behind us. It looks like Manfred and two men from the SS-Kavallerie. Four Alsatian dogs come tearing after them.

We push on down, and now they are gone.

At once, silence, the pouring rain.

The Sturmmann on the stretcher has stopped moving. Is he dead?

The dressing station, a hundred metres on. Perhaps we are in time.

The sleeve insignia of the medical assistant. Totenkopf.

What is Steiner's division doing here? *The naked corpses of Belize . . .*

'You,' I say. 'What unit are you from?'

He pulls hard on the stretcher, I stumble forward, a tight grip on the handles.

When I look up he is pointing his gun at me.

A jolt goes through me.

'Goga?' I blurt out. 'You're Goga?'

He stiffens for a second, blue eyes staring.

They show no fear.

What, then? *Scorn?*

Now I hear the hooves behind the ridge.

The barking dogs.

Goga turns his head slowly towards the sound.

He turns back to face me.

Something strikes my neck, and I fall back.

– – –

'Did you see him?'

Manfred, dismounted, shaking me.

'Yes, he . . . am I hit?'

There's a searing pain at the side of my neck, and adrenalin courses through my body.

'Here,' Manfred says, handing me a cloth. I press it to my skin.

By the time I get to my feet Manfred is already back in the saddle, catching up with the two other horsemen on the other side of the dressing station, the heavy, loping beasts in the tall grass. One of the dogs spins in the air, hit as it reaches the vegetation behind the operating tent.

Then more shots.

Cries.

Two, three rounds.

I sit down and try to steady my pulse.

– – –

Five minutes later Manfred comes riding up.

Behind him he drags a man with a noose around his neck, hands tied behind his back.

They have wiped the black paint from his face, and stripped him of his shirt. When they reach me I see the tattoos in the small of his back.

Two great eyes that look like butterfly wings. And on his shoulder a cockerel depicted with an earring, just beneath the shoulder blade.

The girl from Belize was right.

Etke.

His face is swollen, but the resemblance to the stuffed head of his brother is striking.

Only the eyes are wrong.

They are not green; they are blue as dust.

Manfred bends down and pats me on the cheek.

'Didn't you get my message?'

'No. What message?'

'That he'd slipped through – they were disguised in German uniform.'

'No. I went to help him . . .'

Manfred sits up, tugs on the noose and spurs his horse on. Goga is in his grip.

'Hey,' I shout after him.

'What?' says Manfred.

'I need to interrogate him,' I say.

'You?'

'Yes!'

'Since when did you have the stomach?'

'I was the one who found him!'

Manfred swivels in the saddle as I come up alongside him.

He raises my chin with his whip, which he draws across my throat.

'How's the wound?'

'What?'

'Your neck?' he says. 'Did he hit the bone?'

'It's nothing,' I say. 'I need to interrogate him, it's my job after all. It might not even be him!'

'It's him,' says Manfred. 'But come and watch the perform-ance, by all means, after I've finished with the little faggot . . .'

He jerks his head in Goga's direction.

Entertainment

My house in Lida, the next day.

I spend the day at home, most of it in the bath.

My Masja comes in intermittently and scrubs my back with a brush of boar bristles, cleaning and dabbing the wound in my neck; the bullet chipped my collarbone, I am yellow, orange and blue. Masja empties the tub, reaching down between my legs, and fills it up with fresh water from the big jug. She has rolled up her sleeves, and draws an arm across her brow. Her neck is moist, hair plaited like Etke's.

If only I could reach out to her.

Does she hate me?

Does it matter?

I reach for the squat bottle on the table next to the tub instead.

I think about Goga, what Manfred is doing to him in the basement. The Ukrainian who severed the windpipe of the Jew from Zaludok. Has he unrolled his cloth of instruments, selected his knives, his tongs, his shears? What secrets is he extracting from him? How did he know Steiner's route? Did he witness Steiner wipe out his family? Was it revenge? Or merely an absurd accident? *A joke told by an idiot*? Why was I not allowed to question him?

And all the time: Goga, pointing the gun at me.

What lay in that moment?

Scorn, anger . . . what?

'Herr, why are you laughing?'

'Sorry?'

'You are laughing, Herr.'

Masja wrings the sponge and scrubs my back.

'A man was going to kill me, Masja.'

'What is funny about that, Herr?'

'Nothing.'

'Then why did you laugh?'

'I think I am rather angry with him. He seemed so . . . indifferent.'

– – –

The foyer is buzzing with people as I enter Manfred's white hospital.

I finish my cigarette, hesitate for a moment at the top of the stairs. But I have questions for Goga, and descend into the basement. On the landing I bump into Michael on his way up.

'Oberleutnant der Polizei,' he says, placing a hand on my shoulder as I try to pass.

'I want to see Manfred,' I tell him, turning to face him.

'I'm sure you do,' he says.

His hand stays put.

'I'm here to question Goga,' I say, and place my hand on his. 'Manfred said . . .'

He steps up close, the stench of his breath in my face, and I can see his eyes swimming with inebriation.

'Fuck off,' he says. 'Or . . .'

'Or what?' I say, and twist free.

'Or else we'll come after you,' he says with a smile.

'We?'

'Yes, *we* . . .'

Later, when I telephone Manfred from the mess, it is Michael who answers and hangs up.

– – –

I am sitting in the park again with my Kirsch.

I never found out what the young telegraphist girl I slapped was called.

It feels like an infinity ago. I want to apologise, but no one comes down from the offices of the regional commission, only soldiers on leave from the front, bandaged, hobbling, leaning into their crutches, silent.

I stare at my photograph of Eline, but the moist gleam of her lips has no effect. Her half-turned face.

It is growing dark by the time I get to my feet.

I am drunk and immeasurably tired as I sit down again in the half-empty theatre that is the Wehrmacht cinema.

The mood is shiftless as the curtain goes up to the tramp of marching feet in the *Wochenschau* newsreel. No more mention of Kursk, all Belgorod now, and *Raum Orel*, conquered Soviet tanks and downed Ilyushins, prisoners sent back down the line. *Are we losing?* When the map comes up, Kursk is way behind the front line. We *are* losing. A Hauptmann of the Luftwaffe turns round and asks for a light, and I do the honours for us both. Does he not realise that we are being swept off the court, that the

Russians are coming? Will they be forgiving? Does he not know a single fucking thing? He shushes me when I lean forward to pursue it with him, and the curtain goes up for the main film.

I shrug and sit back, slouch into my coat and drink.

Intoxication topped with the tart taste of cherry.

I yawn.

The first strains of *Ich Weiss, es wird einmal ein Wunder geschehen*. I Know One Day A Miracle Will Happen. I sit forward in my seat, the titles passing over the screen, a background of foliage. *Die grosse Liebe*. Zarah Leander is the singer in the Scala cabaret. Viktor Staal is the fighter pilot on leave. She looks like Eline in her black dress. The Hauptmann in front of me applauds vigorously as she finishes *Mein Leben für die Liebe*. He twists round to look at me, but all I do is stare while Viktor Staal follows her through the streets after the show and an airraid warning throws them together outside her building.

Leander opens the windows of her apartment as a precaution against wayward shards of anti-aircraft and Staal turns off the lights at the other end of the room. Then suddenly she turns towards me in the darkness and whispers:

Is it true what they say?

She holds my gaze.

Is it?

I close my eyes tight and open them again. She is still looking at me.

They say you don't do what we tell you to . . .

I glance around. She *is* speaking to me.

All I can do is move my lips.

'What?'

They say you eat our rabbits . . .

'What? Me?'

They say you were gentle. Aren't you gentle any more?

She does not wait for me to answer, but turns again towards the film, because now Viktor Staal comes up to her and puts his hand on the railing, they stand for a moment and look out upon the Berlin blackout and the first bursts of flak. His face and his perfect hair fill the screen, as he speaks:

'Wow, it's beautiful!'

'Hm, like a fairy tale.'

'No, much more beautiful. Like reality.'

I look around me in the darkness. The Hauptmann in the seat in front slaps a fly on his neck and emits a sigh into the barren theatre.

He applauds again.

– – –

The next morning Manfred telephones with a place and a time: the hospital courtyard, 4 p.m.

I am to be there before the others.

I put down the receiver and ask Masja to get my dress uniform ready.

I shave, trim the hair at my neck and temples, groom in the Nazi style.

I sit down on a stool and polish my boots with a soft brush. They gleam, black.

I fetch my pistol holster, slide the PPK into the black leather and fasten it to my belt. I have no medals, no copper.

I pomade my hair in front of the mirror, form a parting with the comb, and adjust with the tip of a finger.

it . . . almost as much as he hated the Jews . . . Let the festivities commence!'

The microphone squeals out a descant. Nothing happens.

'Begin!' Manfred shrieks.

An entrance door of the hospital opens and Goga emerges.

Manfred has made him a Thracian. His costume is finely woven willow and flax, decorated with feathers: a solid helmet, gladius and parma, a small, round shield.

Michael shoves him on through the passage, kicks him from behind, knout in hand.

Goga stumbles and loses the helmet, Michael lashes him with the whip, and Goga scrambles to his feet.

He looks down at the ground.

Michael puts the helmet back on him, grips him by the neck and hurls him into the arena.

The sun is raw, abominable.

– – –

Goga stands in the middle of the arena.

A wound has opened up in his thigh.

His feet are bloodied, misshapen in the sandals.

He has no control of his knees, they knock against each other.

Urine trickles down his leg.

Bach-Zelewski points and glances at the man seated next to him. They laugh.

In a moment they will enter. The two beasts.

I know that Manfred has been starving them since they killed the deaf boy.

When Michael kicks open the gate of the improvised stall at the end of the long passage, I see that Manfred has laid his hands on some more. They batter against the fencing, perhaps a dozen in number, a many-headed goods train charging towards the arena.

There are too many of them, making them panicked and aggressive. The passage is a bottleneck – a heaving frenzy of meat, and they are at each other's throats. Then suddenly they are out, the arena is theirs, snouts rooting the sand.

For a moment they are confused.

Silence.

Then they see Goga.

'I haven't got my binoculars,' I say to the man next to me, an officer I haven't seen before.

'You're not borrowing mine, that's for sure!' he says, putting them to his eyes.

I turn and go down the steps, and hear the first clash as I leave.

Cheers.

Mirth.

– – –

Reaching the park, I change my mind and go back. I have to see it – his final moments – only then I think better of it, the whole thing is just too grotesque. I go back to the park, sit down on a bench and stare up at the civil commission offices again.

I sit for a while and wait, and then dash back.

The entrance to the hospital yard, the one I used twenty minutes ago, is locked so I must walk all the way around the building and in through the main entrance on the other side. I can hear the tumult from within, the screams of the beasts, the clamour of the crowd.

I run into an SS guard at the door and explain my business. He gives me directions and I walk through the great hall, turn right into a long, white corridor and follow the noise. The glass door at the end is locked, I back-track, down into the basement. Manfred's secret room is locked, but the door of the mortuary chamber further down is open. The steel door leading directly out to the seating stand is locked too. I switch left, along a second corridor lined with hot-water tanks, make another turn, and then another, before entering a new corridor in which I find a Sturmmann.

'The hospital yard, is it this way?'

'Yes, just make a left down there and you'll see the stairs, Herr Oberleutnant. You haven't seen a toilet anywhere, by any chance? I've got the most awful diarrhoea . . .'

'Sorry, no.'

I find the stairs, but when I go up I emerge at the other end of the yard, a tiny corner hemmed in between the building's outer wall and the tall boarded fence enclosing the arena, some fifty metres from the entrance and the seating stand. SS are posted all along the perimeter, ready to pounce should Goga attempt to climb the fence, but here I am on my own. I can see only the upper rows of the stand at the far end. I am about to turn back when I realise the crowd is on its feet and looking towards my end of the arena.

Goga must be right on the other side of the boards.

There is an empty chair and a thermos flask.

They must belong to the Sturmmann I ran into.

I can hear the boars, they are so close.

— — —

I stand up on the chair and peer over the fence. I see three muscular beasts, battering, grunting, squealing, climbing each other's backs. And there, less than half a metre below me,

Goga pressed against the boards, upright. He has lost his helmet, his face is chewed open, his eyes closed, neck and shoulders gaping wounds, one arm visibly broken. He staggers, unable to react when one of the animals charges onto the backs of the two others, only to have misjudged the distance, jaws snapping furiously at the air in front of him as it slams its weight into the fence. The whole structure threatens to give and I almost lose my balance on the chair as the beast scrambles to its feet again. Then everything goes quiet for a moment.

It lifts its head and looks at me. A small, blue eye.

It is the black one with the spot on its ear, the one that killed the deaf boy.

I cannot keep my eyes from it.

'Kill me . . .'

I am startled to hear Goga speak.

'Have mercy . . .'

Before I can react, Goga twists round, reaches up with his good arm and has me in a headlock. I prise at his fingers in panic. He claws hard into my neck, pressing me down against the fence. I try to push back from the boards with my knees and thighs but find no purchase. I can't get him off me.

'I'll tell you where the gold is.'

His rancid breath is in my face, his mashed features.

'Let go!'

'Steiner had it hidden. He told me to get it out of him . . .'

'Who? Who did?'

'The one who spoke before . . .'

'. . . Manfred?'

— — —

My ears are ringing. Goga's rapid breathing. The snorting animals. Manfred. A great silence from the stand.

I hear footsteps, the Sturmmann from before, but time has stopped. Everything is turned on its head. The edges are burning. Steiner. *Gold*. Manfred? What the hell is going on?

I manage to twist the PPK from the holster with my free hand and point it over the fence.

'Strehling,' Goga whispers. 'Strehling has the gold . . .'

He tilts his head to the gun, his blue eyes look into mine as he closes his mouth around the barrel.

He nods.

The animals panic and disperse when I pull the trigger.

I see Manfred jump, then a moment's indecision.

The Sturmmann hauls me from the fence.

— — —

It happens slowly. It is a play, a ringing fever.

A Feldwebel goes round the arena shooting the animals one by one. They puncture, the pistol fired into their foreheads, brains exploded, legs buckled beneath them.

They have dragged me up in front of the buffet.

The wind has got up.

I have ruined their party.

Manfred's voice is hysterical as he grips my collar.

'What the hell did you think you were doing?'

'He was trying to pull me down, surely you could see that? He was . . .'

Dirlewanger's ghoulish face is stiffened in scorn.

Grünfeldt with that stupid hat, gawping like a simpleton.

Round, incredulous faces, featureless, eyes on stalks, whispering tongues.

'I panicked . . . I didn't know what was happening. I was grabbed by a Jew . . .'

Bach-Zelewski at the buffet table, tablecloth flapping, piled with cakes and pastries, pulls a cream puff from the top of a tall layer cake and lifts the light pastry into his mouth, considering me with indifference. I am still soaked from the bucket of water Michael threw in my face.

'I'm sorry,' I say. 'I'm sorry . . .'

Manfred lifts his cigarette hand to his mouth, tilts his head slightly to the side.

He looks right through me.

Bach-Zelewski stamps out his own cigarette.

'Bloody coward,' he spits. 'Kripos are such bloody *cowards* . . .'

'He's not used to it, that's all,' says Manfred, stepping closer, smiling into my face. 'You should have seen him in the puszcza . . . afraid to get his socks wet.'

He puts his hands on my shoulders.

'But what can be done? He's my friend.'

– – –

Manfred has called the car forward.

'I don't know what got into me,' I say.

He turns towards me, stands for a second with his hands in his pockets, produces a packet of Efkas and sticks a cigarette between my lips.

'Forget about it,' he says. 'I spoke to the camera crew, they got it all on film. You could end up famous, your *coup de grâce* . . . if he'll have it, that is . . .'

'The Führer?'

'No, not on the cards, so I'm told. Maybe Himmler, though. Kaltenbrunner, at least . . . I mean, Hubert got a state funeral, for Christ's sake! You don't think it was too much, do you?'

'What?'

'All this. Maybe you're right. Maybe it *was* too bizarre.'

The car pulls up and I get in. One of the Schwabenland brothers, Michael, is behind the wheel, reeking of booze. The car doesn't move. Manfred knocks on the glass. I roll the window down.

'Heinrich?'

'Yes?'

'Look at me . . .'

'What?'

'What did he say to you?'

'Who?'

'Don't say who, Heinrich . . .'

He holds my gaze.

'I really wish you hadn't said that . . .' he says.

'He spoke German, Manfred . . .'

'And?'

'He did say something, of course he did.'

'What did he say?'

'He begged, for God's sake . . . what the hell do you expect?'

He straightens up, slaps his hand on the roof of the car.

'You know how much I love you, don't you?' he says.

The Opel pulls away.

Gold

The Opel lingers as I unlock the door of my house.

I draw back the curtain slightly in the drawing room. The car is still there.

Michael has his arm hooked through the windscreen, he leans out to pick something up from the pavement.

'Herr?'

Masja stands in the doorway, she looks frightened.

Her sleeves are rolled up, her hands still wet.

I must have screamed.

'Here, I'm sorry,' I say.

I take out my wallet and count the notes, slap the coins down on the coffee table. A little more than twenty marks. A pittance.

'Wait . . .'

I find two fifty-mark notes in the bureau and go over to the desk.

'Take this and get away from here.'

'Herr?'

'Pack some things . . . or is there nowhere you can go?'

Her cheeks blush.

'Gospodin, are you angry? Have I done something wrong?'

'What? No.'

I write out a note to the Hotel Vogel, the place is Nur für Deutsche, but officers use it to hide away their local mistresses, they call it the Hotel Vögeln – Hotel *Fuck*. No one will look for her there. I sign my name, Oberleutnant Hoffmann, tear the page from the pad and hand it to her.

'Go there and wait for me.'

She reads, looks up at me. She is crying now. I press the money into her hand.

'There's no need to be afraid, just go.'

She nods, but remains standing.

I yell: 'Go through the garden. Come on, hurry. *Get a move on, NOW!*'

But still she hesitates.

I watch her scurry through the garden. She looks both ways then disappears down the path behind the hedge. When again I look out at the road my eyes meet Michael's as he puts his foot down and speeds away.

I sit down in the rocking chair and rock, PPK in my lap.

Steiner had the gold.

He told me to get it out of him.

Manfred . . .

– – –

A creak in the hallway.

I am out of the chair in an instant, but there is nothing there. I stand and sway on the balls of my feet, the floorboards beneath me creaking, silence, creaking. But there *is* something, down in the basement, the rattle and turn of a handle. I hold the pistol out in front of me as I creep down the stairs, straining to listen. Nothing. Or rather: a muffled oscillating sound from the floor above, like the heavy ticking of a clock. I steal back up the stairs, edge my way along the wall to the drawing room, release the safety catch from the PPK and pounce into the open doorway. Again, it is nothing: the rocking chair, still in motion. I walk forward, place my hand on its back to stop it. Only it won't stop, for my hand is trembling. And then, behind me: footsteps, halting abruptly as I spin round.

'Masja!'

She stands with her coat over her arm.

'I forgot my *Passierschein*,' she says quietly.

'For God's sake, Masja! I could have shot you!'

'I will go now.'

'No. It doesn't matter. Just stay.'

'What?'

'No, go!'

'What does Herr want me to do?'

'Go. No. I don't know, Masja. I need to think. Bring me the cognac.'

Then, as she turns:

'And Masja. Check and see if anyone's watching us from the street.'

'Herr?'

'A car. Suspicious persons, anyone hanging around, the same car again . . . take down the registration numbers and see if any recur. Do you understand?'

'Herr?'

'Just go, for God's sake!'

– – –

In front of me on the desk: the Hungarian cognac, a box of 7.65s, the PPK.

I have replaced the missing cartridge and filled an extra magazine.

I hold my head in my hands. Be methodical. Deep breaths. Relax. *Think*.

The seconds before I fired.

I jot down the sentences from memory.

Goga said:

Steiner had the gold.

He told me to get it out of Steiner . . .

The one who spoke before . . .

He must be Manfred. Manfred spoke, he spoke *before* . . .

I tap an Efka from the packet and light up, inhale the smoke deep into my lungs as I stare at my notes. I crumple the paper in my hand, ignite it and watch it burn, then pat out the glowing flakes in the ashtray.

Start again.

I write:

Steiner hid the gold.

Strehling has the gold.

Gold. Everyone steals. In the camps, at the mass graves, everyone steals from everyone else. Gold, cash, jewellery. In principle the penalty is death, and yet it is tolerated, as long as the scale is acceptable, and the further up the ladder you are, the greater the tolerance. The peacocks, the senior functionaries, with their ingots and their Rembrandts. Steiner was an Obergruppenführer, he could do *anything*. He gave Manfred that groteque SS ring with the Runic insignia and the diamonds, and Manfred threw it in the river in penance.

(a.) The gold exists.

(b.) Strehling has it. But who is Strehling?

I go on.

Goga said:

Kill me . . . Have mercy . . .

Goga begged. He would have said *anything whatsoever* in order to die. Is that what he did on Manfred's steel bed? Did he tempt Manfred with gold? Manfred was not buying it, he sent him out into the arena.

I smirk and pour myself some more cognac.

Is that what Steiner did too? The great orator, the SS general, the doctor, his *blood and soil*, did he beg for his life in the barn at Belize when his own blood splashed onto the soil of Belorussia? When Goga stood with the *Schächtmesser* and began to cut, did he try to buy himself a pardon? And Etke, who heard it all from the hayloft. Was it *Strehling* she heard, rather than *shibboleth*? Was that just a clever idea of mine after a bit of Bible reading? Or was it Goga's revenge, his own private River Jordan? Or what? I toss my head back and laugh.

Did Steiner think Goga was after his gold when he said shibboleth, and blurted out Strehling? Was it all just some sordid accident, a misunderstanding on the brink of death? Did Steiner think it would save him?

I write:

Strehling = Shibboleth. Passed on in exchange for a merciful death?

I write:

Does Manfred know I know?

— — —

I burn my notes in the fireplace and sit down in the armchair, my dress uniform in front of me on the rocking chair, the PPK in my lap and the almost empty bottle in my hand. I become an ear, turned towards the whistling wind of night.

Am I too to be laid out on Manfred's steel?

Is he speculating now in his white hospital, as I sit here and wait, the glowing end of my cigarette pricking at the darkness?

Who will blink first?

ELINE

Correspondence

Lida, 4 July 1943
Letter 7

Honey, dearest!
  Thank you for the par

Nothing has changed since I left the office two weeks ago.

Only my adjutant is new, a tall, fair-haired boy from Vienna with pomaded hair and a lisp. His lips lingered too long around his tongue for him to control his airflow when he introduced himself. *Freszl.* Does Wäspli now lie shot in a ditch? Blown to pieces by a bouncing mine? Dumped in the rubbish container in Manfred's basement?

I pick up my pen and complete the word:

cel

I throw the letter away, tidy my papers. Stare at the honey jar, *untouched by this raging war.*

Nothing happened in the night.

Masja roused me at five o'clock. The empty bottle rolled across the floor.

I walked here on stiff legs, criss-crossing the cool streets, slipping through a gateway, into a garden, down a path with mildewed roses, out onto the boulevard again.

No shadow. Not a soul.

If Manfred was out to get me he would have collected me last night.

Conclusion: Be yourself, a coward. Tidy your papers and smile.

Let Manfred have his Jew gold.

The last case is still on my desk. The killing of Feigl the Jew. I can hardly remember it.

Two SS men get into a drunken brawl, the Hauptsturmführer Breker and Kindler, Breker shoots Kindler's pet Jew, Feigl, to get back at him. Breker's version is still in the case folder, *an accident*, but Breker died with Steiner. I remove the portrait of the Führer from the wall, turn the combination and take out Kindler's report, which happens to be the truth, *Case number LZ 512–A, – GHETTO LIDA/A. Feigl, in conclusion.* I read the closing lines again:

It is therefore to be concluded that the shots that killed the Jew Jozef Feigl were fired by SS-Hauptsturmführer Heinz Breker, attached to SS-Dienststelle Lida. Pursuant to regulations re. impunity within the administrative boundaries of the Reichskommissariat Ostland, the case is deemed not to be encompassed by sections 211 or 212 of the German Penal Code. Charges will not be brought.

Case closed.

H.H. Oberleutnant d.P., Lida District.

I place the report uppermost in the case folder with the other documents pertaining to the case, witness statements and photographs, and close the folder with an elastic band.

'Frezl!'

'Herr Oberleutnant,' he says, standing to attention in front of me.

I hand him the Feigl report in its green folder.

'One for the archive and one for Sturmbannführer Kindler. Have a dispatch come and collect it,' I tell him.

Then, when his eyes remain blank:

'SS-Dienststelle Lida, 3rd Office.'

'Yes, Herr Oberleutnant.'

'That's all,' I say, and he turns and leaves.

I lean back in the chair. *That's all.* At once, I am content with myself and ravenous for food. I dip a finger into the honey, savour the taste, then succumb to greed and scoop into the jar, let the dollop begin to dissolve in my mouth, crush the crisp wax against my palate, slurping the substance inside me, the darting tingle of sugar dispersing about my organism. I empty the jar and lick my fingers, one by one, then lean back into the chair again.

Happy, witless.

It *is* over.

— — —

Lida, 24 July 1943
Letter 7

Dear E

It has been some time since I last wrote, but these last weeks have been – well, hectic. I trust you have not forgotten your little Tulle? I have not forgotten you. In fact, and it is rather a

209

paradox, I suppose – I have never thought about you as much as I do now. As if I miss you any less by sending you a letter. It's silly, I know. But you know that already.

Do you remember when we went skating on the Alster and you pretended not to hear when I said I love you? I went after you, but you kept avoiding me with your figures of eight, and then it was that you fell and broke your arm. It wasn't the best start . . . You were sixteen, I nineteen. And do you remember what you said when we said goodbye at the station? Time to grow up, Heinrich.

I think I can say that during the past eleven months I have done just that. Grown up. Which is why I . . .

I dig out the relevant forms, the ones I ordered a month ago. The *Ariernachweis*, pedigree back to great-grandparents. Statement of financial affairs. Marriage authorisation from the Gesundheitsamt.

Pure of blood, Aryans, financially sound, approved, stamped in blue.

I finish the letter. A handwritten postscript, underneath *Your loving Heinrich*:

PS. Will you marry me?

'Frezl!'

— — —

Young Frezl stops with the letter to Eline in his hand. He turns round:

'Oh, a message came for the Oberleutnant earlier on.'

'A message?'

'Yes. Or rather, a little letter. I forgot.'

He darts out, returns and puts it down on the desk in front of me. The lilac envelope is blank. I pick up my letter opener and send him a glance. He withdraws.

Has Eline stolen a march on me? A little game, perhaps? The girlish colour, the thickness of the writing paper. Has she had someone bring it with them from Hamburg? Ingo, for instance, from the infirmary? The envelope is unscented, not a hint of lavender. Perhaps there is a pressed flower inside.

I pull out the letter, the paper is folded down the middle. I unfold it.

A scream goes off inside my head.

– – –

'Who delivered it?'

'I don't know!'

The blood has rushed to Frezl's head, his transparent skin.

'It was . . .'

'WHO?'

'No, I didn't see him . . . he . . .'

'SS . . . Wehrmacht . . . SD . . . Who was it?'

Frezl sighs. I leap down the stairs, my pulse racing.

The street is empty.

Frezl is blowing his nose when I come back. He is about to say something, only I dismiss him with a wave of my hand.

– – –

I stare at the telephone. Is it some sick joke? Manfred's shock therapy. Confuse the victim. Lilac envelope, a little message . . . a token of fondness, a slap in the face.

Manfredism. *You're not to know if I'm coming to kill you or not.*

The letter is in front of me:

WHO IS STREHLING?

I lunge for the receiver.

'Hauptsturmführer Manfred Schlosser,' I bark at the operator.

'One moment . . .'

I hear the connection being made; his adjutant comes on at the other end.

'This is Oberleutnant Hoffmann. Manfred, is he there?'

'No, I'm afraid he isn't.'

'When will he be back?'

'It could be a few days yet.'

'*Days?* What do you mean?'

'The Hauptsturmführer has gone to Hamburg.'

'Hamburg? When?'

'Yesterday. Immediately after the entertainment. By plane.'

'What? Where can I get in touch with him?'

'You can't . . .'

– – –

'Is the Oberleutnant unwell?'

Frezl puts a hand on my shoulder. I am on my knees.

I must have been gone for a minute, my breathing.

It fills the room.

'What?'

'I heard a noise and—'

I get to my feet, brush something from my jacket.

'No. I'm fine.'

He looks at me, his bright eyes.

'Go,' I tell him. 'I don't know what happened.'

— — —

Once Frezl has closed the door I go over to the window, pull down the blinds, flip the wooden slats and look out. A heavily laden truck rumbles along Falkowska Street, a motorbike with a sidecar turns the corner on the right where a car with darkened windows is waiting in the shadow of the station building. I stare at it. There is someone inside.

I go back to the telephone, there *is* a definite click before I get the operator.

Someone is listening in.

Back to the window with my binoculars.

The car is still there.

Someone has obliterated the number plate. Mercedes, no insignia, it could be anyone. Now I see how it strains, as if the driver has the clutch on the biting point, ready to pull away into the street.

Someone is waiting for me.

If it *isn't* Manfred, then who *is* it?

Everyone knows I was in charge of the investigation. But who knows what Goga told me?

The SS-Sturmmann who hauled me off the fence?

The Schwabenland brothers, Hans or Michael, who loitered outside my house last night?

Who?

It could be *anyone at all who wants in on the spoils.*

Another rush of anxiety as I realise that I am alone, without protection, without Manfred.

— — —

I splash my face at the bathroom sink and stand for a moment in the dim light, hands against the porcelain. I try to steady my heartbeat as I stare at myself in the mirror, but it races away, tears through my nerves, my head screeching, an electric current that jars in my teeth, squeals in my ears, my pupils dilating, eyes wider and wider, chest thumping.

'*It's easy . . .*'

'What?'

I bang my head against the mirror. Zarah Leander again.

'*Killing,*' she says. '*Killing is easy – but hard to forget . . .*'

'Killing is easy?'

'*No, loving is, you fool . . .*'

She is gone.

There is only my round face in the mirror, my rectangular spectacles.

– – –

When I find myself again my legs are shaking.

After a minute I can stand.

I am calm then, only my hands tremble.

My head is clear.

Manfred.

I have to get to him.

He has to save me. He got me into this.

That time he pointed his pistol at me in Koreletjy, *someone trying to pull one over on us*. Generalkommissar Kube, who put his people on me in Minsk. Why? Dirlewanger, who wouldn't speak to Manfred when he brought him the stuffed head of Goga's brother prior to Operation Hermann. Goga, who knew Strehling. A treasure without an owner? What's going on? Have I been drawn into yet another grotesque scheme?

Manfred must have found something out. But *what*?

I must go to Hamburg and find him, but first I need to get past whoever is outside.

I have one chance. It is slight. But it is there.

– – –

Back in the office, I test my voice. An octave too high.

I try again.

'Frezl!'

He appears at once.

'Yes, Herr Oberleutnant.'

'Did you send that report to Kindler?'

'I'm waiting for the messenger.'

'Cancel it, then get me the telephone directories for Göttingen, Frankfurt and Hamburg.'

'Göttingen, Frankfurt, Hamburg . . .'

'Yes. They've got them over at the civil commission, you know where that is?'

'Over by the park, yes?'

'Right. While you're over there I want you to find a telegraphist and bring her back with you. She sits on the second row, second from the window. It has to be her, no one else will do.'

'Second from the window on the second row. Have you got a name?'

'No.'

'No?'

'She's small . . . blonde, I don't know. She may have a slight injury, above her eyebrow. Can you manage that?'

He nods, but is visibly perplexed. I open the cupboard and take out my old travel bag, black, crinkled leather with my father's hiking patches on it from Tyrol, but then I change my mind.

'On second thoughts, just bring the telephone directories in a bag. Don't let anyone see them. And I want the telegraphist here in an hour, on the dot.'

Escape plan

The gun is a prototype, StG 44, Sturmgewehr 44, from the locked arms cabinet by the firing range in the basement of police headquarters, brand new, straight from the factory of Haenel GmbH, firearms and bicycle manufacturers. It is heavy, some five kilos, a metre in length, a colossus of chambers and clicking catches, glistening with gun oil, a model aeroplane, a spaceship, Fritz Lang's Metropolis. I slam the box of ammunition down on the terrazzo table, 8mm cartridges, the Kurz ammo spills out onto the tabletop with a clatter, and I press them down into the curved magazine one by one, thirty in all.

The weapon stutters against my shoulder as the cartridges are deployed into the chamber and launched down the rifled barrel. The cardboard figure at the end of the range disintegrates into paper and dust.

The suction of the mechanics as I reload.

Another volley, howling.

The assault rifle fits in my father's travel bag.

I throw in an extra magazine, eight for the PPK, and ten hand grenades.

I can blow that Mercedes off the road.

Frezl has left the six telephone directories on my desk. Individuals and companies. Göttingen and Frankfurt are consigned to the floor: whoever is in that car can look for Strehling there.

There are eight Strehlings in Hamburg, spread over the city: Heinz, Gerda, Wiltraut, Dieter, Urs, Wilhelm, Rolf and Heinrich. No, he lives in Altona. That would be a possibility too. The same goes for Kiel; Holstein too, for that matter. Christ. But Manfred is in *Hamburg*. His adjutant said so.

He knows the same as me. Strehling has the gold, Goga said.

I note down the addresses. I get out my code book and write a message using the code entries for the 4th of March. My former Kripo partner knows to look up that date whenever I send him a telegraph. Even if everyone knows the code, no one knows not to use today's date in the book. I tear out the 4th of March, fold it four times, roll it hard and pin it to the inside of my collar with a safety pin. I go over to the window again. The car is still there, engine idling. I have the coded message in my pocket.

I fill in the application form for leave, for Frezl's out tray. Under REASON I type:

M a r r i a g e

– – –

'*You?*'

Frezl found the telegraphist.

Her make-up is overdone, but her features are still delicate.

218

The bruise on her cheek cannot be seen, the plaster over her eyebrow is gone too.

'Yes,' I say.

I push a small, stubby glass of Kirsch across the desk.

'I want you to help me,' I say.

'Why should I? Remember what you did last time I tried to be nice?'

She reaches for the glass and looks at me with her green eyes, the perfect youth of her face, the wide cheekbones and garish red lips that curl around the glass, bird's wings of lipstick left on the rim after she knocks back the contents.

'Why did you do it, anyway?'

She tilts her head, she *is* a flirt, and rather nervous too.

Suddenly all I want is to kiss her, to forget everything that is about to happen. She reaches across the table and pours herself another Kirsch. At once I despise her. I could hit her again.

'Don't look at me like that!' she says.

I put the application form down in front of her. Marriage automatically means three days of leave.

'What's this?'

'Look and see.'

She leans forward, picks it up and skims through.

'Marriage?!'

Her cheeks blush at once.

'It's important to me that you're the one to do it,' I carry on.

'Me?'

'Yes.'

She lifts up the glass and puts it to her lips, only then to think better of it.

'And here I was thinking you were going to say sorry . . .'

She thrusts out her arm as I reach over the table, and jumps to her feet.

'Don't you touch me. You make me . . .'

Her eyes are a moist film.

'You make feel me dirty . . . I don't know what it is.'

I want to kiss her again. She is so young.

I take out Eline's photograph and hand it to her.

'Here,' I say. 'That's her.'

'Zarah Leander? You're marrying *Zarah Leander*?' she says, giggling now.

'That's Eline. It's the only one I've got . . . she dyed her hair . . .'

She takes the picture, studies it, studies me. Her eyes are play-ful all of a sudden, provocative.

'You're mad, do you know that? You've got a screw loose! And now you want to go off to Hamburg and see if your fat fiancée really *is* Zarah Leander!'

'Something like that.'

'And why should I help you?'

'Because you're *nice* . . .'

She tilts her head again. I could drink from her green eyes.

'You really are mad.'

I pour two more glasses of Kirsch and hand her one.

'Cheers,' I say. 'Wait a minute, I don't even know what you're called.'

'Greta,' she says, picking up the glass and sitting down again.

'Weissbecker. And yours?'

We chink.

'Staal. Viktor Staal. Zarah's already accepted . . .'

— — —

She stands, draws her hands down over the small of her back, smoothing her grey skirt, twisting herself into place.

'There was something else,' I say, rising to join her.

'Yes?'

I take the note with the coded message from the pocket of my uniform jacket and hand it to her.

'Will you send this for me?'

'What is it?'

She hesitates, suspicious.

'For the Kripo in Hamburg? You're not going to get me into trouble, are you?'

'It's best you know nothing about it.'

I lean forward, cup my hand to her ear and whisper:

'Zarah has a problem, a women's matter. You know . . . *hush-hush*.'

I put an index finger to my lips.

'Hush-hush?'

'Hush-hush.'

We stand there for a moment, next to each other. I can smell her perfume. I want to kiss her again. She draws away from me and puts the note in her pocket.

'Has the whole world gone mad?' she says.

'Yes,' I say.

– – –

He is a big man. Hauptsturmführer Kindler, my ticket to Hamburg, the size of zu Gutenberg, my superior who is on leave in Stuttgart, at the manor house on the Neckar, with its pollarded poplars, the old baron to be put in the ground, eaten away by bone cancer, or is he still on his deathbed? I have forgotten.

He is a 56.

His police uniform hangs in his cupboard, behind the desk, three offices down.

Frezl smokes a long, pink cigarette as I walk along the corridor, inhaling in a concentrated sort of way, as though he has never done it before. Is that make-up on his eyelashes?

I pat the pockets of the uniform. Nothing untoward. Or rather: a photograph of a girl, ten or twelve years old, in a grey skirt, ankle socks and patent leather shoes, feet splayed out. She curls in front of the camera, a scatter of teeth and freckles. In the background a vast lawn, and a horsewoman in a jacket in the distance.

I fold the uniform up, put it in the bag with the StG 44 and toss the cap on top.

It would fit an oil drum. And zu Gutenberg is a Hauptmann d.P.

But it will be dark.

— — —

Kindler bursts in through the door a few minutes later, open leather coat, heavy boots, throws himself down in my chair, arms wide, bellowing:

'So what the hell am I here for . . .?'

'Because of this,' I say, and shove the folder containing the Feigl report across the desk to him.

'And what might that be?'

Kindler snatches up the folder, leans back, opens it and narrows his eyes. Is he short-sighted, too vain to wear spectacles?

He starts laughing.

'I knew it! It *was* Breker . . . the bastard . . . Was that all?'

'Yes. I thought you might want to know.'

'Indeed!'

He rises, sways slightly, a tower of flesh, a rumbling roll of laughter.

'I thought you were too scared, when it never came.'

'I was on another case. Goga, you know . . .'

He lifts a paw and wipes his nose.

'Lunch on me! Say where!'

– – –

The mess, later.

'*Nobody* touches my Jews . . .'

He jabs a finger at me, then swipes the air with his great mitt. Small, thick-bottomed schnapps glasses litter the table, a battery of yellow shots, he picks one up and hurls it down his throat, the waiter pours a dozen at a time, appears again with the bottle, scatters the alcohol over the glasses, soaking the table in spirits, a fuming swamp of booze. Kindler leans forward, piggish eyes swimming, a thick curtain of smoke in the iris, copper-coloured spots. He runs a finger inside his collar and loosens his tie.

'I'm telling you . . . fucking . . . *whores* . . . Ha!'

They cannot touch me as long as I am protected by Kindler.

Nobody touches Kindler. They are not going to gun down a Hauptsturmführer in the middle of town, for God's sake.

Saliva dribbles from his mouth, his head is on the table.

He sweeps the glasses to the floor.

He falls asleep.

When I collect my jacket from the cloakroom, one arm around Kindler's shoulder, there is an envelope sticking out of the pocket. I slide a finger inside and tear it open. Kindler supports himself with both hands on the counter, devouring the cloakroom girl with his eyes, jaw hanging open.

It is from Greta. On the last page: *Approved*.

A seat on the train to Hamburg tomorrow morning at five.

Greta . . .

There is a reply too from my colleague, Kripo, in Hamburg.

I put them in my bag. Now I have all the documents.

All I need to do is get through the next four hours until the train leaves.

I pick up the bag with the uniform and the StG 44 in it and put it under my arm.

'We'll go and have some more,' I say, patting Kindler on the back. 'And let's find some *whores* . . .'

Kindler sighs.

'I forgot my . . .' He belches. 'Left my tablets at the office... dicky heart.'

The sky is a scream of crimson as we emerge from the establishment. The Mercedes pulls away from the kerb and crawls along behind.

– – –

Between the road and the pond, a couple of hundred metres beyond the station, a grainy *terrain vague*, amid the rumble of the drinking houses, the squealing whores, the needle snatched from a gramophone record, dance music, they must be playing musical chairs or strip poker, or the floor is made of lava.

A man roars.

A musty shed at the pond's edge. The girl is sixteen, seventeen perhaps. Her mother or aunt, a small, tightly packaged woman, receives us. She withdraws, and we are left on our own: bed, table, cupboard, samovar.

Kindler is huffing and blowing. His enormous frame fills the place.

'Do you speak German?' I ask the girl.

She nods and looks at the floor.

'*Bonk, bonk* . . . A bit of . . .'

'Hey!' Kindler belches, staggers, lurches towards me. 'You!'

The girl looks up. Her face is pale, hair jet black, freckles dotted about her mouth.

'Heads or tails?'

He fumbles in the pockets of his leather coat. He finds 50 pfennig, turns it between his fingers, the coin held up in front of his face, and lays it in the palm of his hand.

'Tails,' I say.

He slaps the coin down on the back of his hand. His drooling mouth.

'Feeling lucky, are we?' he says.

'Maybe,' I say.

He narrows his eyes, squints at me. His eyeballs are tinged orange. What is that? Liver disease, heart disease? He tilts open his hand.

'Ha!'

Removes the hand in a flourish.

The angular eagle, the swastika in the wreath. *Deutsches Reich 1943*.

Heads.

He steps up to the girl, leans into her, slobbers in her ear and straightens up again.

'Are we on?'

The alcohol is rank on his breath.

– – –

Kindler's dick.

She sucks it erect. It is red as fire, a dog's dick.

– – –

Kindler holds her knees together with one hand, presses them upwards to her chestbone and bats aside the flaps of his coat. His boots are by the bed.

He crumples her up, flattens her, grinding away inside her.

He slaps her in the face a couple of times and increases his cadence.

Her neck is stretched, her head turned towards me, but she is not looking at me. At first there is only her rhythmically jolting head and the slap of flesh against flesh, then a trickle of blood from her left nostril, and Kindler opens his mouth, a torrent of obscenity, groans and stiffens, empties himself inside her.

My Efka has burned out between my fingers.

– – –

Kindler is asleep, his breathing ceases, then from the darkest depths a sudden eruption as he heaves in air like a man drowning.

The girl is seated on the bed with her hands between her knees.

The tartness of cold and semen.

I stand up and lift my father's travel bag onto the table. I take out zu Gutenberg's uniform and hold it up in front of me, judging the size against the sleeping Kindler. The girl follows my movements with her eyes. I arrange my weapons at the bottom of the bag and place it by the door, hang the uniform over the back of the chair, put the cap on the table.

I pick up the jug from the washstand and fill up the samovar.

'Have you got firelighters?' I say to the girl. 'Firelighters?'

'Gospodin?'

'For the samovar . . . come on!'

She gets up from the bed, takes her top from the bedpost.

'Don't put your clothes back on.'

She fails to understand. I snatch the top from her hands, lead her to the samovar, my hand around her neck.

'Tea,' I say.

Her hands tremble as she gathers kindling and a couple of firelighters. She cannot hold the match still. I squat down too, and now we are next to each other.

I snap the dry twigs into smaller pieces and insert them under the samovar, get a flame going and stare into it. The flame is blue, it licks and devours, it leaps in the darkness.

'Are you cold?'

'No, gospodin.'

Do you understand pee . . . *piss*? Do you need to . . .?'

I gesture with my hand.

She shakes her head. I nod, indicating the samovar.

'Tea first,' I say.

The water boils. I open the tap and fill the little teapot, then pour a small cup and hand it to her. It steams in the cold of night.

The girl raises the cup to her lips.

She is afraid. She smiles. I put a blanket around her.

'What's your name?'

She says nothing.

'Your name? *Sjto tebja zovut?*'

'Irina.'

'Heinrich. *Menja zovut Genrikh . . .*'

She empties the cup, looks up at me.

'I think I need to now,' she says.

'Drink some more. We'll wait.'

– – –

'No, not me. Him . . .'

I point at Kindler. His mouth is open. The bridge in his lower jaw has dislodged, a verdigris copula on which he chews, a skeleton, a roll of barbed wire transversing his gaping mouth, he sucks and chomps, his tongue around the metal, slavers and mutters, chokes and splutters.

'Gospodin . . .?'

'It's all right,' I say. 'I know him.'

She goes over to the bed, looks back at me.

I nod and she straddles Kindler's face, the open jaws, hesitating still.

'Yes, yes!' I say.

She presses a hand to her crotch, the muscles of her abdomen tense, and then it comes, a couple of ragged splashes at first, then a forceful, unsteerable cascade into his face, into his mouth. I step up and put my hands on her hips, steering as she drenches him, pisses all over his uniform, his leather coat, his hands, his filthy hands.

Only gradually does he come to his senses, reach a hand between her legs, fling her hard against the wall.

'What the *hell* . . .!' he bellows, his feet on the floor at once. 'What the . . . *fucking hell* . . .!'

He rises from the bed, bewildered for a moment, grabs his P38 and racks the slide, turning towards her. She has curled into a ball, hugs the wall, hands cupped around her neck: the serrated ridge of her spine, her jagged knees, her scrawny body. I am across the room in one movement to knock his hand away. He lashes out, I swivel and lock my arms around his stomach.

'Sigmund . . .!'

'I'll fucking . . . *fucking* . . .!'

'Sigmund! You told her to yourself. You told her to, only you can't remember!'

His eyes are so close to mine. He could destroy my face with his bare hands.

And then he starts to laugh.

'Fucking hell! Did I really?'

'Yes.'

'Fucking hell. She's pissed all over me . . .'

– – –

Zu Gutenberg's uniform fits him perfectly. I adjust the collar. Kindler sways gently as I place the cap on his head. He takes out his little box and shakes a pill into his palm. He opens his mouth and I place the small, round tablet onto his tongue.

'You look much better now,' I say.

'I'd better be off home,' he says.

'Yes,' I say. 'You better had. Come on.'

– – –

We step out into the alley in front of the shed. Kindler stands for a moment looking forlorn. I guide him up to the road and shove him onwards before turning back down the alley on my own. He staggers out into the road, his legs unsteady. Reaching the pond, I drop the bag and take out the StG 44, click in the magazine and follow the structures that line the water's darkness, cutting back up to the road again. Kindler walks alone through the thin light some twenty or thirty metres in front of me, the street empty, zu Gutenberg's police uniform standing out in the night. The Mercedes pulls out of a side street, brakes hard at Kindler, the door flung open, Kindler's cry. I pull the cocking handle, it snaps back and I step out into the road.

I hold the trigger in until the firing pin clicks, change the magazine and fire off another volley as I approach the vehicle. The driver collapses over the horn.

I dump the StG in a garden and shout:

'HELP! Partisans!'

The horn blares.

– – –

In the car.

I take in the shredded remains of a uniform, purple epaulettes and gold braid – Grünfeldt's arm is broken, his head buried in the back seat. Haber is in seizure. I take hold of his collar and haul him away from the horn, and then everything is quiet. Frezl has been slung halfway out of the vehicle, his arm is draped across Kindler's gut. I stroke a finger over his cheek, close his eyes, close his mouth.

His last breath against my hand.

A fair-haired boy.

Only now do I realise that I have killed Kommissar Kube's men.

The first of the Wehrmacht come running, braces dangling, Mausers cocked at the ready, a clamour of voices.

'Police,' I say. 'I'll get help.'

My watch says eleven minutes to five as I duck back into the alley to pick up my bag.

Eleven minutes until my train.

The train

I can see the train as it comes in across the great shunting yards.

Kube's men.

When Kube finds out he will kill me . . .

Severe searchlights beam out from the engine sheds, the doors open with a clatter, and troops spill onto the ramp. In front of me a sandy pathway opens up through the darkness, a luminous track.

A woman turns onto the path a few metres further on, she comes straight at me, her face a veil of smoke, swirling smoke in the grey darkness.

She staggers, veers off to the right, clutches her throat, and falls towards me.

'Masja!' I shout.

I catch her. Masja's hands are around my neck, the taste of blood in my mouth.

'Masja!'

A tall, thin man steps onto the path.

'Should we stop the bleeding?' he says calmly.

'What?'

'She'll die in your arms. Do you want her to die?'

'Do something, for Chrissake!'

'Where are you going?'

The thin man grips Masja firmly in his hands and lays her down. Someone else steps from the bushes, inserts his fingers into the wound in Masja's neck and applies a tourniquet. He is shorter, stockier than the first man.

I have seen him before. Who is he?

'Who are you?'

'I asked you where you were going,' says the thin one.

'Should I let go?' the stocky one asks.

'No!' I shout. 'Hamburg!'

'Hamburg?'

'Yes. Strehling is in Hamburg!'

'Thank you.'

Dirlewanger's deathly face emerges from the darkness. He places his tongue against his upper lip, spits out some shreds of tobacco. He walks up to Masja with a pistol in his hand.

'Are you fucking her?'

'What? No, for God's sake!'

He empties the P38 into her face. Blood splatters his hands.

The stocky one, crouching at her side, releases the tourniquet and gets to his feet.

'Oscar!' he says. 'I'm drenched.'

'You said you weren't fucking her,' says Dirlewanger.

'What?'

'We're coming with you,' he says, and offers me a handkerchief. 'Here. You're covered in blood.'

'I'm not going anywhere,' I say.

He stands there, holding the handkerchief in the air.

– – –

The stocky one has his fingers in my mouth, he is trying to tear off my head. Dirlewanger kicks me in the stomach, I try to bite into his fingers, they're gagging me, and I am dealt a blow to the forehead.

'I can't hear what he's saying . . . let go, Klaus . . .'

I sit up, spitting earth from between my lips.

'What is it you want? Did Kube send you?'

They laugh.

'No, you shot them, remember? Kindler, as well. Rather well thought out, for a nobody,' says Dirlewanger. 'Quite spectacular, in fact.'

'Manfred will be coming to get you. He'll . . .'

'We'll deal with Manfred.'

'Michael and Hans . . . the Schwabenland brothers . . .'

'Hush . . .' says Dirlewanger, index finger to his lips. 'Don't tell anyone . . .'

The thin one laughs.

'. . . or else they might come after us.'

Now Dirlewanger laughs too, laughs as he rips off my rank insignia with his penknife.

'She tasted rather nice, by the way, even if she was oblivious . . .'

'Who?'

'Your little telegraphist cunt . . .'

– – –

Dirlewanger's mouldy face as he raises his hand and the train sets in motion.

I sit in the murky carriage with my hands folded around my knees, handcuffed. Dirlewanger's men guard me – the stocky one with his fat legs dangling out of the door. He rifles through my wallet. Klaus.

234

'Tossing off to Zarah Leander, are we?' he says when he sees the photograph of Eline.

The other man says nothing, two green cat's eyes in the dim light.

'And what have we got here?'

He unfolds the reply from my colleague in Hamburg.

'A code?'

I stare back at Dirlewanger as the train pulls away: he dwindles to a speck and is gone.

'No,' I say.

'We'll find out, don't you worry,' says Klaus.

'It makes no difference,' says the thin one. 'What we want to know is inside his head. If he won't talk, we'll cut it off.'

Klaus stuffs my wallet into his pocket.

I remember him now.

The man from Dirlewanger's zoo.

I never did report him for Rassenschande.

The Jew lover with the whip.

– – –

The tall, thin one with the sallow skin is called Rainer. He shovels stew into his face straight from the primus. He has opened the little aluminium spoon from the cutlery set and holds it at the join, his meagre mouth tight as he attacks the food.

We hold back as the troop trains slowly clatter by.

A company of the Wehrmacht clambers in at Navahrudak.

Klaus has been out in the shunting yards looking for booze.

He lifts a leg sideways into the wagon and hauls himself inside.

'I got the biscuits you were wanting.'

Rainer says nothing.

'How much do you want for the packet,' another man asks, a corporal of the Wehrmacht who sits smoking in the corner.

'They're not for sale,' says Rainer, and snatches the packet out of Klaus's hand.

Klaus sees me looking at him, the humiliation in his face.

'What are you staring at?' he says.

'Nothing,' I say. 'Is there any water?'

'Not for you, there isn't, you stupid fuck,' says Klaus. He glances at Rainer. Rainer bites into the packet and spits out cardboard.

It is early evening already.

They are going to die. Both of them.

Sallow or ruddy, it makes no odds.

The Wehrmacht company leave us at the next stop.

After an hour the darkness is total, and we are on our own.

— — —

Later, somewhere in western Polesia.

'Psst . . . Klaus . . .'

'Shut up and sleep . . .'

'I need to piss . . .'

'Ssh . . .'

'But I need to piss . . .'

'Shut your *fucking*—'

'Do you want me to wake Rainer?'

'What?'

'I'm bursting here. Do you want me to wake him up? OK, I will . . . Hey, Rainer!'

'What . . .'

'Shut up, for God's sake . . . *it's OK, Rainer, nothing* . . . All right, come on, then.'

'Can't you tilt the bucket a bit?'

'Tilt it?'

'That's right, tilt it.'

'Like this?'

'That's it. You're scared of Rainer, aren't you?'

'What?'

'You heard.'

'You mind I don't punch you in the face.'

'Go on, then. But what would you do with the bucket?'

'Just *shut it*. Are you finished?'

'Not quite. That's it. Here.'

'Chuck it out yourself.'

'Aren't you worried I'll jump off the train?'

'Give it here!'

'Ssh, you'll wake Rainer.'

– – –

'What *now*?'

'I've seen you before,' I say. 'You look after Dirlewanger's zoo. You're the one who likes to watch things grow.'

'What?'

'That's what you said. You like to watch things grow.'

'And?'

'I can understand that . . .'

He snaps a thumb at his lighter, a flame flares madly in the dark. He cups his hands around it as he lights up a cigarette, his face emerges in the glow.

'I understand why you fuck her as well . . .'

237

He stops in mid-movement. I hold his gaze. I hold his gaze, and he knows I know.

'What?'

'The redhead . . . you know who I'm talking about . . . the *Jewish* girl.'

It is instinctive and sudden, an elongation of the body, the flash of his fist. I duck to my left, he draws back his arm, lunges and grips me tight in a headlock.

'*You shut it*,' he hisses. He holds the blade of a knife to my eye. 'I'll kill you like a pig, I'll cut your throat!'

'Rainer,' I say. 'Rainer . . . if you kill me . . . let go.'

He releases and shoves me against the rear wall.

'You keep your mouth *shut* . . . or *else* . . .'

'Or else what?'

'*Shut up over there!*'

– – –

I double up in the dark, curling into a tight ball at the first plunging kicks to my abdomen, unable to keep the breath inside me. Rainer twists my handcuffed arms up over my head and steps on my wrists. Klaus straddles my legs, fists pummelling at my stomach.

'Now keep your fucking mouth shut!' Rainer yells. 'Keep your fucking mouth shut, do you hear me!'

My mouth is bleeding, my teeth feel loose.

'Nnn!'

Rainer steps away.

'One more peep . . . do you hear?'

'Nnn!'

'That goes for you, too, Klaus. Not one peep . . .'

'Right.'

– – –

'Argh . . . I think I've broken a rib . . .'

No answer. The wheels clatter against the tracks. Rainer breathes heavily, snoring. Not a sound from Klaus. In the flare of the lighter flame, I see Klaus turned away, staring out into the darkness.

'You got turned in . . . he shafted you . . .'

Silence. Attentive silence.

'I wrote the report yesterday, before I left . . . I can stop it . . .'

He says nothing. I can almost smell the thoughts as they turn inside his hideous little head. He exhales; the peppery smell of smoke lingers for a moment and is sucked out through the door. The orange dot of his cigarette flickers in the darkness.

'I could have a word with zu Gutenberg, my boss,' I tell him. 'It's on his desk . . . he's on leave. He'll be home in four days . . . if I don't get back before, it'll be passed on. Rassenschande, what's that . . . death penalty, penal unit? And what about the girl?'

'Shut your mouth. Why would anyone tell *you* anything?'

'Because you SS are always at each other's throats.'

'And where did you get all this?'

'Do you think I'm stupid?'

'So tell me who snitched.'

He inhales, pleased with himself.

'Who do you think?'

'Just tell me, you fucking liar . . .'

'How much did they tell you about Hamburg?'

'Tell me, you *bastard* . . .'

'I didn't think when the complaint came in last Friday . . . Rainer stabbed you in the back, Klaus . . . I'm going to die in Hamburg, and when you get home they'll be waiting for you . . .

execution, penal unit. You'll be clearing mines, Klaus, if you're lucky.'

'Shut it. Just shut your *fucking* mouth.'

– – –

'I've got a lot of friends in Hamburg,' I say a while later. 'We could get away, no bother. If only . . .'

'If only what?'

'You know what you have to do, Klaus.'

'What?'

'I don't know you. How would I know anything about a complaint?'

'You're bluffing!'

'Use your head. You look after Dirlewanger's little zoo. You're a nobody, Klaus. You're expendable. Like me. We're little fish, spokes in a wheel . . . you wouldn't get a single gram of that gold.'

'Gold?'

'Yes, gold. Didn't they tell you?'

He looks at me blankly.

'They didn't even tell you!'

'What should I do?'

'We'll be changing wagons at Brest-Litovsk, different gauges, it'll take an hour. Get Rainer to go with you for some coffee . . .'

'Coffee . . .?'

'Yeah, coffee . . . some good coffee.'

'I can't . . .'

'Yes, you can . . . *coffee* . . .'

'Shut up about bloody coffee!'

'They'll do you in, Klaus . . . a steaming cup of good, hot coffee.'

'And then what?'

'Get his papers.'

'His papers?'

'That's right.'

Another blank look.

'Now's the time, Klaus . . .'

'How do I know you're not going to do a bunk in the meantime?'

'Cuff me to the stove. I'm done in . . . you beat me to a pulp, for Christ's sake.'

— — —

Brest-Litovsk

The gigantic station is made up of sixteen tracks, it's the heart and arteries of logistic operations: weaponry heading east, spoils west. The blackout is total, everything happens in the dark, a clamour of noise like fifteen factories, an ear-splitting screech of wagons and rails, trains laden with tanks. We roll into the sidings and wait, a sudden fountain of welding sparks, cries and shouts, sounds so very near, and yet oddly muffled, as though we were kilometres under the sea, as though this were the Mariana Trench, and then the rumble of RSOs.

Klaus stretches, he digs the toe of his boot under Rainer's right buttock and kicks it about.

'I'm fucking freezing. Let's get something to warm us up . . .'

'What about him?'

'I've cuffed him to the stove.'

Rainer gets to his feet and comes over to me, gets down on his haunches and lifts up my head.

'We worked him over, didn't we?'

'We did.'

'Five minutes,' says Rainer.

— — —

I count the minutes, I count the dead in the darkness, try to recall their names, their faces. Etke. Greta Weissbecker, who died for being *nice*. Steiner, Breker, Goga, Wäspli, the Czapski family, Zaludok's entire ghetto, the Schwabenland brothers, Kindler, Grünfeldt, Haber, Frezl. The deaf boy. The ones who got blown to bits. The nameless. The mad Russian with his tin of peaches. The Jewish girl who spat semen in her hand.

Masja. Already, her heart stopped, her body barely cold, the blood sinks inside her organism, dark pools settle at the bottom of her organs and muscles, livid islands rising up to the surface of her skin, *livor mortis*, and soon, in the morning, now, come the first of the blowflies to deposit their eggs, the fat flesh flies, the beetles, a scabby fox, a dog, and in a few days she will be unrecognisable, an emaciated object, a bundle of bones, a memory only, in my searing brain.

I hear footsteps in the gravel outside the wagon. They come to a halt.

'Right,' says Klaus, and clambers inside. He tosses me Rainer's wallet. He lights a cigarette, his face blank. 'You keep your mouth shut!'

— — —

The train starts moving.

In a moment it will halt at the station itself and the wagon will fill with troops, men heading home on leave, wounded, an unfamiliar multitude.

I have a couple of minutes, at most, but the darkness is on my side.

'Get these off me.'

'As if . . .'

'Come on. A police officer cuffed to a stove. How are you going to explain that?'

He ponders for a second, then steps up and uncuffs me.

'One wrong move . . .'

I get to my feet and try to shake some life into my hand.

'Aren't I supposed to have a pistol?'

'You show me where the gold is, then maybe . . .'

I sit down with a sigh.

'I'm starving. Haven't you got anything?'

He rummages in his rucksack, produces a tin and rolls it towards me.

'Tin opener? Have you got one? Or would that be too risky?'

It lands in my lap. The tin sighs as I press the blade into the lid. I scoop up the congealed goulash and press handfuls into my mouth.

'Thanks,' I mutter.

He is over by the door, looking out.

I come up behind him with the tin, the sharp, jagged lid.

'Want some?'

'What?'

He half turns, a sudden warmth in his voice.

I grip his chin, wrench back his head and cut into him below the jugular. The artery is impossible to pin down. He flails his arms, and strikes my ear, launching my spectacles into the darkness. He twists to face me, a hand already clutching at my neck, and then I slice open his larynx. He stiffens for a second as air squeals from his lungs, as I chop at the artery.

Then comes the blood.

I hold him upright, as it pumps out.

He collapses at the knees, and I allow him to fall to the floor.

His pupils are already fixed.

The moist film of his eyes glistens a moment in the night, then it too is extinguished.

I retrieve my PPK, pat him down and find his papers, his and Rainer's *Soldbücher*, the three wallets, and dump his body onto the shunting ground.

I rinse my hands in the piss bucket, then throw that out too.

I am shaking uncontrollably, and I have to use both hands to put my spectacles back on.

– – –

'Ah, company at last! I've been sat here freezing on my own since Minsk,' I exclaim as the first hands grip the wagon door and men begin to clamber inside.

'Dieter Horn,' one of them says by way of introduction, hand raised in salute. 'Panzergrenadier. Where are you heading?'

'Hamburg.'

'Hamburg? Me too. Whereabouts?'

'Hamm.'

'You're joking.'

'No, no joke.'

'Where exactly?'

'Rumpffweg . . .'

'Small world!'

'All he can talk about is bloody Hamm,' someone says. 'You'd think everyone who was anyone had to come from Hamm.'

'It's true!' I say, and laugh.

I still can't stop my hands from shaking.

Home

We come to a standstill somewhere in Vorpommern, in a haze of pollen and summer heat, on a siding, half hidden by a flourish of birch trees. Above us a rumbling swarm of American bombers, USAAF, are out daylight bombing, their white bellies flying fortresses of aluminium, shining serpents in the sky.

Are they heading for Rostock? Berlin?

I move my bowels, crouched on the edge of a gravel pit.

I have emptied the wallets and dispersed the documents, the two Soldbücher, identification papers, photographs. Coins too, and a safety pin. I stare blankly at a small knotted keyring from Rainer's wallet, embellished with ceramic beads.

Klaus Maier, Rainer Fuchs, short and tall respectively. *Missing in action*, as the letter will say, the notification that will be sent in a week's time to a village in Westfalen, to Rainer's wife, a pudgy woman with a low hairline and a surly mouth, when Rainer fails to return from Navahrudak. And the daughter who knotted his keyring will forever inhabit the wilderness of *missing* and will place flowers and small ceramic items on an empty grave without ever learning that her father was a bastard.

Perhaps it is for the best.

Requiescat in pace.

I light up an Efka for the child I do not know, and spit tobacco shreds.

Klaus has a pocket album with small photographs of animals and massacres, a long-eared owl on a branch, the shaven-headed Jewish woman from Dirlewanger's zoo together with a fox, others of her with assorted fauna, goats, a scarf wound around her head, a feeding bottle held to the mouth of a hedgehog. Camouflaged keepsakes, rather inventive. A blurred image of a mass grave, corpses like stacked logs in a muddy pit. Atrocity tourism and sex. Or did he love her? Have I killed *her* too, by leaving her alone without his protection?

In the coin compartment of Rainer's wallet I find a small handwritten note. *Peter 0134, Hamburg.* The puerile flourish of the hand. Is Dirlewanger dyslexic? This is an internal number, SD. *Sicherheitsdienst.* Dirlewanger must have given it to them before he sent us off. Peter must be their contact. What will he do when they fail to call him and report?

Who is at the other end besides Dirlewanger? Kube, Gottberg, Bach-Zelewski? The entire SS?

Can Manfred get me out of this?

I unfold the telegram Greta gave me, from my old friend in the Kripo in Hamburg, homicide department. The coded message was in Klaus's wallet, a garble of nonsense. I find the page from my code book, a taper pinned behind my collar, unroll it, lie down on my stomach and spell my way through:

No trace of M. Schlosser. Man B. Winther found dead today,
24 June. Signs of torture. ID B.W. stores manager STREHLING

```
G.M.B.H.  engineering  works.  Address  Peute  Hafen  4-8.
No admittance. Belongs SS. Can get no further. Live well.
Hugo.
```

The 24th of June was two days ago.

Answer: Strehling is not a man, but a company. Not a who, but a *what*.

Manfred went directly after this B. Winther, tortured and killed him, and left him somewhere to be found. This was not Koreletjy or the death zone, but Hamburg. Germany. Perhaps he is counting on Kripo panicking once they realise the SS is involved. Even so, he is running a risk. And if a stash of gold vanishes from an internal store it will be found out. You can fill your pockets in the occupied territories, but get it back to Germany and everything will be itemised and registered like it had never been anything but ours. Unless the gold *wasn't* registered, and Manfred knew that.

I pinch an Efka between my fingers and flick it into the gravel pit.

The time is just after two.

It is all beginning to come together.

You do not kill a man in Hamburg because a partisan spills a name under torture to save his skin. Manfred must have known Steiner had the gold. And why? Because the two of them knocked it off together! *He taught me everything*, Manfred said. When he threw the ring in the river it was no gesture to me, he knew there was much more where that came from.

Goga said: *Steiner had the gold hidden. He told me to get it out of him.*

Manfred did not go to Hamburg to unravel some plot.

He *is* the plot.

I don't want to carry the thought through to its logical conclusion.

I must get the gold.

Taken from the teeth of Jews. Prised up by tongs, dissolved by acid, melted into bars.

Pecunia non olet. Maybe I can buy myself free? Maybe I can survive this after all.

My stomach is in knots.

What will Manfred do if I find him?

If I find him, he will kill me.

Eline. Why am I thinking about her now? Is she involved in this?

She is pure. She has to be pure.

When I return, the train is already in motion. They see me running, the shouting bodies inside the carriage, and a forest of arms extends from the open door of the wagon. I grab one and am pulled inside.

— — —

Tuesday, 27 July

Hamburg is nothing but smoke. We see it even as we approach the city from the north, late in the evening , a thick, black pulse of explosions, a veil of gases and particles drifting towards the Elbe, towards the sea. It is no longer a city. It is the earth on fire.

A railway worker.

We call out, he turns, lowers his shovel, cups his hand behind his ear.

'What?'

'Is Wandsbek hit?'

'Is Hamm?'

'St Pauli?'

'Altona?'

'What?'

We yell, a single larynx, and he draws a dark, calloused hand across his mouth.

'No,' he shouts as we pass. 'It's . . .'

'What did he say?'

'The docks,' someone says.

'It must be Howaldtswerke.'

'It's Howaldtswerke.'

'It must be. The docks. He said the docks . . . Surely they wouldn't bomb . . .'

'They would. There's nothing those bastards wouldn't bomb . . .'

'Look, you can see . . . it's coming from the docks, not the city . . .'

'You're imagining things . . .'

'No, look!'

We refuse to believe it. We see flakes of ash descend upon us like malicious snow, a leisurely precipitation, like feathers, like paper, a gossamer of burning wool.

– – –

The railway lines are intact as we near the centre in the grey rain of ash.

I omit to say goodbye as I jump down from the wagon at the Hauptbahnhof, the smoke and the stench filling my nostrils, panic screaming in my brain; at once there is only Eline. I run, barging my way though the weary faces, the whites of their eyes, colliding head on with a family, my bag ramming a child, Eline, the mother's suitcase bursts open, clothes, shoes, brushes spill out, why a fur coat in the middle of summer, in this heat, in this oppressive heat, Hamburg has never been so unbearably hot, I nod and smile my apologies, a tornado, a typhoon, an earthquake, white inside my brain, Eline, I tumble out onto Steintordamm: thick banks of smoke; black, shimmering mountains tearing at the lungs; firefighters battling; throngs of soldiers and children; Eline; I run towards the water, follow the railway east, seeing nothing, running, running, Nordkanal, Eiffestrasse, I reach the Mittelkanal, the low bushes, the gravel paths, the lazy water.

I stop, hands on my knees.

My breath, a tentacled mass heaving from my lungs.

I am in Hamm.

I look around. Benches. A stretch of bushes and trees. Apartment buildings beyond, wrought-iron balconies facing north. The docklands. The tenements to the south, their proletariat. The backyards of my childhood.

A schnauzer twists in its collar.

Suddenly frantic, I pat myself down, spinning round, but I am *not* on fire.

It is the docks that are burning. Not Hamm, not Hammerbrook!

'Why is that man laughing . . .?'

He is no more than five or six years old, in short trousers and long stockings, a cloth cap. What is he doing out so late? His hand extends into his mother's. She pulls him away, her other hand steers a pram laden with suitcases and oddments, a child in a grubby bonnet. Is the city being evacuated?

The boy is right.

I am laughing, silently, without an audience now, mouth curled in a grin, grimacing like an idiot, only now do I emit a sound.

It is Tuesday, 27 July 1943. The time is twenty-one minutes past eleven in the evening.

I can see right through the hole in the sky.

To the blue of night.

Is it this simple? Do I love her? I start to whistle.

I am twenty-seven years old.

Eline Schlosser is twenty-four.

Am I spontaneous?

Do you like me now?

– – –

Now I am here, in the growing darkness. The ash as it settles on Dimpfelweg.

There are no lights on at number six, but no lights are allowed. *Verdunkeln! Der Fiend sieht dein Licht.* I climb the step, the brass nameplate next to the door: 3rd *Floor – Prof. Schlosser.* Are they gathered there inside, the professor and his wife, and their blonde-haired daughter, or have they retired to bed? Have they gone down into the basement, have they packed their air-raid bag, their sandwiches and toothbrushes?

Why do I not ring the bell?

I step down and go back onto the street, stand at the wrought-iron railing and peer up at the windows in case a chink of light has escaped from behind the blackout curtains.

But there is none.

Did she get my letter? Has she accepted? Will she marry me?

I look down at myself. The brown stains on my uniform, Klaus Maier's blood. My filthy hands. My shame.

I panic as the front door opens.

I dart into the garden and duck behind a clematis.

My mind is short-circuiting, my pulse is screaming inside my head.

A trap! Manfred is inside waiting for me . . .

I hear voices from the stairway within, a dark female voice: Gerda Schlosser. And a brighter, ringing inflection, that familiar hint of irony: Eline.

A gentleman appears, in a dark coat, a civilian with a fresh complexion, a fawn trilby hat.

It is *not* Manfred.

Eline comes out as well, at the man's side.

She too is wearing a coat. They exchange remarks.

They leave together!

— — —

'Do you think we'll make it?' Eline says.

I can see her hand, from the knuckles down, her long fingers extending from her sleeve. She is *not* holding his hand.

'Yes, but we haven't got much . . .'

He halts directly in front of me. I can hardly comprehend that they can fail to see me behind the clematis.

Should I step forward?

'I thought I heard something,' he says. 'Didn't you hear it?'

Her face. Her chin is a chalk-white triangle as she stretches her neck and tilts her ear towards the sky.

'No, Ernst. There's nothing there. Come on . . .'

And now her hand slips into his.

My breathing stops.

Her hand flutters from his again to brush ash from his lapel, to smooth the cloth.

'Best get a move on,' she says. 'Otherwise we'll be late. And you wouldn't want that, would you?'

'Certainly not.'

'Have you got your shelter card?'

They head along Dimpfelweg.

'Yes,' he pats his breast pocket. 'It's right here.'

They pass the Wagner home, its forbidding ivy.

The whitewashed kerbstones stand out in the dark.

They pause at the showcase outside the cinema, then continue on.

No, suddenly they veer off.

By the time I turn the corner they are gone.

The rumbling darkness, the oil blazing in the docks, the long shadows.

No smoke, only the reek of it.

There they are, already a good way along Hirtenstrasse. She looks up at him as they walk.

His fawn trilby hat.

They pause again, to look at the advertising pillar in front of the church. She laughs.

I cross over, and they turn again.

– – –

Eleven thirty-eight.

Kleinalarm over the loudspeakers on the street corners: *Enemy aircraft over German Bight* . . . I start to run as the third signal sounds soon after. The streets fill up, and at once the sky is illuminated.

I run in the glare of the searchlights.

– – –

I am halfway along Hammer Hof when the *Fliegeralarm* sounds, followed by the distant rumble of the planes. There must be hundreds, thousands. The first bombs fall, miles away yet, the searchlights poke into the night, scanning the darkness. In a moment the first of the bombers will be bathed in light.

Anti-aircraft on the ground, 88s.

A heaving swarm of people on the corner of Meridianstrasse. There must be a shelter there. No one says anything as I edge my way into the queue, all that exists is the noise of the engines, the surge of the throng, jostling citizens with grim faces, an infant wrapped in a shawl, expressionless. All of Hamburg burrowing into the ground, down into the catacombs – why couldn't they give us more notice? – and there, some twenty metres further on, *his* bobbing hat.

'Get a move on, for God's sake!' I yell, clawing my way forward. 'Gangway!' But I am making no headway through this wall of flesh, this teeming swamp of human beings, and at once the searchlights begin to sweep without direction, randomly, feebly, and now I am able to see what it is that's causing the radars to fail: a glittering snow of brilliant confetti descends upon Wandsbek and Hammerbrook, shimmering shreds of silver, a shower of aluminium.

And then, high above our heads, captured in a beam, further illuminated by crimson red explosions of flak, the master bomber, scattering iridescence from its belly, a series of lazy, green, phosphorescent flares.

Christmas trees.

People look up, hypnotised.

A rain of festive baubles.

The plane breaks to the left, its right wing disintegrates, it descends into a spin, fuselage torn apart in a flickering blaze of light.

Immediately, panic breaks out, people are screaming, there is an immense surge, while a policeman beats back the crowd with his baton. I lose my footing and scramble amid legs, a knee jars against my cheek, I tear at a thigh, haul myself forward and up, shouldering away a frantic, scrabbling man as I rise, he stumbles and falls, the air is filled with the stench of fear, and I am punched in the face, expelled from the pack, to stand and gasp, to look up at the leisurely green lanterns as they float down from the sky towards us.

There is a thud as the first green weight lands only metres away, followed by another, and another still.

A mesmerising sparkle of phosphorus.

Smouldering circles of light, inextinguishable.

They are dropping their markers here.

We are the target.

— — —

And now they are upon us, a crashing wave of heavy British bombers, Avro Lancasters, Halifaxes, Wellingtons.

The drone of the engines, millions and millions of flies, rattling cogs, the roar of the pistons, the first fragmentation bombs descending through the air, plunging.

The sky is streaked with incendiary bombs, my gaze sucked towards the blazing light.

I cannot move. My head bent back, I stare up into the night.

A piece of sky breaks off, a roof splits open, black, flashes of light, glittering glass.

Everything is on a new scale.

I am ripped from the air.

– – –

Only a moment has passed when I come to my senses. Total silence. There is the entrance to the shelter. They are closing the steel door. Rubble, figures staggering, muffled sound now, a rush of noise in my ears, my eardrums must be ruptured. My shoulder is numb. Explosions, a hail of glass. I duck, and reel with each blast. The buildings shudder. At once I am alert, and now I run, through a storm of incendiaries; their slush of rubber and burning petroleum. The leaping flames of phosphorus as a tree ignites into a web of blazing white. Sounds become clearer to me, I am at the door and am stopped by a square-jawed warden. I shout out, but am unable to hear my voice in this screaming pandemonium. I yell through the noise: POLICEMAN HERE! He nods to someone inside, turns to find me again. A woman comes running towards us, gripping a little girl by the hand. Abruptly she is hurled through the air, speared by flying debris – the child is flung across the street, and then I too am let inside, the door pushed shut, bolted, while something outside slams against the steel.

The woman's body?

'The child . . .' I say.

'She's dead, you didn't see,' says the warden calmly.

He places the flat of his hand against the door. I grip his wrist.

'No, she fell, that's all . . . it was the mother . . . You must let her in, for God's sake! She wasn't hit. She *wasn't* . . .!'

I am thrust down the stairs, the space is crammed with people. I feel a blow to my jaw, someone holding me down, a hand pressed against my neck. My frenzied breathing.

'No more to be admitted!'

I stare into the barrel of the warden's pistol. Two men grip me under the arms.

'Are you going to calm down?'

'Yes.'

'Are you?'

'I . . . am . . . quite . . . calm.'

– – –

The sign down the stairs: *Luftschutzraum*, max. 200 persons.

Grey, silent faces. There must be more than a thousand.

All of them looking up, listening.

We can hear the explosions, the dull pounding.

Someone turns the handle of the air filter. It wheezes, like lung disease, an ice generator.

I cannot see Eline in the tightly packed mass.

I cannot move.

'Is it here?' someone whispers behind me.

'No, it must be Wandsbek.'

'Nothing can happen to us here. There are gas filters.'

'But they cast their markers here . . .'

A couple of minutes and they are silent again.

It *is* here. The ground trembles. Plaster and dust fall from the ceiling.

'Eline . . .' I breathe. Then louder: 'Eline, are you here? Eline Schlosser!'

'You shut up, *now* . . .'

'Eline! Eline Schlosser . . .'

The filament flickers, the light goes out.
The luminous walls sway. Waves of light.
It is now.

— — —

The earth shudders. Hands over ears, sheer noise rips through
my body. I curl up, arms clutched tight around my torso. The
barrage of my heart, the quaking structure, and now my head,
breaking, noise searing in my brain, I *am* the noise, it tears
everything out from within, everything I am . . .

— — —

From somewhere far away, someone finds my hand. The cold of
a wedding ring, an elderly hand, the pulse of a woman's fingers.
Ninety-three, ninety-four, ninety-five . . . The only sound in a
world torn asunder.

She is crushing my hand.

She cannot help it.

'*Can you hear it?*'

The voice of Zarah Leander, whirling within the storm.

'What?'

The words are wrenched from within me, shredded, they come
to nothing.

'*Can you hear my heart?*'

All I can do is move my lips, without a sound.

'*Yes . . .*'

'*Can you hear something else, too?*'

'*Something else?*'

'*Listen.*'

Her pounding pulse. And now, within: a beat still faster,
another heart.

'*What is it?*'

'*It's yours, silly . . . your heart inside my own.*'

The blast as the bomb hits the shelter. The hand is torn from mine. A deluge of bodies engulfs me, a hail of shards, dust enshrouding.

Face peeled away.

I cannot move my legs.

The woman is gone.

— — —

A moment later I see Eline over by the entrance.

She does not see me as she staggers through clouds of dust.

'Eline!'

Blood trickles from her ears. She reaches the street and begins to run.

'It's me, Heinrich!'

I too emerge and see the fleeting grey of her shadow amid whirling flame.

The wind is a storm. It howls.

— — —

I hug the fronts of the buildings so as not to be sucked into the firestorm. Roofing flies through the air. The asphalt is bubbling, I see blue flames of burning oil. A young woman scuttles for the other side of the street. It is *not* Eline. Her shoes stick in the molten surface, she steps out of them and tries to go on, comes to a standstill and stiffens as she ignites.

— — —

And then I see her. She has crossed through a burning court-yard and is running along the house fronts, her upper body bent forward, holding her long hair in one hand, the other clutching a handkerchief to her mouth. As she reaches the corner of Hammer Hof she is slammed by a gust of wind, loses hold of her hair, a sudden whirl of blonde, and then at once a flourish of sparks, her coat lifts in the wind and she is already aflame, a fiery gash in the air, gone. I yell, but my voice is gouged from my mouth, I edge my way through the storm towards her, I *must* . . . A Mercedes, the curve of its front wing strikes the boiling asphalt, rear end hurled forward, somersaulting as it smashes against the wall to my left, a scream of twisting metal, trees thrust through the air, figures cast about, dolls or people, waving walls of fire. I squirm my way to the corner on quaking knees, a blitz of magnesium bombs, and emerge into the open, the heat a searing blow, a shot, instantly deadening the side of my face. I collapse, bury my head in my coat, curl up tight, the storm sucking me into its maelstrom, I flail, twisted in the air, my coat ignites, flame, heat, now, my time . . .

– – –

A pop as something explodes, a cork, a bottle-top, and something hits me, a hard, wrenching pain. Are my ribs broken? And then at once, there is water everywhere, a fire hydrant uprooted, and I am in its fountain, a pluming geyser ejected into the sky. Its showers collide with the heat above, condense and turn to steam, but here in its midst a torrent of icy cold water on my skin, I scramble to my feet and stand upright, enclosed within a cylinder of sea, fire all around me.

– – –

When I come round my eyes pick out a passage close by, a darkness leading away towards the ruins of what had already burned to the ground the day before. I make a dash for it and emerge onto a boulevard, cross towards the storm and reach the bridge over the canal, my strides, long as a giant's, reverberating on the cobbles.

The drowned and the drowning, a tangle of limbs.

I have forgotten them.

I am in the park now, on the great lawns. Bent double, hands on knees. It is already so much cooler here. The heady rush of pure, refreshing air. The green grass. I look around me. People, blanketed by dust, burnt, coughing, saved.

Hardly ten minutes have passed.

A densely populated island of white-eyed survivors.

'Do you mind if I sit here?' I ask a young woman with her arms around a small boy. I try to smile, but have lost all expression. My face remains stiff when she replies with a *not at all* and makes room.

It is an exchange from a different world.

– – –

'Would you like some, Herr . . . *Herr* . . .?'

The little boy gives me a nudge. He is almost hidden in his mother's arms. He holds a jar in his hand.

'What?'

'My mummy made it, it's jam. Plum.'

'Cherry plum,' says the woman, looking at me, gleaming eyes in a sooted face, and at once I am awake.

'I carried it all the way,' says the boy and hands me the jar. 'I held on tight, even when I fell in the water. I didn't drop it.'

'I couldn't, really,' I say, and yet my eyes devour it, my throat is parched, my entire body overheated, screaming for liquids.

'Please, have some,' the woman says. 'You don't have to eat it all.'

I accept with a nod, and feel immediately embarrassed. I weigh the jar in my hand as I unscrew the lid, the sweet aroma of the heavy mass inside. I slobber as I suck the viscous jam into my mouth, as it runs down my chin.

'Oh . . .'

'I'm sorry, I'm so sorry . . . I don't know what got into me . . . I . . .'

'Emma Biermann,' she says. 'And this is . . . say hello to the gentleman, Wolfie.'

'Hello, Herr . . .?'

'Maier,' I reply without thinking. 'Klaus Maier. That's the best jam I've ever tasted . . . hardly the right time to say so . . .' I add with a vacuous smile, throwing out my hand to indicate the scene, as though everyone here were redeemed while the fires rage about us, as though I were buying a round for the whole crowd down at the Beim Schwarzen Ferkel, which must also be gone, as though all this were *pleasant*, and I throw out my hand again, as if to test the feeling. And indeed, it *is* pleasant, we are on top of the world, looking out on the burning city that is so oddly distant, as though it were all a film, a cabaret, a circus of leaping flames and flying elephants. 'Would you care for a cigarette, Frau Biermann? That would be nice, don't you think? A Greek one to puff on. Don't you believe me? Oh, but I can assure you they are indeed from *Greece*, what's the place called, Thessaloniki, that's it! There you go!'

I extend my German Efkas, and both of us stare at the packet.

She giggles, quite as vacuously as myself, shameful.

'No, thank you. No more smoke for me, thanks.'

She begins to sob.

KLAUS MAIER

So it goes

There is no morning. The sky is black with smoke. The sun is a small, furious pinhead. The city looks like the moon, made of nothing but minerals. The stone is burning hot. Everyone else in the district is dead. So it goes.

— — —

The mother and her son are asleep, clutched together. I take off my coat and cover them up, then stand and stare. The boy's lips are blue with cold, but he is alive.

I study them for some time before going back into the ruins.

Long shadows, drifting. Someone says Moorweide. Behind the Hauptbahnhof, near Dammtor, the university.

'They say there's water there. Survivors.'

I must have scraped my watch against one of the house fronts, the glass is whitely opaque and roughened with scratches, but I can make out the hands. The time is just gone ten. It was on Hirten-strasse I saw her, and now I descend from the smouldering park.

— — —

Lumps of coal. Porous, pulverised.

Some of them still breathe.

I call out her name.

– – –

It is late afternoon when I find Eline on the steps leading down to Landstrasse.

I *know* it is her. The shoe one step down is hers, the cream-coloured silk, the discreet red strap, its fluid beauty, cream and red. *Where is the other one?* I glance around, but see only rubble, shards of stone, ash, a charred birdcage, broken items covered in soot, items that are no longer items, only remains, rubbish, unrecognisable, a wrought-iron balcony in the middle of the street, destroyed.

The shoe is almost pristine. One hundred and ten Reichsmark, from Paris, Rue Saint-Germain, Balmain. I had to force her inside, we had hardly any money. The old gentleman with the pigtail, high heels and silk jacket slipped the shoe onto her little foot.

'*Such fine and dainty feet . . . Madame . . .*'

'Mademoiselle *Schlosser.*'

I sit down next to her, but cannot bring myself to touch.

'It's me, Heinrich . . .'

I want to say *darling*, but I am unable.

Her terror as she was cast into the firestorm, as the flames took hold of her hair. I, who could not save her. Now she screams, but makes no sound, everything inside her is cremated and gone, she has no lungs, no mucous membrane, she is this charred crust and a hollow crackle from within.

Her trembling arms.

She is neither woman nor man.

She is mineral.

Carbon.

All of a sudden I hate her. I am consumed with rage, and yet helpless.

'Who was he?' I demand. 'The man you were with. The one at your door. Who *is* he?'

Her blackened skin flakes away as she tries to speak, the corners of her mouth fall open, the pink tissue inside, her lips as they break apart, the pinkness of her tongue. I cannot hear what she says, I put my ear to her mouth.

'No one. It was nothing, darling . . .'

– – –

I sit with her, my hands on my knees.

I have placed her shoe in front of me.

I speak to her, I have no idea what I am saying.

I pick up the shoe, exploring it with my fingers, as if it were her body they explored, the perfect curve of the topline, the click of the buckle, *caressing*.

I rip out the insole, breathe in the smell of the leather to escape the stench that is all around me, an intimacy amid destruction, pulling the shoe apart, piece by piece, kissing it.

I realise I am humming. What am I humming?

When I look back at her she is still. I put my hand to her mouth. Nothing.

I put my ear to what remains of her face.

There *is* something.

A murmur.

I hear it now. Everywhere.

The murmur of all things.

The heat of the blaze, ticking in the stone.

– – –

I get to my feet and stare at the heap of shining patent leather, silk and paper.

There is a folded piece of card. How did it get there? Was it in her shoe? Her charred clothing? I pick it up and open it, *Deutsches Reich Kennkarte*, the eagle on the front. Her photograph, fastened by a rivet in a punched hole. Her solemn face is put on, an attitude, an exterior about to crack, she is struggling to keep the mask together. Underneath is the way she is, blonde, vibrant, alive . . . *Non-distinguishing features: Wears spectacles.* Her fingerprints, right and left index fingers. The stamps of the Polizeipräsident. *Distinguishing features: Slight deformity of right wrist due to Colles fracture, little finger stiff, crooked.* Our skating trip to the Alster, my ugly mark.

I was banned from their house for the three weeks she was in plaster. I sent little letters she never returned. When eventually I was allowed to visit, the whole family was there, in the third-floor apartment at Dimpfelweg 6, in the crowded parlour, its plush satin and tassels and the professor's carnivorous plants, the hum of the thermostat, the sense of being in an aquarium, the funnel-like crowns of the flowers sucking in the heavy, moist air, looking like ears directed towards me, and Eline, reading my letters out loud, making a quiz of my quotes for her brothers and sisters and cousins, while Manfred studied his fingernails with a malicious little smile on his face.

I had indeed quoted them all: Goethe, Schiller, Novalis, Morgenstern, Rilke, J. P. Jacobsen. And then, when it all got out of hand with Tristan and Iseult, *a tale of love and death*, and she was proceeding to my own dabblings, I burst out:

'*Am I never to be forgiven?*'

'*What do you say, Eline?*' the professor's wife inquired.

Prolonged silence.

Then whistles and jeers:

'*No!*'

— — —

I take Klaus Maier's *Soldbuch* from my inside pocket (*Non-distinguishing features: Tendency to overweight, Distinguishing: N/A*) and stare at his thick jaw. The photograph is attached with ordinary staples, the stamps are SS. Why this hierarchy, rivets and staples? Switching photos is easy. Does no one tamper with their *Soldbücher*?

I prise the staples open with my fingernail, twist and remove them, repeat the procedure with my own photograph, which I then affix to the corresponding page in Klaus Maier's book, pressing the staples back into place. The stamps almost match up.

I flick through my new identity.

I have served in Croatia and have been decorated: EK (Second Class), close combat awards.

Dental records: upper teeth removed in '37.

Wounded in the groin at Smolensk, nothing visible.

Wedding tackle intact.

The photo has me looking shrunken, my neck is like a lizard's.

No tendency to overweight there.

Hello, Klaus.

I get up and walk away.

— — —

Dimpfelweg 6.

The clematis reduced to ash. The broad steps leading up to nothing, down to nothing. A pile of rubble, a carbonised garden. 'House'. 'Garden'. 'Steps'.

The door of the basement is blocked by charred beams and rubble.

I hold my handkerchief to my mouth as I crouch down and enter.

They are intact, a small cluster, two adults, two children, red-brown, amalgamated, *heart-coloured.*

The professor is curled into a ball, his hands around his knees, head between his legs, at the air pump.

His wife, still with her heavy earrings, the solid purple crystal in the silver setting. Her skin is a dry and withered parchment, shrunk back over her skull, her face is too small for her head, her lips fall short of her teeth.

The gaping hole of her mouth.

She is clutching the two grandchildren. I recognise only one.

Before I vomit I count the dead.

By the stadium, Hamm:
1. Eline Schlosser (24 yrs)
Dimpfelweg 6:
2. Gerda Schlosser (61 yrs)
3. Friedrich Schlosser (68 yrs)
4. Reinhardt Hubertus (13 yrs)
5. Child, probably Frida Hubertus (9 yrs)

I go out again, into the light.

I walk in the direction of the docks, alone in a world emptied of people.

– – –

A few minutes later, on the corner of Borstelmann.

A man picks his way over the rubble, through the gigantic gateway, NASIUM still legible, in imposing Gothic lettering, once gilded. His legs are uncertain, a small, crooked man in a large, dusty cap, he too alone in the world. A clacking and grating of stone; the entire building spat out through the gateway. A chunk of masonry wobbles beneath his feet and for a moment he stands quite askew, on one leg, an arm held out, the bottle in his hand, and then he loses balance, careers and flails, carried forward by his own momentum, and stumbles past.

He picks himself up, stands for a second as if to recover his bearings, walks a few steps towards me and stops.

He turns his head slowly in the direction of sound, eyes white, milky cataracts.

He rubs his mouth.

He moves left, but stares right.

'Why don't you say something?' he says. 'Are you injured? Can't you speak?'

He extends the bottle towards me.

'You can have some of this. There's more. Look . . .'

He shakes the bottle gently, amber schnapps sloshing inside.

'Do you need help . . .? Is that you, Beate . . .?'

He scrabbles in the rubble with his hands, feeling the stones, heaving them aside, clawing.

'Beate . . .? Are you there?'

I take my Efkas from my breast pocket, flick open my lighter, light up and blow smoke out into the empty air. He pauses.

'Why won't you help me?' he asks.

'Help you do what, old man?'

'Help me find her . . . I can only see to the left . . .'

I step to my right.

'Is that better?'

'Yes, that's better. I can see you now! Lothar . . .'

I stare at his extended hand.

'My wife is . . . She was holding my hand. And then . . . Lothar. My name's Lothar . . .'

'Yes, you said.'

— — —

He sits down, his clouded eyes staring up at me. Now and then he lifts the bottle to his lips. I have scaled the mountain of rubble. In front of me are teetering walls, barely upright; to my left what remains of my old *Gymnasium*, the right side intact as far as the third floor, classrooms dissected by an Allied bomb: desks, blackboards, cupboards of splintered glass, the pale colours of a map of Europe. I step onto a beam, balance my way across a ten-metre drop and lever myself into a space that used to be a room.

Manfred's classroom.

He was a year above me.

The main hall is gone, the corner where I spoke to him for the first time. He was leaning against one of the columns, in the midst of his group, smoking, a king in perfect tweed, handing

274

out his orders. Peter with the ginger hair, his fat messenger boy, came up to me and said:

'*Schlosser wants to speak to you.*'

'*With me? Why?*'

'*Because.*'

When I went to him the others were still chattering, but Manfred needed only to raise his hand and they were silent.

'*You're Hoffmann.*'

'*Yes.*'

'*I hear you wiped out Hartmann in the Aeneid.*'

'*I suppose.*'

'*He had to stop you halfway through Book Six. You've got a photographic memory, haven't you?*'

'*Remembering is easy for me.*'

He took a piece of paper from his pocket. Held it up in front of me for a few seconds, columns of figures, then crumpled it up and tossed it in the wastepaper basket.

'*What was yesterday's share price for Howaldtswerke GmbH?*'

'*114.2.*'

'*Told you,*' fat Peter said.

Manfred put out his hand.

'*Manfred, Manfred Schlosser. Would you like to come bird-watching with me this afternoon?*'

I cross the swaying floor to the blackboard. There are pieces of chalk on the ledge. I take two and make my way down to the ground again.

'Here,' I tell him, handing him a piece. 'What did you say your name was?'

'Lothar . . .'

'Lothar what?'

'Brylla.'

'Lothar Brylla. And your wife's name?'

'Beate . . .'

'Right.'

I write *Where is Fr. Brylla?* on the wall. Then underneath: *Lothar is alive*.

'Come on,' I say. 'Let's find you something to eat.'

– – –

On what used to be Eiffestrasse:

'My grandchildren, Arno and Wilfried, are with my sister in Neumünster, she—'

'Do we have to talk?'

'What?'

'Can't we just walk?'

'Of course . . . all I was saying was . . .'

'Don't.'

– – –

Near Spalding, we traverse the smouldering tumuli of debris, then abruptly a little path cleared through the rubble.

'Aren't you coming?' Lothar says when I stop.

'No. Just keep going straight on. A hundred metres, perhaps. There are some people there. Policemen. Perhaps they have food. Perhaps your wife might be there . . .'

'What about yourself?'

'Don't worry about me.'

'I don't even know your name.'

– – –

At the canal, walking south.

The pale flesh of the corpses, like boiled fishmeat, their loose, jointless limbs, mealy faces dip and bob in the water, drifting with the suitcases, like soggy bread, dumplings in soup, driftwood, rubbish, the drowned piling up beneath the Luisenbrücke, gently changing places, in motion, as though the Elbe were simmering.

They must have jumped in and been unable to get out again.

Few burns.

The rest of Luisenweg is gone, all the way down to Süder and Bille.

Hansaburg, far to the south, is still there. Towers and embrasures.

The wind picks up.

I carry on towards the docks.

– – –

The docklands are empty, not a soul to be seen. I climb aboard the wreck of a ferry jammed in the harbour under the destroyed railway bridge, step onto its tilting deck, the side of the vessel peeled away, the hold and saloons gaping below, shining brass and varnished wood, a direct hit. I hold onto the gunwale, the boat is keeling over, I cross the deck, grab hold of a rope, the ladder is still intact and I am on the other side of the channel.

I am standing in Peute Hafen.

– – –

The heat is unbearable here as I wander through the docks.

I pull my handkerchief from my pocket once again and cover my mouth.

The coal heaps are burning.

STREHLING GmbH is a cathedral in cast iron and rubble.

The heat has been so intense the great hall has melted, its structure buckled.

I find my crumpled packet of Efkas, tip it on its head. Two cigarettes drop into my hand. I tuck one into my breast pocket and light the other.

I unbutton the flap of my holster as I enter the building.

'Anyone here? Hello . . .?'

No answer. Everything here is dead.

I stand open-mouthed, staring at the glazed surroundings, looking up through a roof that has dissolved ten metres above me, into disorderly stalactites of purple glass.

Boilers, piping, exploded into scrap. Lingering heat. I kick through the debris. In the midst of it all is a locked safe, untarnished and sublime. Krupp steel. I clamber and scrabble, an imbecile in search of a key. I gash my hand. The filthy, blistered skin of my hands. I return to the safe, brace my legs and wrench the handle in vain.

I stare down the length of the factory floor. At the far end is a car, crashed into the end wall, a convertible.

When I get closer I see that only the steel body remains intact, the windows and everything perishable are gone. Inside this singular meteorite, it too purple, are the remains of a human being, motor car and corpse amalgamated, the skeleton a loose collection of charcoal sticks encased in a brittle glass of slag and variegated dross, rubber and shards of something that glitters.

I gasp as I realise I have found the gold.

I come back with an iron bar I find lying around. I tear my undershirt into pieces and wind the material around my hands.

– – –

Reconstruction: Manfred must have thought he had time to get out with the ingots. He had the engine running, but something sent him off into the wall. If the building took a direct hit, a thousand-pound bomb would have brought the roof down on him.

On top of his head, in his open car.

He loved convertibles.

Only after that, when the incendiaries came through the gaping hole above, did the car burst into flame. First the leather seats and upholstery, his clothes. Then the rubber tyres. His skin withered, the fat of his body began to boil, his muscles to burn, the petrol in the tank exploded, and everything after that must have gone so quickly – the wood of the dashboard, the bakelite and the glass, the suspension and the soft metal – and then, when the temperature reached 1063 degrees Celsius, the ingots became liquid and swam into it all.

– – –

I climb into the wreck through the open roof and begin hurling away the rubble, hacking and digging with the iron bar, a heap of stone and soot and small, grubby lumps of gold, my fingers bleeding, another gash in my hand, I am sweating profusely, amid this fat sheen of gold and filth, the stench of rubber, sulphur and death. I scrabble away until the bones are laid bare, femur, radius, the shattered socket of a hip, a rib that crumbles in my hand. My fingers follow the spine, and at the front of the vehicle, below the place where the steering wheel would have been, the gold finally came to a halt.

I have found Manfred's head.

The vertebrae of the neck break away as I struggle with it. Eventually it comes free and I am left holding a shapeless bulk some five or six kilos in weight, a blackened stump of bone protruding from one side, and when I turn it over a piece of the frontal bone lodged in the metal's flat underside. Only the uppermost part of the eyebrow ridge is visible. In the middle, approximately where the mouth should be, a length of metal juts out. It looks like part of the brake pedal.

The stench is foul. I pull on the metal protuberance, but find it is stuck fast, and the smell worsens.

I sit down, take my handkerchief from my pocket and begin to polish, spitting on the agglomerated lump until it starts to shine.

I hold it up in front of me with two hands and put my ear to it, imagining a grumble from within.

'Sorry, what was that, Manfred? What? Speak up, I can't hear you.'

I start to laugh, witlessly, nodding frantically and without a sound.

'You don't say! Is this funny, Manfred? Are you having *fun* in there?'

When I realise I am sobbing, I let go and dump it.

Report

Shortly after, I pick up the head and wrap it up in my coat.

I have to get away, out of the city, I need to hide before they come after me. Kube. Dirlewanger. SS, Gestapo, Wehrmacht. The entire fucking war machine . . .

I start walking south, away from the docks.

Klaus Maier, Sturmmann, with a skull of gold, survivor of the firestorm.

I memorise my report as I walk.

June 1941: Manfred Schlosser is appointed adjutant to Hubert Steiner, who as head of Einsatzgruppe B wipes out Jews in the wake of Heeresgruppe Mitte. They plunder their victims, seizing anything of marketable value – gems, cash, gold. At some point Steiner breaks the agreement, gets greedy and pulls a fast one, makes off with the spoils and hides them away on the premises of Strehling GmbH, an SS warehouse in Hamburg's dockland.

Spring/summer 1943: Manfred finds out and wants his share. Or maybe Steiner wants rid of him. Manfred realises it is only a matter of time before Steiner has him sidelined. He has no chance against an Obergruppenführer. He takes a desperate step, makes contact with the partisans, enters into an agreement. Or maybe Goga is taken prisoner on a hare hunt, Manfred finds out he is a survivor from one of his and Steiner's operations and hatches a plan. There is a common interest. Goga can have his revenge, Manfred gets the key to the gold and does away with Steiner. Manfred invites his old friend and mentor, Steiner, and his wife Gisela, who is on a tour of the front, to Lida.

July 4, 1943: Manfred has picked out the escort and decided on a route. His friend Hauptsturmführer Breker does the driving. I later identify him by the gap in his front teeth. At Belize, Goga and the partisans are waiting. They kill everyone and torture Steiner. Goga gets his revenge, extracts the name of Strehling GmbH and makes off, reneging on the agreement. And that is where I enter the picture. Manfred's old friend and confidant, whom he could rely on *not* to ask the wrong questions. I could find Goga and make it all look good. Only Kube smelled a rat and sent Grünfeldt and Haber after me.

— — —

Presently there are people. I have come to a gathering point where there are water trucks, food and supplies, so many suit-cases and hats, so many tins of food, people in nightshirts and slippers, holding children by the hand, all saved from the flames.

On a table: sandwiches made from white bread, black coffee, lemonade, jugs of water.

Salami, pork crackling, blackcurrants.

The cool water in my throat.

I wipe my mouth on my sleeve, my bundle wedged tight between my feet, and fill my pockets.

A little girl stares at me with wide eyes. I begin to cry. I stand there for a moment. I have a human head wrapped in a coat between my feet. I fill my mouth with food and sob. I cram my pockets. The girl is pointing at me now. Her mother is dabbing ointment on her burnt brow. She looks at me too.

Black and pink.

— — —

I carry on in a southerly direction. I am picked up by an army truck.

Grave faces. No one says a word. A boy eats from a tin.

The vehicle sways.

July 23, Manfred's Forum Romanum – that was supposed to fool them all. Goga, bereaved and vengeful. Goga divulges his secret, and I reward him with a panicked *coup de grâce*.

July 24, that terrible day Manfred took the train to Hamburg. Kube sending his note to make me break down and reveal all. And Dirlewanger, waiting until I stepped into action.

Did Manfred betray me?

Did he leave me to the wolves so he could get away?

When we get to the moor, the soldiers let me out.

Someone tosses me a packet of cigarettes and a water bottle.

I trudge off into the heather. All I have to do is follow the path.

After a while I am gone.

A dot on the landscape.

— — —

Like confetti. They are everywhere, small burnished strips of foil. They must have been what I saw yesterday, a silvery shower disrupting the gunfire. I pick one up, it is shiny on one side, black on the other, like a spinner for catching fish. They crackle beneath my feet.

Not a soul on the horizon. An expanse transected by the brows of hills, occasional gravel pits.

Empty, and silent.

I pause for a second and stare in every direction. There is nothing here.

A piece of the puzzle remains.

The note: *Who is Strehling?*

Why did Kube send it to me?

Why did he not follow the scent himself instead of going through *me*?

He could have just gone to Hamburg. Manfred's adjutant told me straight out where he was.

He didn't need to play detective.

It doesn't make sense.

The adjutant told me. Because I asked him.

It hits me like a hammer.

Kube didn't know! He just had his men follow me . . .

The note was from Manfred, sent after he left for Hamburg.

He knew Goga had spoken to me. He knew I was lying when I told him Goga hadn't mentioned the gold. He said: *You know how much I love you, don't you?*

He was telling me he knew.

He couldn't take me with him to Hamburg, it would have given rise to suspicion, but he was banking on me coming after him. He instructed his adjutant to tell me: *Schlosser has gone to Hamburg.* The right name, the right destination, only the one small error as regards Strehling . . .

A crossword puzzle for a child.

Have you proposed to my sister?

A way of getting to Hamburg without arousing suspicion: *Marriage.*

You're malleable, like clay, he said.

Soon you'll be like me.

You're easily fooled.

Was he leading me on?

A sordid little labyrinth?

Was that *it*?

I sit down in the heather. I put the head down in front of me, straighten it so the brow and the sockets are turned towards me. The brake pedal protrudes like some obscene lollipop. I stroke Manfred's brow, the bone is cold and dead, but the gold is faint electricity.

I put down Maier's open *Soldbuch* next to it.

I stare out from the page, my wire-rimmed spectacles, the roundness of my face.

There is not a sound here.

Even now, after I have solved the puzzle, the pieces fail to fit.

A tiny filament in the conflagration.

All the dead.

All those I killed. Etke, Goga, Greta, Masja . . .

Why should I be saved?

I am a criminal, a beast.

Eline's *Kennkarte* is bent.

She looks at me, her head turned slightly to the side, about to laugh.

Her hair is a fountain of flames.

Fear not

And then the birds.

I am on my knees in the midst of teeming nature, a cacophony of cheeping, chirping and cooing, little legs scurrying over sandy earth, a berry in a beak delivered to a hole, an industry of feeding and crapping, humping and hatching. My PPK is snug in my hand.

An extension of my hand forged in steel.

Ballistics: Fired only twice.

Into the neck of a child. Into the mouth of a Jew.

I put the pistol to my head, curl my finger.

I close my eyes and see Eline.

Her trembling arms.

'*It was nothing, darling . . .*'

My head, struck by a crowbar.

Thunk.

– – –

'*Here I am . . .*'

Blistering pain, my head rings. I get to my feet, dazed and unsteady.

'Hello?'

There is no one here. There is *nothing* here. Only rugged landscape.

I hear the babble of a stream, the hum of the moor. A bit further on there is a thicket of hazel, a fat, croaking wilderness of summer, the trampled ribbon of an animal track.

I blink.

'Is anyone there?'

'*Over here. Come.*'

My blood runs cold, the powder burn from the shot searing my skin.

The bullet must have brushed my temple and whistled on.

I smell of residue, the smouldering wound.

'Where?'

'*You didn't think you'd get off that lightly, did you?*'

The voice is Zarah Leander's.

She is very close, I can hear her breathing, but I cannot see her.

I stand and listen, but there is no one there.

But there *is*.

A glimpse of hair over by the twiggy hazel bushes, hidden by the tree.

'*Fear not . . .*'

'Fear not?'

I pick up my bundle and am there in a few strides, a tangle of little paths, moist and dark. I hear only the sound of running water.

'*Here . . .*'

I stumble in the direction of the voice.

'*Here . . .*'

But she is not there either. Where *is* she? A shudder of leaves, I thrust myself sideways through the undergrowth, branches flick back in my face. I emerge, and *again* she is gone, but I am in the light. In front of me, the steep slope of a gully disrupts the horizon.

She is standing with her back to me, some ten metres ahead.

Now I've got you.

As she turns her head I stumble.

I pick myself up and she has vanished. I claw my way up the slope.

– – –

When I get to the top I see the railway, the sweeping curve left across the moor and the gullies. A hundred metres on, the line is broken by a gaping void, tracks jutting into thin air, a pounding of heavy pistons.

I run along the line and now I can see crumpled goods wagons in a haze of stone dust, ragged holes torn in their sides by the artillery guns, yawning craters, the engine flat on its side after the air strike.

'*Come on . . .*'

She is there again. Somewhere up ahead.

Her voice at once coquettish.

'*. . . little man . . .*'

I slide down the other side of the slope and get to my feet among thistles.

I walk among the dead.

Those blasted to pieces, and those who seem almost unharmed. Half-naked, clothing ripped away.

I go through the wreckage, crouch down beside a body, the curiously real appearance.

The waxlike face, the pleasing curve of the mouth, the expensive dentures.

Her head is shaven.

'*Don't look at them . . . The dead . . . are . . . no fun . . .*'

I straighten up. I look around, but cannot see her. I go on.

'*Here . . .*'

I stop in front of a wagon that as if by miracle has remained upright. There is no sound from inside.

'What do you mean, here?'

'*Here I am . . .*'

I pull on the door, it is bolted and padlocked. Barbed wire at the ventilation openings, barbed wire on the roof.

I grip the handle with both hands and put all my weight into it.

Release, pause, pant.

'*Come on! I thought you were . . . strong . . . little man . . .*'

'I can't . . . it's locked!'

'*No, it's not. Come on . . .*'

'Look,' I say, and heave once more. The door opens like a breath of wind.

They are piled in a heap at the far end, entangled in the dark, in their furs, they smell already. Stiffened jaws. So many mouths.

'What?'

'*Come . . .*'

I clamber inside, stand for a moment in the dust and the stench, trying to get my bearings in the dim light.

A hum of flies. No one is alive here.

'*Hold me . . .*'

I turn. She is standing with her back to me at the other end of the wagon.

She is in a long coat, her hair tied up.

I step towards her, put my hand on her shoulder.

She turns her head slowly towards me.

The darkness of her eyes.

'Will life be wonderful, do you think?'

— — —

I am struck hard on the head. I black out. Pistol shots. Someone grabs my feet. I see stars. My mouth is bleeding. Sound returns. The engine, still turning over. People.

'He's stolen a uniform . . .'

'What the hell happened to his face?'

A kick to the head.

A young lad, his face close to mine.

He prods at the side of me that is numb, the roughened skin at the temple.

'Get a look at this . . .'

The crouching figure speaks again, there must be someone else in the wagon, someone he is talking to.

'He looks like he *melted* . . . Heinz, I think he fucking shot himself in the head!'

He pats me down, his hands travelling down my legs, searching me.

In a moment he will discover Manfred's head.

He is Wehrmacht, hardly more than a boy. They swarm on the slope.

Kübelwagen, trucks.

'All dead . . . I reckon,' another voice says, a voice barely broken by puberty. 'Do you want me to give them a round to make sure?'

'What?' says the one at my side, and turns his head away from me for a second. 'Yeah, give them a—'

His voice is disconnected by the elbow I thrust into his larynx. He is stunned, sways a moment on trembling knees like a top, a preposterous snake who gapes at me open-mouthed. I slap him in the face, twice in quick succession to stop him passing out, already on my feet with his Mauser in my hand. I flick the safety catch, slam the butt hard against his cheekbone, blood spurts from his nose and eyebrow, and still he has yet to grasp what has happened.

He is a child now, he snivels and looks up at me.

Blood runs from his nostrils, a figure eleven traced dark red on his lip.

'I want the woman,' I say without raising my voice.

The other man emerges into the light, his pistol is pointing at me.

'What woman . . .?' he says slowly.

'*Her*, for Christ's sake . . . her!'

He looks scared when suddenly I yell:

'I'll shoot him!'

I thrust my boot into the crotch of the one on the floor. His eyes roll, I wave my gun. The others stare at me in bewilderment. They are children.

Hair cropped close.

Thin.

'I was on the train, for Christ's sake! SS!' I shout at them. 'Klaus . . .'

I choke on my own voice, the stutter of SS, it is not my voice, the thick accent of the Rhineland.

'Klaus Maier . . . Idiots! If you've . . .'

I stop in mid-sentence, her voice again.

I glance around, but the woman from before is nowhere to be seen.

'*Psst . . . over here . . .*'

But she is there, with her hands in her pockets, a bit further away, looking down at the floor.

She is still in her long coat.

And now an officer comes towards me, with long, purposeful strides.

Too thin for his uniform, like all the rest.

– – –

'I can't just give it to you . . .' he says, a Leutnant with sun-bleached hair. He stands with my *Soldbuch*, unable to make up his mind. He looks me up and down.

'I need that fucking Kübelwagen. I was supposed to have been in Neuengamme this morning.'

I throw out my hand at the chaos of corpses.

'For Christ's sake, man,' I continue. 'Look at this *shit* . . . two thousand prisoners . . .'

'I don't know . . .'

I go up and take hold of the woman's arm, march her over to the car. The soldiers stand and look on. They step aside for us.

– – –

I put the head down on the back seat. It feels warmer now, there is a rumble in the air. The woman says nothing as I start the engine.

Who is she?

The Leutnant stands gaping as I tear off up the hill. A moment later we join a wider unmade road. I put my arm over the seat and look back. They are gone.

Neuengamme is twenty kilometres to the west.

'Say something,' I say.

Nothing.

I grip her chin with two fingers and turn her head towards me, but change my mind.

At the next junction I take a right and head south.

Shortly after, I pull off the road.

The car is quiet, the heather brushes against the undercarriage.

I can hear her breathing.

The house

We reach the Schlosser family's country house in the early evening.

I leave the car a few hundred metres away, in the darkness of the fir trees.

The woman wakes as I step out and slam the door.

'Come on,' I say.

A few minutes later and we are up on the ridge behind the house. She stands with her hands in her pockets and shudders from the cold. I lie down in the grass and put the binoculars to my eyes: the white gable, half of the main house, the fence, most of the garden, the barred white of the greenhouse. The shutters are closed, the place unopened for summer.

The net was strung out between the two apple trees then.

Badminton and lemonade, chinking ice cubes.

Eline, engrossed in *Malte Laurids Brigge* on the swing seat, and me, smashing all the time in her direction just to go over and retrieve the shuttlecock. She, reading on, lifting her legs, looking the other way, her finger on the page.

'*Manfred's friend needs to work on his badminton . . .*'

'Heinrich . . . I, we . . . it's, ha!'

'Manfred? . . . Maaaanfreed . . .'

'Yes . . .'

'*You must help him, anyone would think he hadn't a tongue in his head . . . it's a shame, he might have something interesting to say.*'

I change position, crawl forward. Now I can see the rest of the house, the shed at the back.

Nothing moves, only the windows glint in the dying sun.

'We're here,' I tell her.

– – –

I hesitate for a moment on the wooden veranda and listen before breaking a small pane in the French window and twisting open the lock. I nod and she steps inside.

I light the carbide lamps on the tables and the windowsills, one after another.

I put the bundle with the head in it on the floor next to the fireplace and sit down at the desk. The professor's desk. I put my PPK down on it.

'Look at me . . .'

– – –

'Who are you?'

She is thin as a dog.

She stands with her hands clasped in front of her, staring at the floor.

She wears a man's coat, the cut is English, a trench coat from before the war, the belt pulled tight and tied with a knot, her waist no thicker than a fist, strangulated by hunger, but rather than hiding the fact she displays it, as if, perhaps, to deride me, *der Reichsdeutsche*?

She does not answer my question.

'Come here.'

She stares at me.

'Come here, I said!'

Nothing.

'Sit down.'

She sits.

'So you do understand . . .'

Still nothing.

'Put your hands on the desk.'

They are scarlet, hungry. Her nails are dirty.

'Look at me. Keep your hands on the table. Turn them over.'

Visible scars across both wrists, the right more pronounced: she is left-handed. I moisten my finger and trace her heart line, her fate line, the rough scar tissue.

'Turn your head.'

'Look at me again.'

'Stand up.'

'Show me your tongue.'

'That's it.'

'Say aah.'

All the time I am staring at the knot of her belt. Now she looks at it too.

I stand up and face her.

'Why did you speak to me? Why didn't you just let me *die*?'

She raises her head, her eyes are completely dark, no more than pupils.

'Look at me, for pity's sake!'

I lunge forward. She recoils, terrified.

'You've no idea what I'm talking about, have you?'

She hesitates.

'You just want to live, right?'

'Yes . . .'

A hint of an accent. What, Italian? French?

'No matter what?'

'Yes.'

– – –

We are in the basement. Her clothes are on the floor next to the bath.

She sits in the scummy water as I work the soap into her hair, her thin, thin hair, piling it up and massaging, working up a lather, smoothing out the strands.

I rinse it through with water from the jug on the washstand.

Her skin is unhealthy, starved of nourishment, sallow. Her breasts are small, nipples large and dark.

I nod and she gets to her feet, water dripping from her. Her pubic hair is black, all her joints are visible, muscles knotted beneath the skin.

Her eyes are quite without expression as I pick up the towel and begin to dry her.

She is seated on the chair in a bathrobe, hands between her knees, her hair wrapped in the towel. I open the door where the professor kept his chemicals. I find the peroxide amongst a profusion of vessels.

It is more than half full. A simple formula.

H_2O_2.

– – –

Eline's unruly flaxen plait.

The *Kennkarte* shows her with what looks like short hair, her head slightly turned. It must be in a bun.

This woman has thin, dark hair. It lies in tufts on the floor. I am unable to cut it straight.

I make some adjustments, the tip of my tongue between my lips as I cut round her ears.

The fringe is a nightmare.

Our eyes are centimetres apart.

There is something egg-like about the whites of her eyes, drawn over into the brown of the iris.

Eline's eyes: blue with flecks of orange, but eye colour is not a category of the *Kennkarte*.

Distinguishing features: Slight deformity of right wrist due to Colles fracture, little finger stiff, crooked.

I lift her chin with two fingers.

'Say after me: My name is Eline Schlosser.'

'*My name is Eline Schlos*ser.'

French.

'Schlosser,' I repeat.

'*Schlosser . . . My name is Eline Schlosser.*'

'This is my house.'

'*This is my house.*'

'I played in the garden when I was a child.'

'*I played in the garden when I was a child.*'

'I am a refugee from Hamburg.'

'*I am a refugee from Hamburg.*'

'There is no one else left in my family.'

'*There is no one else left in my family.*'

'I am on my own.'

'*I am on my own.*'

The strands of her hair react at once to the peroxide that devours all colour.

I pour it onto her scalp, my gloved hands working the pungent chemical into her hair.

When I have finished it is white.

Like fake snow.

Vivid.

I crouch down and look into her eyes.

'Good girl.'

– – –

I am in the basement again. Bottles, jars and tins. The professor's neat hand on the labels. Letters and small figures. I have forgotten the formula.

Back in the time we strolled at Kronprinzenkoog, the professor with his hands behind his back, in his long coat in the balmy air of summer, nodding his head at the sandy fields: *Lime is a catastrophe, I've always said so. They use lime, but lime is no good here. And why?*

Eline, intentionally, vanished in the dunes.

My first encounter with the professor.

'Because . . . it's . . .'

He paused, as if he had only just noticed me.

Peering over the top of his spectacles, the bushy eyebrows.

'You've no idea, have you?'

'No. But I would very much like to know, Herr Professor.'

'Would you indeed? I'm not sure I believe you.'

'No, really . . .'

'Lime acidifies, kills any soil that is rich in salt. So what would it need instead?'

The formula, I can't remember the formula. Something with a C in it. I go through the jars and bottles, the combinations mean nothing to me, they could be number plates, anagrams. Or was it an L? P to the power of 4? *Come on . . .*

Eline, who had come up behind me and squeezed my hand, patted my palm with her perfect little finger, then fluttered away again.

'Don't be so tiresome, Daddy . . .'

'Tell your young friend the answer . . .'

'CaSO$_4$.2H$_2$O . . .'

'And that's German?'

'Gypsum . . .'

'Gypsum, of course! The farmers should be using gipsum here. Gypsum gives off sulphur . . .'

And there it is! A big tub of the stuff, CaSO$_4$.2H$_2$O. Enough to put an elephant in plaster.

– – –

In the basement corridor is a lime-spattered sledgehammer, propped up against a painter's bucket, from the lip of which hang two grubby, stiffened cotton gloves. I pick up the hammer, and test it in my hand. It is too heavy, too unwieldy. I take the gloves with me.

The toolbox under the lathe is a mess. It surprises me. I would have thought he would have been tidier, a board on the wall with nails to hold each tool in place, their outlines perhaps traced in pen.

There is a knife, some rusty screws and nails, a screwdriver, a fretsaw, a hammer.

It will have to be the hammer, though the head is loose.

– – –

Back in the kitchen.

The dressing case in the cupboard is all but empty.

A bottle of iodine, a rusty pair of scissors. A thin roll of sticking plaster. No hypodermic.

The professor's old underpants, torn into strips.

'Put some music on!' I shout into the living room.

I hear the scratch of the needle, followed by Beethoven, the Diabelli Variations, while I boil the right glove and cut a couple of centimetres from each steaming finger.

'Who's the pianist?'

'. . . *Kempff.*'

I place the strips of material from the dressing case next to the gloves, mix the plaster in a tub and slowly turn the glove in the solution.

'Come out here,' I shout.

— — —

Her wrist trembles as I press her arm down on the kitchen table.

I mark the spot with a drop of iodine between the uppermost joints.

I pick up the hammer.

The trembling, moist, purple spot.

The joint capsule shatters with an audible crunch, her ring and little fingers part.

She stands and stares at her hand, as if she has never seen it before.

Then she screams.

— — —

Her wide-open eyes as I manipulate the joint and fix the fracture, winding the strips around her fingers, drawing the cotton glove over her hand. I apply the bandage, smoothing plaster into the material.

'That's it . . .' I say when it is done.

She takes the glass of apple schnapps I offer.

'It's what they call a *Colles fracture* . . .'

— — —

'Choose . . .' I say with a nod towards the dining table on which I have laid out Eline's dresses.

I found them upstairs, removed the mothballs, brushed the dust from them. Old, faded summer frocks. I turn round as she steps into a white one with little red dots.

I wind the handle of the professor's gramophone and pour two apple schnapps into the fat glasses from the cellarette.

She looks nothing like Eline. She is a sallow, emaciated woman with shocking white hair and her hand in plaster.

'Try the blue one . . .'

— — —

We drink schnapps. Beethoven crackles.

I powder her face white. I add kohl with the little brush.

It is a mockery, intoxication.

'Dance with me . . .'

— — —

Back to the chair.

She sits at the table, painting the nails of her broken hand.

A red rash has come up on her cheek and down her neck.

I go up and place a large hat on her head, decorated with imitation grapes and a trail of tulle, pins and faded ribbon.

It must have belonged to the professor's wife.

I am drunk. Suddenly, desperately.

I spray her all over with perfume from the bottle in the upstairs bathroom.

Her smell.

Eline's.

I lift her chin.

'Say *butterfly* . . .'

'Butterfly . . .'

Her French tongue, unable to manage the consonants.

My words, that struggle on her breath, my words in her throat. Two translucent lips, her small, French mouth.

I grow hard.

To own her.

Small, hungry butterfly.

– – –

The alcohol rouses me.

Sumptuous, fleshly words of German: *Hagebutte, Alpenrose, Edelweiss, dickflüssig, Bruch, Ruhe.*

I: in the armchair, with cognac and the semi-automatic pistol tapping out the beat on my thigh.

She: in the bathrobe, naked underneath.

I get up and tear open the knot of her belt.

Her starved features, lines and shadows; protruding ribs, bony feet.

On the gramophone: the Diabelli Variations still, from another world.

I close my hand around her breast.

Her soft, white flesh, nipple erect against my palm.

The scent.

My hand between her thighs.

'Hold me!' I yell at her.

'Like this?'

'Yes, that's it.'

I bury my face in the hollow of her throat, kissing, licking, biting, my hands all over her. She does not move.

I stop.

My coat has fallen away from Manfred's head on the mantelpiece. His skull and glaring eye sockets. The shimmering hum of gold.

There we stand, arms around each other, awkward.

I pull away.

'Put some clothes on,' I tell her.

— — —

'Come here.'

She stops in mid-movement, one leg inside one of Eline's dresses.

'Finish what you're doing first.'

I go up to her and button the dress at the back.

'You look wonderful.'

She turns, without daring to look me in the eye. I take Eline's *Kennkarte* from my trouser pocket.

'Here, take this.'

'What is it?' she says.

'Just take it.'

I put it in her hand. She opens it and looks up at me. Looks at it again.

'Is that her?'

'Yes. That's Eline.'

And then:

'I want you to do it.'

I hand her the PPK. She takes it, hesitantly. She holds it pointed at the floor.

I put both hands around it and lift it to my mouth, curl her finger around the trigger.

'When it's done you can go,' I tell her.

'I don't understand,' she says.

'I killed a child with this. Do it!'

She is startled.

'Do it!'

I force the barrel into my mouth.

I close my eyes.

'No,' she says, and withdraws.

She tosses the pistol away, it spins across the floor, halted by the leg of a chair.

We stand looking at it.

'I won't help you,' she says. 'I want nothing to do with you.'

– – –

'Come here.'

'What now?'

I go over to the mantelpiece and pick up the lump of bone and gold.

'You're going to help me.'

'Help you do what?'

'Just come with me. I'm not going to hurt you.'

– – –

In the basement, the professor's
storeroom again.

Shelves of vessels, flasks and laboratory beakers.

'Look for HNO_3 and $3HCl$.'

'H-what?'

'HNO_3 . . . Is that all there is?'

'Yes.'

'And HCl . . . how much of that?'

She shakes the bottle in her hand. A bit more than a litre, perhaps.

I take the big six-litre crucible and two beakers, one-litre capacity each.

There are no tongs in the workshop, I look everywhere.

– – –

I get a fire going with some sticks in the professor's little smoke-house in the garden.

I have erected a table on which I place the apparatus: crucible, beakers, two bottles, nitric acid and hydrochloric acid, a measuring cup.

I find a pair of gardening gloves in the shed. They are stiff, but will do.

She sits on the wooden veranda with her plastered hand in her lap.

I measure out four decilitres of nitric acid, twelve of hydrochloric and mix them together in a beaker. The colourless liquid turns orange within seconds. I lower Manfred's head into the crucible, which I place on the hot stones of the smokehouse before adding the solution.

'Come here and look at this,' I say to her.

'What is it?'

'Aqua regia. Royal water. The only solution that can dissolve the noblest of metals: gold.'

I crouch down. She does likewise.

We can see the gold in the skull, the skull in the gold, immersed in the royal water, which after a moment turns dark purple and gives off a suffocating cloud of smoke.

'Mind, it's burning hot.'

'What is that on the top?'

'The calotte.'

'Calotte?'

'The uppermost part of the skull. It's called the calotte.'

We watch as the gold separates, the brake pedal turning loose, oxidising and falling apart, garish green flakes descending to the bottom of the vessel.

Green and black, gold and fire.

'Alchemy,' she says.

The skull breaks up, the jawbone drops, the teeth of the mandible already a powder, chemical snow, the forehead collapsing, a seething and bubbling mass.

'There we are, Manfred,' I say when all that is left is sediment. 'It's over now . . .'

'Did you know him?' she asks.

'Yes, he was my friend. My only one, I think.'

'How did he end up here?'

'It's a long story. We need to filter this now.'

— — —

Gold chloride, dull, speckled flakes in their hundreds, swim in the beaker.

A film of perspiration covers my brow. I thrust the spade into the ground next to the pit I have dug. I fill it with firewood, which I then douse with petrol. I fetch the tongs from the fireplace and a pair of bellows. In the basement I find a small earthenware crucible but nothing in which to mould the ingots. After some rooting around I come across some bricks at the far end of the garden with core holes in them.

I strike a match on the sole of my boot and at once the fire leaps in the darkness.

I form a rectangle of twenty-four bricks, pull off the gloves, help her put one of them on and show her how to hold the tongs with the crucible in the middle of the fire, where the heat is most intense.

I stoke the pit with firewood and work up the temperature with the bellows.

After some minutes the chloride is a glowing orange, it loses form, collapses in on itself and melts.

'Now,' I tell her, and she removes the crucible from the fire, steadies herself for a second before lifting it over to the bricks and pouring the gold into the holes.

'Again,' I say.

The sweat pours from us.

'Again.'

— — —

She rolls firewood to the pit, hampered by her plaster cast, she keeps stepping on the hem of her dress, her face is black with soot. I maintain the temperature, furnishing the fire with blasts of air, we fill the last of the bricks with the molten gold.

We sweat, and the work makes us blind.

I go inside and fetch the schnapps while the stones cool. We sit in the moist grass in silence. The fir trees sway as the flames crackle. I hand her the bottle, she drinks and wipes her mouth on her sleeve. I see the smear of make-up and soot drawn across her face. She looks nothing like Zarah Leander. She looks nothing like Eline. Her teeth are dreadful.

I realise I have not thought this through.

I have no plan.

I have no idea what is supposed to happen.

I get to my feet and pick up the hammer. I bring it down on the bricks and break them into pieces. I remove the small, ribbed ingots and pile them up.

One hundred and twenty-two of them.

'I'm hungry,' she says, and rises. 'Is there anything to eat?'

– – –

She sits in the living room. I empty my pockets in the kitchen: two curled-up sandwiches, blackcurrants wrapped in a paper napkin, pork crackling, lint, some squashed berries. I go down into the basement, find the key above the door of the larder and discover pickled vegetables and preserves, a rusting, dented tin of fish balls, some soft biscuits. My hands are full, a jar of pickled cucumber under my chin.

When I come back into the living room she has put on her trench coat again, knotted the belt tightly and wiped her face with a cloth.

She is smoking.

I put the food on the table and go over to the gramophone. I put on the Diabelli Variations again and sit down.

I nod at the food and indicate that she can have what she wants. She takes one of the sandwiches and lifts the bread.

Egg, butter, cress.

'You needn't be scared,' I tell her, and smile when she hesitates. 'It's not poison.'

She does not smile back.

Beethoven fills the room, Kempff's subtle phrasing.

She devours the sandwich, gulping it down.

She eats noisily.

'Diabelli . . . was that a random choice?' I ask after a while.

'What?'

'Just before . . . the Diabelli Variations.'

'Before what?'

'Before . . . earlier . . .'

'No,' she says, and licks her fingers. For the first time, she looks me in the eye. 'It was one of the first pieces I learned.'

I take some crackling.

'Did you know,' I say, suddenly cheerful, the roasted pork rind popping inside my mouth, 'that in his Harmonielehre Schoenberg calls it Beethoven's most adventurous work?'

'No,' she says. 'It was just there, that's all. I hoped perhaps you would hesitate if I chose something you liked.'

I stop chewing.

'Did you think I . . . was going to kill you?'

'Yes. And I was right.'

She looks me in the eye as she speaks, articulating the words quite calmly, now twisting slightly to her left and rummaging for something in her pocket, something she finds.

She puts my PPK down hard on the table.

'Tell me how to be her . . . Eline.'

'And if I won't?'

'You will. You want to.'

Her fingers latch onto the gun. 'You so want to be forgiven.'

She has fine hands, I notice now, as she nurses the magazine.

A burnished light has come to her eyes.

Was that a smile, as the needle reaches the end and idles harshly in its groove?

She gets up and lifts the tone arm.

She has her back to me as I speak.

'We were engaged to be married. This is her house.'

'Just tell me what to do,' she says and turns to face me, the gun still in her hand. 'Date of birth, education . . . information to get me through the checkpoints.'

'Don't you want me to tell you about her . . .?'

'No. Do you want me to tell you about my dead sister, my daughter . . .? Elsa, Marion . . .?'

'No.'

'About how it felt when you broke my hand? If it hurt?'

'No.'

'Before . . . when you were going to rape me? How *that* felt . . .?'

'No.'

'Did it thrill you?'

'No.'

'Did you like me being scared of you?'

'. . . Yes.'

Now she has no response. She sits down again, engages the safety catch of the PPK and puts it back in her pocket.

I pick up the bottle of schnapps and take a good swig. I am prickling with shame.

'The whole of Hamburg is being evacuated,' I say, and put the bottle down on the table again, only to change my mind and gulp down another mouthful. 'Hundreds of thousands of people. No one will give you a second look. All they're going to look at are the most superficial features . . .'

'Like a Colles fracture?'

'Colles fracture, short hair . . . and tell them who your brother is if you get into trouble. Manfred Schlosser.'

311

'The man in the gold?'

'The man in the gold, yes. He was a Hauptsturmführer, SS. There must be a photograph of him here somewhere. Hang on a minute.'

I get to my feet and go into the other room in search of photo albums, but find none. And then I remember, there was one of him in uniform in his mother's bedroom on the first floor.

– – –

When I open the door of the bedroom I hear a record being put on the gramophone downstairs. It is no longer the Diabelli Variations, I know the piece, but cannot recall what it is. I go to the window and open the curtains, look out at the garden as I hum the tune. There is a thin band of light behind the trees now, and there, on the dresser next to the bed and the vase with the dried lavender in it, is the photograph in its frame. I unfasten the clips of the cardboard backing and Manfred drops into my hand. I had forgotten that I am in the picture too. It was taken just before we went away, over by the roses, the table can be seen behind us, set for tea, laden with cakes. Manfred in his black uniform and jackboots, laughing in my direction while I look at the photographer, Eline.

A moment later we started on the cakes, a cornucopia of confection.

Eline, wiping some whipped cream from my lip with her index finger and dabbing it on my nose.

She was bursting with laughter.

That little squeal of hers.

'*I love you,*' she said, still giggling.

The tip of my tongue curled towards my nose, mouth crammed full of cake.

'Till death thdo uth paaart?'
'Mmm . . .'

— — —

When I go back down again the gramophone is well into the andante of Mendelssohn's Violin Concerto in E minor.

The woman lies reclined on the sofa.

The trench coat is pulled tight around her. One hand rests on her stomach, clutching the pistol, the other grips the material of her coat.

She is asleep.

I go over to lift the needle amid an abrupt blare of horns, but instead I remain standing, staring at her. I can see into her sleep, but it feels too intimate and I cover her up with a blanket. She stirs slightly, whimpers and turns onto her side. I manage to grab the pistol before it clatters to the floor.

I go back upstairs, find a suitcase in Eline's room and pack some of her clothes: a brush, a mirror, toothpaste, pillbox. She is still asleep when I go into the garden to collect the gold and arrange the ingots in the case. Back inside, I leave the case by the sofa, place the PPK on the table next to her and sit down in the wicker chair over by the French window.

I stare at her foreign face as morning comes.

I cannot be done with it.

— — —

For a moment I am confused, I sit up with a start, wide awake.

I don't know how long I have slept. It must be well into the morning.

She stands looking down at me. The suitcase is on the floor beside her.

Her arm is raised. She has the PPK.

She racks the slide with her injured hand.

I made the cast too tight, the tips of her fingers are purple.

I have never been this calm.

'Are you leaving?' I say with a nod towards the case.

'Yes,' she says. 'There must be more than a hundred million francs in there . . .'

'And what about me? Am I to die?'

'It's what you want, isn't it?'

'Yes.'

A silence.

'Do it, then.'

'Don't smile like that . . .'

'Am I smiling?'

'Yes.'

'I'm sorry.'

She turns her head away from me. Her hand is shaking.

I close my eyes, listen. Nothing happens.

'I can't!'

'Yes, you can.'

'No!'

'Do you hate me?'

'No . . . not any more.'

'Come here.'

I place my hands around the pistol, drawing it to my forehead, holding it there until her own hand is still. 'Now do it . . .'

I close my eyes tight, and this time I do not open them again.

I can feel her trembling, the cold sensation of the muzzle against my skin. Or perhaps it is me trembling? Our nerves screech in the darkness, *come on, get it done*, my bloodstream a slow whisper, *like a caress* . . .

'*Darling* . . .'
  '*Yes.*'
  '*Come, take my hand.*'

When I rise the world has become transparent.

All sound has been turned up. I can hear everything.

And there she stands, at the end of the garden, beside the swing seat by the roses.

She gives it a push and the hinges squeak.

As I come closer I see they have put the table up.

A large dish of cream cakes.

She is wearing her black dress, the one with the stays, and the puffed sleeves.

Long, black gloves.

She waves to me.

She is Zarah Leander.

She says life will be wonderful.

NOTE

Reference has been made to the following:

Curt von Gottberg: 'Order of evacuation, 1/8/1943'; Hugo von Hofmannsthal: 'Ballade des äußeren Lebens' ('Ballad of the Outer Life', translated by Margarete Münsterberg); Carl Schmitt: 'Das gute Recht der deutschen Revolution'; The Bible: Book of Judges; Georg Trakl: 'Am Rand eines alten Brunnens' ('By the Rim of an Old Well', translated by Alexander Stillmark) and 'Psalm'; *Deutsche Wochenschau* 7 July 1943; Wilhelm Müller: *Die schöne Müllerin*; J. W. Goethe: *Faust*; Bernward Vesper: *Die Reise*; Hermann Rauschning, *Wenn Hitler siegt! Politische Gespräche mit Hitler über seine eigentliche Ziele*; Kaing Guek Eav (aka Duch): 'Manual of interrogation from S–21'; Aeschylus: *The Eumenides*; Heinrich Himmler: 'Orders of the Day No. 160/43/ 10.7.43'; Ernst Jünger: *Das abenteuerliche Herz* ('The Adventurous Heart', translated by Thomas Friese); *Deutsche Wochenschau*, 21 July 1943; Wolf Biermann: *Die Lebensuhr blieb stehen*, one of Erich Andres's photographs of the aftermath of Hamburg's bombing; Kurt Vonnegut Jr.: *Slaughterhouse-Five, or The Children's Crusade*; Hans Erich Nossack: *Der Untergang: Hamburg 1943*.

LIST OF REAL PERSONS AND EVENTS

Erich von dem Bach-Zelewski, 1899–1972, SS-Obergruppenführer and General der Polizei, HSS-PF of Heeresgruppe Mitte 1941–43, in charge of anti-partisan operations in Belorussia from 1941 and the entire Eastern Front from July 1943. Led the suppression of the Warsaw Uprising in 1944. Was never convicted of any war crime.

Oscar Dirlewanger, 1895–1945. Oberführer, head of Sonderbataillon Dirlewanger. Took part in anti-partisan operations in Belorussia and the suppression of the Warsaw Uprising in 1944. Presumed beaten to death by Holocaust survivors in a prison camp, June 1945.

Curt von Gottberg, 1896–1945, SS-Gruppenführer and General der Polizei, deputy for Bach-Zelewski, Generalkommissar of Weissruthenien, head of anti-partisan operations, Heeresgruppe Mitte. Led the Kampfgruppe von Gottberg, which took part in the majority of anti-partisan operations between 1941 and 1944. Committed suicide in May 1945.

Wilhelm Kube, 1887–1943. One of the first members of NSDAP. Gauleiter for Brandenburg. Generalkommissar of Weissruthenien 1941–43. Assassinated in September 1943.

Zarah Leander, 1907–81. Swedish actress contracted to the UFA film studios from 1936. Leander became one of German film's biggest stars due to her roles in films such as *Die grosse Liebe* (The Great Love), 1942. She appeared in a number of Nazi propaganda films. She left Germany in 1943.

Operation Gomorrah, the RAF's night bombings of Hamburg, 24 July to 3 August 1943. The exact number of dead has never been ascertained, but estimates suggest that the eleven days of bombing cost in the region of 40,000 German lives, some 30,000 alone in the firestorm of 27–28 July. The district of Hamm remained uninhabitable until the 1950s.

Operation Hermann took place in the Naliboki forests between Lida and Minsk, 13 July to 8 August 1943, an anti-partisan operation with the additional purpose of rounding up forced labour. According to the German reports, 4,280 bandits were killed and '20,944 imported to the Reich' as labour, 9,065 of these being men, 7,701 women and 4,178 children. Kok-saghyz was never planted in the area.

GLOSSARY OF TERMS

Ariernachweis: Aryan certificate, document certifying membership of the Aryan race.

Armia Krajova: The 'Home Army', the Polish underground resistance army.

Christmas tree: German term for flares parachuted by Allied bombers to mark out target areas.

Death zone: Area evacuated during anti-partisan operations. Hundreds of villages were razed to the ground, their inhabitants either killed or deported from the zones.

Einsatzgruppen: Special deployment units, death squads under SS command, responsible for the systematic killing of Jews behind the front.

EK: Eisernes Kreuz 1. 11 Klasse. Iron Cross 1st and 2nd Class.

Feldwebel: Non-commissioned officer of the Wehrmacht, equivalent to a British company sergeant major.

Flak: Anti-aircraft guns (from the German Flugzeugabwehrkanone, 'aircraft defence cannon'), or the fire from these guns.

Generaloberst: 'Colonel General', rank superior to British general and immediately below field marshal.

Gesundheitsamt: Health Department.

Gymnasium: German upper secondary school, preparing students for advanced academic study at university level.

Heeresgruppe Mitte: 'Army Group Centre', strategic army group of the Wehrmacht operating on the Eastern front.

Hiwi (Hilfswilligen): Local 'voluntary' assistants enlisted in the occupied territories.

HSS–PF: Höhere SS- und Polizeiführer, Higher SS and Police Leader. Command authority for SS and police units in a given region, directly responsible to SS leader Heinrich Himmler.

Jägerbataillon: 'Hunter Battalion', special forces unit.

Kennkarte: Identity card.

Kok-saghyz: Also known as Kazakh dandelion, kautsjuk, a perennial dandelion plant with a high content of rubber.

Kolkhoz: Soviet collective farm.

Kripo: Kriminalpolizei, the Criminal Police.

Kübelwagen: Jeep-like light military vehicle.

Lebensborn: 'Fount of life'. SS-initiated breeding programme with the aim of propagating a master race.

Machtergreifung: Hitler's seizure of power, 30 January 1933.

Master bomber: Pathfinder plane among bombers, whose task it was to find and mark the target.

NKVD: The People's Commissariat for Internal Affairs, Soviet law enforcement agency, ran the Gulag labour camps.

Obersekunda: Upper tier of the German Gymnasium.

Orpo: Ordnungspolizei, the 'order' police, regular police force.

Passierschein: Official safe conduct pass.

Puszcza: Polish word for large forest.

Rassenschande: 'Racial defilement'. Nazi term for sexual relations between Aryans and non-Aryans, punishable by law.

RKFDV: Reichskommissariat für die Festigung deutschen Volkstums, the Reich's Commission for the Strengthening of the German People. In Belarus, this body was charged with ascertaining the racial value of orphans or children of German soldiers. If such children were found to be Aryan, they were sent to Germany and brought up there, often in the children's homes of the Lebensborn project.

RSO: Raupenschlepper Ost. Lightweight caterpillar vehicle often used to transport artillery to the Eastern Front.

Sanitäter: Medical attendant.

Schächtmesser: Knife used for kosher slaughter (German: *Schächten*, cf. Hebrew: *shechita*).

SchuMa (Schutzmannschaft): Local police auxiliary in occupied territories.

SD (Sicherheitsdienst): SS intelligence arm, 'security service'.

Sd.Kfz 222: Light armoured reconnaissance vehicle.

Slavic campaign of 928: The East Francian king, Heinrich der Finkler (Henry the Fowler), waged several wars against the Slavic people of present-day Poland, Ukraine and Hungary, during which he enlisted bandits, poachers, etc. who were granted safe conduct during battle and allotted land following conquests. As such, they were a kind of medieval cossacks.

Soldbuch (pl. Soldbücher): Identity document of German military personnel.

Sonderkommando 1005: Facetiously termed 'special commando' of labourers. A number appended to the title of Sonderkommando referred to a specific task. Sonderkommando 1005 thus carried out Sonderaktion 1005 (more simply Aktion 1005), the 'special action' of systematically removing all trace of the mass killings of Jews by exhuming their corpses and burning them in mass graves. Also known as the 'corpse commando'.

SS-Dienststelle: Administrative entity of the SS.

SS-Hauptsturmführer: (Hstf.) SS Head Storm Leader, SS commissioned rank equivalent to British captain.

SS-Oberführer: SS Senior Leader, SS commissioned rank between British colonel and brigadier.

SS-Obergruppenführer: SS Senior Group Leader, SS commissioned rank equivalent to a British lieutenant colonel

SS-PF: SS- und Polizeiführer, SS and Police Leader, rank immediately below HSS-PF.

SS-Rottenführer: SS Band Leader, non-commissioned officer of the SS, equivalent to British corporal.

SS-Scharführer: SS Company Leader, non-commissioned officer of the SS, equivalent to the short-lived British WWII rank of platoon sergeant major.

SS-Schütze: Private of the SS, 'rifleman'.

Stalag: Stammlager, prisoner-of-war camp for Russian rank-and-file soldiers and non-commissioned officers.

SS-Standartenführer: SS Standard Leader, commissioned SS rank equivalent to British colonel.

SS-Sturmmann: 'SS Storm Man', stormtrooper, rank equivalent to British lance corporal.

Stützpunkt (pl. Stützpunkte): Military support point.

Tante Ju: 'Iron Annie', nickname for the Junkers Ju 52 transport aircraft.

Totenkopf: 'Death's Head'. Skull emblem worn by the SS. Unit name of the 3rd SS-Panzer Division of the Waffen-SS, whose skull insignia differed slightly from the regular emblem.

Trawniki: Concentration camp guard trained in the Trawniki camp.

Untersekunda: Lower tier of the German Gymnasium.

Window: Later known as chaff (German: *Düppel*), small, thin pieces of aluminium dropped from bombers during air raids in order to disrupt radar signals. First used during Operation Gomorrah.

Acknowledgements

Thanks to Naja Marie Aidt, Niels Beider, Karen Vad Bruun, Eigil Bryld, Benni Bødker, Christian Dorph, Helle Ann-Britt Grubert, Poul Hæstrup, Kasper Pasternak Jørgensen, Birthe Melgård, Gita Pasternak, Johannes Riis, Anna Sandberg, Jakob Sandvad, Therkel Stræde, Jenny Thor, Sofie Voller.

Martin Aitken is the acclaimed translator of numerous novels from Danish, including works by Peter Høeg, Jussi Adler-Olsen and Pia Juul, and his translations of short stories and poetry have appeared in many literary journals and magazines. In 2012 he was awarded the American-Scandinavian Foundation's Nadia Christensen Translation Prize.